Out of the Frying Pan

Out of the Frying Pan

JANET E. GREEN

Out of the Frying Pan

Janet E. Green

Copyright © 2021 Janet E. Green

ISBN 9798742644453

Cover design and typeset by www.greatwriting.org

The author thanks and acknowledges Jim Holmes of
www.greatwriting.org for assistance in preparing this
book for publication.

A
HABARI
PUBLICATION

www.janetegreen.org

Contents

This book is dedicated to my sons,

Shaun and Jamie.

❖

1

Nairobi,
Westgate Shopping Mall

Sharba was in one of the toilet cubicles in the ladies' room at the Westgate Shopping Mall in Nairobi when she first heard what sounded like muffled explosions outside. Idly wondering what was happening, she emerged and went to wash her hands before moving to face a mirror where she started to fix her hair and makeup. Behind her, in the mirror's reflection, she saw a beautifully dressed African lady of about thirty years of age come out of one of the other toilet cubicles and approach the basins. It was at that moment a huge explosion reverberated through the room making everything vibrate. Startled, Sharba turned to the African lady who also looked confused. Before either of them spoke, a harsh staccato of rifle shots rang out and echoed around the room. They sounded very close.

'Oh my goodness, there must be a robbery in progress,' the African lady spluttered, her eyes looking round and frightened. 'Maybe we should stay in here until things quieten down because those shots seemed to be just outside the door!' Her lips trembled as it dawned on her how very close they were to the danger. 'Let's get to the back of this room and then we can dodge into one of the cubicles if we hear anyone coming,' she suggested, as the need for self-preservation kicked in.

Both women rushed to the back of the room and stood against the wall, listening to the noise outside. There was another huge explosion and more rifle shots, then terrified screams and panicky yells pierced the atmosphere. It was the screams and yells that made the most impact on the two scared women. They conveyed a picture of the utmost horror being witnessed by the people who uttered the calls of distress. Icy chills shot up Sharba's spine as the piercing intonations of terror impinged upon her ears and jarred her very soul. Although they could see nothing from where they were standing, the drama of what was going on outside seemed to infiltrate the ladies room and Sharba felt the tension rise as they cowered in the half light against the back wall.

'It's got to be more than a simple robbery,' Sharba said rather shakily. 'It sounds more like a war!'

Things didn't quieten down and the two young ladies became more and more apprehensive as the time went on. The smell of cordite permeated the room and everything shook as further explosions occurred.

'I can't bear not knowing what's going on,' whispered Sharba at last. The uncertainty of their predicament was torture and she felt she just had to try and get a better idea of what was happening. 'I'm going to go to the door and have a peek.'

'Be careful,' said the African lady, who was obviously too scared to move.

Sharba went cautiously to the door and eased it open a crack so that she could peep out. 'Oh my goodness,' she whispered as she witnessed a horrific scene.

'What is it? What's going on?' the African lady asked unsteadily; she was still flattened against the far wall looking absolutely terrified.

'There're people will rifles,' Sharba said, her voice cracking with fear. 'They look like jihadi fighters.'

'It must be a terrorist attack!' The African lady's face was a mask of horror. 'Don't let them see you!' she urged in a whisper.

Sharba stayed by the door for a few more moments, horrified by the scene unrolling before her eyes. She could see two men with rifles, and they seemed to almost causally throw grenades in all directions and then use their rifles to pick off the terrified people fleeing from the carnage as the grenades exploded. There were women and children among the men, all all running for their lives. Some of them were bleeding from gunshot or shrapnel wounds and many of them were screaming. Another jihadi appeared on the scene and joined in the shooting and Sharba noticed the grin on his face as his finger gripped the trigger. She closed the door and retreated to the far wall next to the African lady.

'We're in real trouble,' she whispered shakily. 'They're killing everyone they can and if they come in here, they'll kill us as well because there's no way of escape except through the main door.'

'I don't want to die!' The African lady's voice began to rise with panic. 'I only came to the mall to buy my mother-in-law a birthday present; I didn't come here to be killed! I have a little girl; she's only three and she needs a mother!'

'It's okay,' said Sharba. She could see the African lady was getting hysterical and she needed her to calm down if they were to have any chance of escape. Somehow the other woman's panic was helping her to keep her own terror in check.

'My name's Sharnique; what's your name?' Sharba had been known by that name for some years now, so it seemed natural to introduce herself that way.

'Angela.'

'Okay, Angela, let's keep calm and we'll make a plan to escape. At the moment, the jihadi fighters are close by, so we'll stay here and hide in the toilets if we hear them coming in. We need to be very quiet—and we'd better turn off the ringtone on our mobile phones because we don't want them ringing and drawing attention to us. When things quieten down a bit and it feels safer, we'll leave here and try and find a way out of the building. Are you alone or did you come to the mall with someone?'

'I'm alone; Wanjiku, my daughter, stayed with her father while I came here. Are you also alone?'

'No, my partner went to Nakumatt supermarket and we arranged to meet in the Java Coffee Shop in about fifteen minutes.'

Sharba wondered briefly if Oliver was okay. She felt sure that he must be, because he was the sort that always managed to wriggle out of trouble no matter how bad things were.

'I'm going to take another peek,' Sharba told Angela after a while when things had quietened down a bit. 'If I think it's all clear, I'll give you a wave and we'll make a break for it together.'

Sharba went to the door again and opened it a crack. She could see bodies on the floor and pools of blood which had also spattered up the walls in places, but the jihadis seemed to have moved on for the time being. For a moment, the sight of violent death and the smell of the blood brought back unwelcome memories from the past that Sharba had banished from her mind for many years. She felt her resolve wavering momentarily, but then she impatiently pushed the memories out of her head and turned to Angela.

'Come on,' Sharba waved to her, and the African lady came rather hesitantly. 'Now just follow me,' Sharba instructed. 'Don't look at anything or it'll upset you. I'll run from place to place where we can take cover if they come back, and we'll try and make our way out of the mall.'

Sharba sensed Angela hesitating as soon as she saw the carnage, so she grabbed her hand and pulled her along as she made for a counter behind which they could duck if a jihadi appeared. Pausing there for a second, she moved on, darting from one place to another while detouring around bodies and trying not to step in the pools of slippery blood. They had only gone a short distance from the ladies' room when they were brought up short by a hissing noise. Looking in the direction from which it came, Sharba saw a brown arm beckoning to them from out of what looked like a cupboard. She made her way towards it pulling Angela behind her.

'Come, come...we can all squeeze in,' said a voice when they got to the arm. The door opened wider and Sharba could see it was a dimly lit broom cupboard and a small Asian woman was urging them to join her inside. The Asian lady shut the door when they had all squeezed in.

'You mustn't move around outside or you'll attract the jihadis' attention and they'll come back and start searching for survivors to shoot,' she told them, her tone urgent.

Sharba noticed that the Asian lady looked about fifty and her black hair was shot through with threads of white. Her face was tense and pale, but she was in control of her emotions and her rather severe expression indicated she would not tolerate any foolishness.

'We wanted to find a way of escape out of the mall,' said Sharba.

'No! That's much too dangerous! You'll bring them back, and those who've been able to evade them will be shot! Just wait here for the security services to regain order.' The Asian lady then pressed her lips together in a way that signified that the subject of escape was not up for discussion.

It was stuffy and hot in the dim cupboard and Sharba, who was the closest to the door, opened it a crack and peeked out. She could just see the entrance to the toilet block from which they had come and suddenly she stiffened as she saw a jihadi appear and open the door to the ladies' room. She heard him shout something and then there was a long burst of rifle fire. She shuddered as she quickly closed the cupboard door because she realised that the man had not bothered to check if anyone was in the toilet cubicles. Instead, he had instead fired into each and every one of them, and had she and Angela been in there still they would have been killed.

'Are you all right?' whispered the Asian lady, noticing Sharba's face. 'Put your head between your knees if you're feeling faint.'

'No, I'm okay,' said Sharba. 'It's just that I've seen one of those bastards shoot up the toilets where we were hiding a few minutes ago.'

'Yes, well you're safe here for the time being,' said the Asian lady. 'My name's Myia. I own the flower shop.'

Sharba and Angela introduced themselves and then they sat in silence for a while. After a bit Angela got her mobile phone out to call her husband. It was then that Sharba realised that she had left her own mobile phone next to the basins in the ladies' room. She had put it there when she had turned off the ringtone and forgotten to pick it up when they had left.

'If you're going to use your phone, keep you voice down and make sure the ringtone is turned off as well,' Myia instructed Angela.

When Angela's husband answered her call, she told him in hushed tones what had happened. But as she related to him the events that had occurred, she became more and more agitated, her voice starting to rise to a frantic wheezy whisper and tears splashing down her cheeks.

'Quiet now!' said Myia sternly.

Angela ended her call quickly. 'My husband is very worried and he says I must stay where I am until we get rescued,' she told the other two ladies with a sniff.

'Quite right!' said Myia.

But Sharba wanted to try and get away from the mall, away from the violence and the blood and the atmosphere of malevolent hatred that seemed to seep into their hidey-hole. As well as everything else, she was experiencing claustrophobia in the hot cupboard, and could feel the perspiration breaking out on her face when she thought of what would happen if they were discovered in this small space. They'd be trapped like rats in a barrel and not even have the chance of running for their lives. However, the other two convinced her that she would be endangering them all if she made a run for it, so she sat quietly trying to control her emotions.

'Earlier, one of those men was shouting, "Muslims, get out of here!"' Myia told them. 'He was letting go the ones who could prove they were Muslim. When he went away, I saw a Muslim woman take off her niqab and tear it into strips which she handed to the women around her to wear as Islamic-style headscarves. She is a good woman, very brave.'

'Maybe we should try and make ourselves look more Islamic,' suggested Angela. 'I bought three lovely scarves for my mother-in-law, so maybe if we wear them Islamic style we'll be less of a target.' She dug in her bag and brought out the scarves.

The three women put the scarves around their heads in an Islamic fashion, hoping it might just help them to evade being singled out as infidels.

'You need to hide your eyes,' Myia told Sharba. 'They have an oriental look about them that's a dead giveaway. Have you got any sunglasses?'

'No, I'm afraid I left them in the hotel,' said Sharba.

'Well, have mine then,' said Myia. She got them out of her bag and gave them to Sharba. They had very ornate frames which were heart-shaped and surrounded by flowers, not the sort of sunglasses Sharba would ever choose to wear, but this was not a time to be fussy and when she put them on they not only hid her eyes but also half covered her face.

'I heard one of the jihadis asking a man to name the mother of the prophet; the man claimed to be a Muslim and he was asked that question to prove it. But he hesitated before answering and so the jihadi shot him!' Myia told the other two women.

'Do any of us know anything about the Koran?' Sharba asked the others, but they both shook their heads. 'Well if we're asked, we'd better just make something up quickly,' she said. 'I bet those murdering bastards don't know much about the Koran, either!'

They sat cramped on the floor of the cupboard listening to the noise of shots and explosions going off in other parts of the building. Surely the security forces should have come and intervened by now, Sharba thought. But she couldn't discern any different patterns to the shots going off which would indicate that there was a battle between two sides. Then she wondered where Oliver was, and she found her thoughts drifting back to Australia where they had first met.

2

Holidaying in Australia

O liver had first spotted Sharba, or Sharnique as she called herself then, when he had been on holiday in Australia. He had booked a daytrip to the Pinnacles Desert and had noticed her immediately as she climbed aboard the coach that would take them there from Perth. She appeared to be travelling on her own, as was he, and she had on red shorts and a white sun-top covered with a loose blouse. The cloth hat on her head matched her shorts. Her figure was superb, but no better than dozens of girls he'd come across in Australia. It was her exquisite face that first attracted his attention.

There was definitely an oriental look to her almond-shaped, sparkling black eyes, but her hair fell in soft black ringlets and her completion was rosy and touched with colour rather than being the rather sallow tint of someone from the east. Her full, sensuous lips parted in a smile of thanks as she sat down next to another woman who moved her bag to show the seat next to her was vacant, and Oliver noticed that the girl's teeth were very white and that she had rather endearing dimples in her cheeks. She was obviously of mixed race, but it appeared that she had been gifted with the very best aspects of each of the ethnic groups in her makeup.

Oliver had got to the stage in his life where he was actively looking for a woman to make his wife. His mother, who was now deceased, had taught him to live an organised life. She had impressed upon him that he should embark on a career of his choice and establish himself properly before he even thought about marriage. Then she had cautioned him to look for someone special, someone who would enhance his life and help him to achieve his dreams.

'You only have one life,' his mother had told him. 'And you need to make sure that the woman you choose looks up to you—you must be the centre of her life and she must do everything possible to please you and make your life happy.'

'Is that even possible?' Oliver had asked doubtfully. 'Most women I know have their own agendas!'

'Of course they do; that's human nature. But you must be sure to pick a woman who's malleable, so that you can mould her into a wife that will suit you. You're the one who matters Oliver, you must never forget that!'

Oliver thought his mother's words were wise, but he also had some ideas about the woman he would choose to be his wife. He had decided that she must be so beautiful that every man who saw her would be envious of him, and when he first set eyes on Sharba, he knew that she was the woman that he wanted because she was absolutely perfect. Covertly, he feasted his eyes on her for a while and the more he looked, the more he wanted her for his own. His mother had also taught him that if there was anything he wanted in life, he should go out and get it—no matter what it took.

'There's always a way,' she had told him. 'You just need to be persistent and never give up and then you'll always get what you want in the end. Sometimes you'll need to employ methods that are not conventional, but that's all right. What's important is that you achieve your objective!'

And now Oliver knew that he wanted the beautiful woman who had caught his eye. It was the right time to find a wife, as he had established himself as a very successful architect—a career which enabled him to live a very comfortable life. He had his own house and plenty of money in the bank, so now was definitely the time to get the perfect partner for life. Luckily, he had some good tools in his box for getting what he wanted; he was handsome and could be very charming. He was well-spoken, educated, and knowledgeable on many subjects. He also was full of confidence and was sure that any girl would be happy to link up with someone who had money and a big house. Then it would just be a matter of moulding her into the woman that he required to make his life perfect.

Oliver decided that he would introduce himself to the beautiful lady that he had been admiring when they got to their first destination, Caversham Wildlife Park, and then take things from there. Already in his mind he had an unerring conviction that he and this girl were destined to be together. He had never felt like this before and, although it was a strange feeling, he couldn't deny that it was there, and he knew he must act on it and make the woman who had captivated him his own.

In keeping with his mother's guidance, Oliver had always pursued the things he desired with single-minded determination, not giving up until he had what he wanted. Now his eyes took on a rapacious glint as he scrutinised the woman who had attracted his attention. She was not wearing a wedding ring and she was travelling alone—which surely meant that she was single. This was a relief to Oliver, because the one thing he would never do was to make a play for a married woman. He decided that he would befriend this beautiful lady at the first opportunity that he had, and then slowly but surely draw her in until she felt at one with him.

When they arrived at Caversham Wildlife Park, Oliver allowed the girl to disembark first and then followed her. She, along with the others, was looking forward to feeding the kangaroos and he fell in alongside her as she offered a handful of food to one of the willing recipients who knew only too well that visitors meant food!

'Oh, you're absolutely gorgeous!' The girl laughed delightedly as the kangaroo nibbled the food out of her hand. 'I wish I could take you home with me; you're such a cutie!' She was so intent on feeding the kangaroos she was taken unawares when a gust of wind blew her hat off. It was Oliver's chance to swing into action and he deftly retrieved the hat, and, dusting it down first, he gave it back to her.

'Oh, thank you.'

'It's a pleasure,' Oliver said laughing. 'I'm guessing from your accent you've come all the way from England?'

'Quite right,' she replied, giving him a dazzling smile. 'And I'm guessing from your accent you come from England as well!'

They introduced themselves to each other. Sharba told him her name was Sharnique Wellby and he said he was Oliver Naughton. The rest of the coach party was made up of Americans, so it seemed natural for the two single Brits to pair up for the day. Sharba noticed that Oliver had a strong masculine face and he looked fit and healthy. His honey-blond hair hung to his shoulders and his greenish eyes were direct and penetrating under very dark straight eyebrows. His expression sometimes appeared almost arrogant, but somehow this added to his attraction.

Oliver made sure he sat next to Sharba on the coach when they moved on, and they chatted together easily as they headed for their next destination. Oliver needed to find out as much as he could about her, but he had to do it in such a way that she didn't realise she was being hunted. He told her he was an architect and this was the first time he had been to Australia. She told him she had been saving for this trip since she was eighteen and it had taken her two years to get enough money together. Now she was back-packing around Australia on a shoestring, with the intention of seeing and experiencing all that she could of the country before her holiday came to an end.

'And you're doing this all alone?' Oliver asked.

'Absolutely,' Sharba answered a little defensively. 'How about you?'

'I'm doing the same,' Oliver replied, but his answer wasn't strictly truthful. Although he was having a holiday in Australia, he wasn't back-backing and it wasn't on a shoestring. He was staying in expensive hotels rather than in back-packer accommodation and his budget wasn't restricted in any way. But he didn't want to tell Sharba that at this stage, because he sensed in her an independent spirit and decided that she would be drawn to him more readily if she felt they were more or less on the same level.

Sharba was quite happy to holiday in Australia alone, but during the barbeque that they enjoyed on the beach when they next stopped, she realised she was having more fun sharing this day with Oliver than if she had been alone. He was very good company, he made her laugh, and there was no denying that he was stunningly good looking.

Oliver discovered that the girl he was so drawn to was an intelligent young woman who had very definite opinions of her own, but she made it clear from the start that she was not looking for commitment. However, he sensed she enjoyed his company and he decided he would just have to work on her gently until she changed her mind.

After their beach barbeque, they were taken on to the Pinnacles, where rocks rose mysteriously from the desert casting ghostly shadows on the ground. Both Sharba and Oliver thought it was a beautiful place in a different and unique way, but there were myriads of flies that tormented them the moment they stepped off the coach.

'My God, I wish I'd brought some bug-repellent,' said Oliver, brushing them away from his face, but Sharba didn't seem too concerned about them. 'Aren't they driving you mad as well?' Oliver was surprised that Sharba didn't seem worried by them.

'They're only flies,' she laughed. Just then one of the Americans approached Sharba and asked if she would be kind enough to take a group photo of the Americans with the Pinnacles in the background.

'Of course,' agreed Sharba, taking the man's camera. 'Where do I press?'

Sharba took three photos of the smiling group and then handed the camera back.

'Thank you so much,' the American beamed at Sharba. 'Would you like me to take one of the two of you with your camera?'

Sharba and Oliver stood among the rocks with Oliver's arm draped over her shoulders. 'We look like an old married couple,' Sharba laughed when they looked at the photo. Oliver laughed as well—if only Sharba had known what was in his mind!

On the last part of their daytrip, they were taken to the sand dunes where they could go sand-surfing. The golden sand was warm under their feet as they climbed to the top of the dune where the boards were laid out.

'Have you ever done anything like this before?' Sharba asked Oliver.

'No—well, I've done some water-skiing, but nothing like this.'

'I haven't either, not even water-skiing.'

Some of the Americans had done it before and they were quick to get on the boards and go hurtling down the dunes. Some sat on the boards, others lay on them and went down headfirst, while the ones who were really experienced among them stood on their boards as if they were surfing the waves.

'I'm going to sit on my board because that looks the best way for a beginner.' Sharba got on her board and pushed herself off. It was exhilarating to sail down the dune with her hair being whipped up by the wind; it made her whoop in delight.

Oliver was not far behind her, but somehow he managed to upend his board as he got to the bottom of the dune and tumbled off in a shower of sand.

'Are you okay?' Sharba couldn't prevent herself laughing at his undignified landing. She helped him brush the sand off his back as he laughed with her.

Again and again, they trudged up the dune so that they could experience the thrill of surfing down it again. Sharba tried it headfirst and told Oliver to do it as well as it was even more exhilarating than just sitting on the board, but Oliver was happy just to sit. Very soon, they were both very sweaty and the sand that stuck to their moist bodies made them look sugar coated.

'That was so much fun,' Sharba said enthusiastically while trying to brush the sand away when the time came for them to board their coach again for their return trip to Perth. 'But I'm really going to enjoy my shower tonight!'

'Where're you staying in Perth?' Oliver asked Sharba.

'Rosebank Guest House,' she replied. 'It's lovely there and only a ten-minute walk to the centre of Perth. 'I've booked in for a few nights because there's quite a lot to do around Perth, then I'll be on my way again.'

'Do you think they might have room for me?' Oliver asked. 'I've been staying with an old friend that I've known for ages in Perth, but he's married now, and I have a feeling that his missus thinks I've outstayed my welcome. I need to move so that I don't cause any friction between Pete and Anna.'

It was a complete lie. Pete and Anna didn't exist, and Oliver had actually been staying at Pan Pacific Perth, but he didn't think this would impress Sharba. Already he had ascertained that wealth and good living didn't inspire this lovely young woman in the slightest, and he decided it would be better to pretend that he was more or less in in the same league as she when it came to finances. Moving into the hostel in which she was staying would be a good strategy, he decided, since he was determined to get close to her.

'I should think there's room,' said Sharba. 'It didn't seem full to me.'

The next morning Sharba wasn't surprised to see Oliver arriving with a battered old backpack. Unbeknown to her, he had ditched his expensive suitcases and bought a second-hand backpack in which to put his things, so that he looked like an authentic backpacker. She was surprised, however, at how pleased she felt to see him again. Travelling alone hadn't worried her—she was a bit of a loner at heart—but things had been so much fun the previous day and she had really enjoyed the good company Oliver had provided.

Over the next few days, they went to the Perth Zoo, the Aviation Heritage Museum and on Horse Riding Trail Rides. Oliver noted the way Sharba threw herself passionately into everything she did, taking maximum enjoyment from every activity. She was obviously a girl who was determined to make the most of every minute of her life and Oliver was gratified that she had embraced him as her holiday companion, but the more he got to know her, the more convinced he became that he wanted her for life.

The problem was, this beautiful girl on whom he had set his heart was treating their relationship as a holiday affair. Oliver played along with her. He didn't want to scare her off by becoming too intense and he hoped that, with time, he would be able to make her change her mind. He found her to be so generous in so many ways, but when it came to disclosing information about her life outside Australia, she was positively unforthcoming. Oliver wanted them to share their pasts, their upbringings and their circumstances, as it would be the first step to drawing them closer together, but she just wanted to live for the moment and didn't seem particularly interested in his past life.

Sharba was surprised how much she was enjoying Oliver's

companionship. He was totally charming and such fun to be with. They seemed to laugh the days away and when he suggested that they hire a car so that they could do things together, just the two of them, she agreed.

'It makes sense, because we can go further afield and do things in our own good time and more cheaply,' Oliver said.

In the close intimate space of the car, Oliver tried again gently to prise some more information out of Sharba about her background, and she did tell him one or two things which made him realise why she seemed such a self-contained and independent young lady.

'I spent much of my young life in a boarding school,' she told him. 'Then shortly after I had finished my education, my parents died in a horrific motor accident, so I've had to become self-reliant and now I find I don't need to depend on anyone except myself.' After telling him that, she made it clear that she didn't want to talk about her past anymore.

However, in time, Oliver did find out that she was working as a receptionist in a doctor's surgery in Oxford and had been told that the surgery would keep her job open for her until she returned. But the house-share arrangement that she had enjoyed with three other girls would no longer exist when she returned to England as one of the girls was getting married, another was moving to Spain and the youngest had decided to move back to her parents' home.

'Where will you live then?' Oliver wanted to know.

'Oh, I expect I'll find another house-share,' Sharba said airily. 'I'll worry about that when the time comes; right now, I just want to have fun.'

Of her future plans she would say nothing more than she would be saving hard for another holiday as soon as she got back, because she had got the travel bug and wanted to see as much of the world as possible while she was still young and healthy.

Oliver considered telling Sharba that he was really quite wealthy and that they could travel the world together straightaway if she liked, but he hesitated because she was such an independent girl and he didn't think she would like to be supported or have to be reliant on another person. He decided to bide his time and try and win her over slowly.

As the golden days of adventure and laughter trickled away, Oliver knew his infatuation had turned to deep love. The thought of losing this beautiful lady after this holiday was over was intolerable. She was everything he wanted in a woman and more. She was beautiful, funny and intelligent, and their sex life was incredible. Her only fault was that she was too independent, and although he knew she was attracted to him and enjoyed his company, it was obvious she wanted to remain unfettered.

Sharba did enjoy Oliver's company enormously at the beginning of their affair, and to start off with it seemed to her that he wanted the same things that she did—a good time without strings. Then one Sunday, Oliver surprised her by getting up early and telling her he was going to Mass. She had noticed that he wore a gold cross around his neck which he often caressed, but many people wore crosses for decoration rather than for religious purposes, so since he had not come across as someone who had a faith she thought it was just an adornment.

'I never realised you were a Christian,' Sharba said to Oliver when he got back.

Oliver observed her with eyes that seemed to glitter with fervour. 'There's a lot you don't know about me,' he said loftily.

All that day he seemed different to Sharba. He seemed remote and preoccupied, but that night he was more intense than he had ever been, and when they had sex he took her with a fierce passion that surprised her. However, the next day he reverted to being the man she knew. She didn't really care whether he was religious or not; it was none of her business.

They had terrific fun together as they laughed their way around Australia and Oliver got a real kick out of the envious looks he received when he had Sharba on his arm. However, he felt more and more frustrated that he had failed to make the beautiful girl fall head-over-heels in love with him, but he was far from giving up.

Sharba sensed a subtle change in their relationship as the days went past. Oliver seemed to become more needy and the loose and free quality of their relationship changed imperceptibly. It wasn't a change that Sharba welcomed and gradually she became aware that Oliver seemed to be becoming more and more possessive of her. She was sure she could see a covetous glint in his eyes when he looked at her. It concerned her.

Also, on the Sundays Oliver decided to go to Mass, his mood seemed to change and he became aloof and distant. It seeded to Sharba that he became almost resentful of her. Then in the evening when they had sex, he seemed practically to assault her, she felt it was virtually akin to rape and it didn't seem normal to her.

Oliver must have had issues in his past, Sharba thought. His cheery devil-may-care attitude to life must be a front. But she didn't really want to delve into his past any more than she wanted him to probe into hers. Her mother had warned her that men could be complicated—and from experience she knew that they could be brutal as well, so now she decided it was time to move on.

'I have to return to England next week,' Sharba told Oliver, feeling glad that she hadn't mentioned her departure date to him before.

'That's a bit sudden, isn't it?' he replied, his voice suddenly harsh.

'Not really, it's the date that's always been booked for my return,' she told him calmly.

'Well, I'll return to England as well, if that's the case,' he said decisively.

'You don't have to do that, Oliver,' said Sharba. She knew that he was on a more elastic timetable than her and hadn't been planning on returning for some time yet.

'I think Australia will lose its sparkle when you depart,' said Oliver kissing her in what she now felt was a far too possessive way. 'Actually, it's time I got back as well. We'll definitely keep in contact when we get back to Blighty, won't we?'

3

Escape Attempt

Sharba's wandering thoughts of the time she had spent with Oliver in Australia were suddenly curtailed when she saw a movement through the crack in the door. An African man in a security uniform with a pistol in his hand had come within her field of her vision, and he was moving quietly from one place to another. He was alone and his eyes darted all around as he looked for jihadis. Sharba pushed the door open a little more and waved her hand. The man saw it immediately and came to the door which Sharba opened wider as he approached.

'How many of you are in there?' the man whispered.

'There're three of us,' replied Sharba.

'If you come with me, I'll try and take you to a fire-escape so you can get to safety.'

'Where're the rest of the security forces?' Myia demanded.

'I'm sorry, madam, there's only me; I'm Jacob and I work as a security guard for the Watergate Centre. The security forces seemed to be ... delayed. So I have come myself to help people.'

'Will it be safe for us to come out?' Angela asked.

'I can't guarantee you anything,' answered Jacob honestly. 'But I'll do my best to get you to safety. Al-Shabaab could come back here at any time and if they find you, they won't hesitate to kill you, so your best chance is to come with me.'

Both Angela and Myia hung back, too frightened to take a gamble with the lone security guard. They thought that it would only be a matter of time before the security forces stormed the mall and made it safe for them to come out, so they declined to go with him. But Sharba disagreed with them; she was only too delighted to be given the opportunity to get out of the claustrophobic cupboard and take her chances with Jacob.

'Good luck,' she whispered to the other two as she shut the door to the cupboard before following the security guard.

Sharba could feel her nerves jangling as she shadowed Jacob. He dodged from cover to cover and stopped every few seconds to listen for the approach of jihadis. Everywhere there were dead people who lay in untidy and undignified heaps, and the metallic smell of blood invaded her nostrils and made her think of things that she had tried to banish from her mind for ever. With an effort she pushed them away and firmly concentrated on Jacob's shiny, bald head that bobbed ahead of her.

They hadn't gone far when Jacob pushed her behind a counter and gestured to her to keep quiet as he crouched down with her. There were people approaching. Sharba felt terrified and she had to control her breathing as her heart hammered in her chest. They would be hidden from the approaching men, but their cover was scanty and although Jacob had a pistol Sharba, was only too aware it would be no match for an automatic rifle—or a grenade! She held her breath as two jihadi men, walking side by side, approached. They were eating chocolate as they laughed together and strolled past without noticing the couple crouching behind the counter. Sharba let out her breath as the men walked out of sight, but Jacob made them stay where they were until he was sure the jihadis were not coming back before they slipped out of hiding and continued dodging from cover to cover as they made their way towards freedom.

Sharba was glad to notice that they appeared to be heading for the Java Coffee Shop, because she somehow had an idea that Oliver would be there. Suddenly they heard a stifled cry and the security man deviated towards the sound. They found an African woman crumpled on the floor behind a huge freezer. She was obviously badly injured with a gunshot wound and blood was seeping out of her clothing around her midriff. She was cradling a child of about a year old in her arms and desperately trying to placate him so that he didn't make a noise.

'Come, mama, I'll help you,' whispered Jacob. He bent to help the woman up and her relief at being rescued was obvious in her face. But she grimaced as Jacob helped her to her feet and Sharba knew she must be in great pain.

'I'll carry your baby,' said Sharba smiling encouragingly at the woman, and she scooped up the child who was covered with his mother's blood but appeared to be unharmed himself, and they continued on their way to the Java Coffee Shop. The baby was silent now as he gazed with big innocent eyes at the strange face of the lady carrying him. He was oblivious to the fact that he was now smearing his mother's blood all over her blouse.

Their progress was slower now since the woman couldn't move very fast and Sharba could see by her twisted face that every step was excruciatingly painful for her. Fleetingly, she wondered if they shouldn't be giving her first aid, but Jacob obviously thought that their first priority was to get out of the mall.

❖

When the mall had come under attack, Oliver was still in Nakumatt supermarket. He heard the noise of gunfire and then suddenly he saw two gunmen appear who started picking their targets. Without consciously thinking about what he was doing, he ducked behind some shelves in an aisle and, bent double to avoid being seen above the shelves, he ran towards the exit of the shop while shots and screams echoed around him. He felt quite surprised to find he hadn't been hit as he emerged from the shop and ran towards the Java Coffee Shop where he had arranged to meet Sharba.

She wasn't there when he arrived, but there were a number of people there who had run away from the terrorists, some of them wounded. It was a chaotic scene and Oliver tried to remember where the toilets were, because that was where Sharba had been headed when he'd last seen her.

'Don't go that way,' said an Indian man, clutching at Oliver's arm and preventing him from running towards the toilets. 'Two of the fighters are up there and they're slaughtering everyone they see—it's a blood bath!' His eyes were round with horror and the hand that grasped Oliver was made strong by his terror.

'But my girlfriend's up there...' Oliver tried to shake the man's hand off his arm.

'You can't help her if you get yourself killed,' retorted the man, pulling Oliver back to the Java Coffee Shop. 'Come, I know a way out of the mall, and the best thing you can do is get out safely and then the security forces will get everyone else out when they organise a rescue plan.'

The last thing that Oliver wanted to do was leave the building while his girlfriend was still in danger. She meant absolutely everything to him, and he wasn't going to let this little Indian man persuade him to leave without her. He tried to pull away from him again, but suddenly there was a burst of rifle fire that came out of the ladies' toilets. A moment later a jihadi, flourishing a rifle, came out of the door.

'Quick!' The Indian man pulled at Oliver again, and this time self-preservation kicked in as he ran with him towards the fire escape. 'You're doing the right thing,' the Indian panted. 'If you get yourself killed, you'll be no good to your girlfriend or anyone else!'

When they got to the bottom or the fire, escape the Indian turned and grinned at Oliver. 'I think we've made it,' he said. 'Come on, let's find somewhere where we can wait for the security forces to free the rest of the hostages.'

They discovered that the Hindu community were already setting up a place in the Oshwal Centre, where families and survivors could wait for their friends and loved ones to emerge from the mall.

'I'm so sorry your girlfriend is still in the mall,' he said when they had caught their breath. 'This is a very bad business; nothing like this has happened before in Kenya. I'm Fauji, by the way.'

Oliver introduced himself and noticed for the first time that the Indian was not a young man. He was probably in his early fifties and his hair was shot through with grey. His white shirt was soaked in perspiration caused by fear and exertion, and his face still showed signs of the anxiety he was suffering. It was a friendly face and he looked kindly at Oliver.

'We can wait here together,' said Fauji. 'My cousins, Tika and Waida, are also still in the mall, but I'm sure the security forces will soon catch the jihadis and everyone will be able to get out.'

While they waited, Oliver told Fauji that he and his girlfriend had flown out to Kenya for a holiday. They had stayed in the Sankara Hotel the previous night and were due to fly to the Masai Mara later that day.

'We only popped into the Westgate Mall to get some batteries for our torch and some shaving cream,' Oliver said. 'My girlfriend went to the ladies' while I went to do the shopping—and then the attack started.'

'I'm so sorry,' said Fauji. 'Tourism is very important in this country, so when something like this happens, it's bad for everyone.'

For the rest of the day Oliver waited in hope that Sharba would emerge. He hated himself for escaping without her and his guts twisted with anguish as he tried to imagine what she might be going through. He kept on trying to ring her on her mobile but got no response.

'Something very bad must have happened to her if she isn't answering her mobile,' he told Fauji miserably.

'No, not necessarily,' said Fauji optimistically. 'She might have switched it off so that it didn't draw her to the jihad's attention by ringing.'

From time to time, hostages managed to escape from the mall and trickled out. Oliver carefully scrutinised them all, but Sharba wasn't among them. Just as it was getting dark, Fauji let out a shout of delight. He had spotted his cousins and he ran to meet them. They were looking traumatised and spoke of the carnage in the mall is hushed voices, but both appeared to be unhurt.

'Oliver, I'm going to take my cousins home,' Fauji told him. 'Why don't you come with us? You can ring the British High Commission and ask them to let you know immediately when your partner escapes.'

'But I should be here for her when she gets out,' answered Oliver anxiously.

'There's nothing you can do at the moment and this isn't a time for you to be on your own,' said Fauji kindly. 'Come home with me, have some rest and a meal, and then I'll bring you back here and stay with you.'

Oliver felt touched at Fauji's kindness, but it took a while to convince him that it would be all right if he left for a while. They first dropped the cousins off at their house and then Fauji drove to his family home in Westlands where Oliver met his wife, Daly. She was a plump little woman who had put her greying hair into a bun. Anxiety was still etched into the lines on her face even though she was very relieved that her husband and his cousins were now safely home and unharmed. When Fauji explained that Oliver's girlfriend was still in the mall, she became very concerned for him.

'You must definitely stay with us until she's found,' Daly insisted. 'We have a big house with four bedrooms, three of which are now empty since the children have grown up and left. This is a very difficult time for you, and we would like to help you in any way we can.' Her dark eyes swam with emotion because she was a compassionate woman and she hated to see the pain in Oliver's face.

The Indian couple were so kind and supportive that Oliver was persuaded to stay with them. After they had had a meal, Fauji drove him back to the hotel to collect their things and, more importantly, to check that Sharba hadn't somehow made it back there. There had been no call to his mobile from her, but that didn't mean she hadn't gone back to the hotel, Oliver mused. She could be extremely traumatised and not thinking straight.

When he got back to their hotel room, he found it exactly as they had left it that morning when they had decided to pop down to the Westgate mall to buy a couple of things in Nakumatt and have a spot of lunch. They had only booked into the hotel for one night, but Sharba had unpacked her case and hung her clothes in the wardrobe. She had put her spongebag and makeup in the bathroom and, as far as Oliver could tell, everything was as they'd left it earlier. It somehow seemed surreal that her clothes, so fundamental to his beautiful girlfriend, still hung serenely in the wardrobe as though nothing dramatic had happened that day. She must still be in the mall, Oliver thought, and his stomach twisted with the fear that something dreadful had happened to her.

After leaving instructions with reception as to where Sharba would find him should she return, Oliver packed up their things and checked out. After putting the suitcases in Fauji's car, they drove back to the Oshwal Centre in the hope that Sharba would have made it out of the mall, and to find out the latest on the rescue attempt. Unfortunately, there was no sign of Sharba when they got there and Fauji went off to try and get some clarification on the situation.

'It's not good news,' Fauji told Oliver when he got back to him. 'As far as I can gather, the attempt by the security forces to flush out the attackers and rescue the hostages is in chaos. Apparently Kenya's equivalent of a Swat team was sent in. They're trained for hostage and siege situations and they went in to try and pin down the attackers inside Nakumatt. Then the army arrived, but for some reason the authorities had not established a clear command-of-control structure, and there was no radio communications between army and police units. One of the recce group was killed by friendly fire when the army mistook him as an armed suspect and then all units were pulled out of the mall. So now chaos continues to reign while the security forces are arguing among themselves.' Fauji looked disgusted.

'So does that mean there's no-one trying to rescue the hostages?' Oliver was incredulous.

I gather there're a few people attempting to rescue them,' responded Fauji. 'Someone told me a handful of Kenyan officers, an off-duty British soldier, some security guards and an Israeli security agent have entered the mall to try and help the hostages.'

Oliver was horrified at the lack of a cohesive rescue plan by the security forces and he wanted to go back into the mall himself to see if he could find Sharba, but Fauji wouldn't let him go.

'You have no weapon,' Fauji pointed out. 'You have no experience in this sort of situation. You'd most likely become another casualty and then you'd be no good to anyone!'

Fauji and Oliver stayed at the centre for most of the night and then when back to Fauji's home for a few hours of sleep. Later that day, Oliver rang the British High Commission just in case Sharba had been in contact with them, but she had not.

Daly tried to comfort Oliver. He was tired and distressed but she did not let him give up hope. 'I've been speaking to Tika and Waida,' she said. 'They explained to me that there're people hiding all over the mall. Some of them are managing to get out, but the majority have hunkered down and will stay put until they're sure the jihadis have been rounded up. I'm sure your girlfriend will be among their number; she wouldn't want to risk getting shot making a break for it before the security forces made things safe.' She didn't add that Tika had also said there were many people who had been murdered; she didn't want Oliver to give up hope.

Oliver was grateful for her compassion and showed her a photo of Sharba that he had on his mobile phone.

'She's a very distinctive looking girl, very beautiful,' remarked Daly studying the photo. Then she had an idea. 'Why don't we get this photo printed off and then you could show it to other survivors and people working at the centre and ask them if they've seen her?' It seemed like a very good idea to Oliver and they immediately set about downloading the photo and printing it on small leaflets.

At about four in the afternoon, they went back to the mall. Things still seemed to be in chaos, but then they saw some white military men working in teams of three entering the building carrying specialist rifles and Fauji found out that they were Israeli commandos. This gave Oliver hope that people who knew what they were doing was at last helping the hostages.

They showed the photograph of Sharba to all who would look at it—charity workers, those who were waiting for news of their own loved ones, medics and the escaped hostages who were still trickling out from time to time looking very traumatised—but always there was a shake of the head. All through that night Oliver waited, hoping against hope that Sharba would come out of the mall.

In the grey light of the early morning when Oliver was at a very low ebb and feeling sure the worst had happened, two shocked women, an Asian and an African, came out arm in arm, escorted by an Israeli. He gave the women a salute when he was sure they were going to be given assistance at the centre and then disappeared back to the mall.

'Aren't you going to show the photo to them?' Fauji asked.

Oliver shook his head. 'It's no good,' he said brokenly. 'I know she's dead.'

Fauji picked up a leaflet and took it to the women. 'I'm sorry,' he said. 'But one of our friends is still missing and we wondered if perhaps you have seen her?'

The two women glanced listlessly at the picture on the leaflet. Both were traumatised and exhausted and didn't want the hassle of helping anyone else, but suddenly the African woman seemed to focus on the photo and she let out an exclamation of surprise.

'She was with us!'

The Asian woman now looked at the picture more closely. 'Yes,' she agreed. 'Her name was Sharnique and she hid with us in a cupboard for a while and then she went with a security guard who said he'd try and get her out of the mall.'

'Do you know what happened to her after that?' Oliver asked hopefully. He had rushed up when he saw that the women appeared to recognise his girlfriend.

'No,' replied the African lady. 'We told her to stay with us because it would be safer, but she wouldn't. That was hours ago— no, days ago even—and if she hasn't come out yet, I fear she hasn't made it.'

Oliver felt completely deflated, but a least he knew that she hadn't died up until the time she had been with these two ladies. It seemed unlikely, but maybe her luck had held after she had left them.

❖

It was not quite seven o'clock the next morning when the first huge blast shattered the entire Westlands district, followed by bursts of gunfire.

'What the hell's going on now?' Oliver demanded.

No one seemed to know and Oliver and Fauji, red-eyed and exhausted, waited, hoping for some explanation. Just after one o'clock there were four more large blasts and a column of black smoke rose into the sky. Rumour had it that the attackers had at last been killed—but still there was no sign of Sharba.

'I think we should go home now and get some rest,' said Fauji quietly. Oliver nodded. He had for hours doubted that Sharba would be found alive and it was only Fauji that had kept him from giving up all hope. Now he felt he must accept the fact that she was dead, but before he did that he needed to rest—to sleep—and then he would face the awful prospect of never seeing her alive again.

He and Fauji returned to collapse on their beds, completely exhausted. They slept for hours and were eventually roused by Daly who wanted them to come and look at some shaky amateur footage that was being shown on television. It was of the back of the Westgate Shopping Mall, showing a vast crater in the rear third of the building where it was said an RPG-7 anti-tank shell had been fired in an attempt to distract a sniper during an operation to rescue survivors from the mall.

Once more, Oliver and Fauji went back to the mall. They could hear explosions and gunfire going on inside and it was said the troops were mopping up and rescuing the last of the hostages. Oliver didn't dare to hope Sharba would be found alive, but still they stayed all day until ten o'clock that evening when President Kenyatta declared that the operation was over. The last spark of Oliver's hope was extinguished by the president's announcement and wordlessly he allowed Fauji drive him back to Westlands. He felt completely broken.

Oliver stayed with Fauji and Daly for another week, hoping that Sharba's body would be found in the ruins of the mall, but it was not. The British High Commission informed him that only three bodies had been recovered from the rubble caused by shells fired into that part of the mall, but others were missing and it was assumed that they had been completely obliterated by the blast. It wasn't easy for him, but Oliver had to accept that Sharba's body was one that was never going to be found. Oliver was a broken man, but he managed to pull himself together with the kind help of Fauji and Daly and he booked himself a ticket back to England. When he left, he promised that he would keep in contact with his friends. He would never forget how kind they had been to him in his time of need.

4

Bid for Freedom

When Sharba and her little group eventually reached the Java Coffee Shop, her eyes swept around the place looking for Oliver, but he wasn't there. Tables had been overturned, spilt food and blood spattered the floor and walls, and there were three bodies, none of which was Oliver's. The whole area seemed to be impregnated with a sense of evil caused by the pointless killing of innocent people and it made Sharba shudder. She was glad Jacob didn't stop there; he continued to a nearby fire-escape down which they could make their way to safety. They could still hear screams, rifle fire and explosions as they made their getaway.

The relief of getting out of the mall unscathed surged through Sharba in a wave of thankfulness. She could hardly believe that she had escaped from the attack unharmed. After the drama and tension of being inside the mall, the bright sunshine and birdsong outside seemed completely surreal. She could see onlookers gathered on the high ground overlooking the Westgate Mall and news crews had set up live points in the roadside furniture market and were already filming and sending out reports on the situation.

Jacob took them towards the Oshwal Centre where a medical station had been set up. Sharba noticed a crowd of people—relatives and friends of the hostages—standing at the Oshwal Centre, scrutinising them hopefully. All the people waiting were evidently longing to see their loved ones emerge.

As Sharba followed Jacob and the injured woman to the medical station, her eyes scanned the crowd of anxious relatives and almost at once she saw Oliver. Her heart felt as if it did a summersault in her chest. He was obviously unharmed although his face was haggard with anxiety. He seemed to be looking right at her, but, surprisingly, there was no sign of recognition in his eyes. His gaze swept over her and the other members of her group and then he looked away, seemingly resigned to the fact that she wasn't among the latest people who had made it out of the mall.

Sharba had been about to wave to him when she realised with a jolt that seemed to surge through her like electricity, that he hadn't recognised her because the scarf and glasses that she was still wearing concealed her hair and face. Also, blood stains had painted her blouse scarlet and she had a baby on her hip, all of which would have made her look like another person. She refrained from waving to him and made no move to attract his attention as she continued after Jacob who was assisting the wounded woman towards the mobile medical centre. Now Sharba's mind was in turmoil.

The woman was immediately taken into a makeshift sickbay to be attended to, so Sharba ducked inside and handed the baby to one of the attendants explaining that he was the woman's child.

'Are you all right, madam?' One of the volunteers asked Sharba as she was about to leave.

'Oh yes, thank you. This isn't my blood, I'm fine.'

She ducked out of the medical centre hoping to see Jacob so that she could thank him, but he had already disappeared. For a few moments she stood uncertain of what her next move would be. She could still see Oliver, but he wasn't looking in her direction now. Her heart seemed to once more be hammering in her chest as she tried to make a momentous decision. She glanced around at the scene—everywhere was tension and anguish. She still felt caught up in it all, but with one more glance at Oliver who was still looking worriedly towards the mall, she walked down the road to where she had spotted a taxi.

'Can you take me to the airport?' she asked the taxi driver. Her voice sounded breathless and gusty in her own ears.

'Yes, Memsahib,' said the taxi driver hesitantly. 'But don't you want to go to a hotel first to change your clothes?' He looked embarrassed.

'No, I'm due to meet my partner at the airport and he'll have my clothes with him. I'll get changed there,' she responded. Her voice had steadied now.

On the way to the airport Sharba took off the sunglasses and dragged the scarf from her head. She opened the window and let the fresh air blow onto her face, because the horror of what she had been through and the enormity of what she was about to do combined to make her feel queasy and nauseous.

When they arrived at the airport, Sharba got some startled looks because of the state of her blouse, but she ignored everyone and made her way with all haste to the ladies' room so that she could make herself more presentable. She was glad to see the ladies' room was empty when she got there and she quickly washed the dried blood off her hands and arms and then removed her stained blouse and stuffed it in the bin. The blood had seeped through the material and stained her bra, but she couldn't do anything about that. She scrabbled in her handbag and brought out a T-shirt that she kept there for emergencies and put it on. There were also blood stains on her black slacks, but they didn't show too much. Sharba pulled handfuls of paper towels out of the dispenser and, dampening them with water, she sponged her slacks down as best she could. At last, when she had decided she couldn't get them any cleaner, she looked at herself in the mirror.

She could see the strain of the last few hours in her face. It was pale and there were lines around her shadowed eyes, while her hair looked wild and tangled. She retrieved her makeup bag and started working on her face and hair. The familiar act of redoing her face seemed to calm her nerves and eventually she felt that she looked almost normal despite the butterflies that continued to flutter uncomfortably in her stomach. 'Am I going to do this?' She put the question to her reflection in the mirror. 'Yes,' she answered herself firmly. 'This is my chance. I'm no longer Sharnique Wellby; from this day forward I'll revert to my true name, Sharba Lengi, and I'll *never ever, ever,* tell *anyone* of my past. That's what I'll do because it's the only way I'll be able to evade Oliver for ever.'

She pushed her British passport with her name Sharnique Wellby on the front into a little-used compartment of her bag and retrieved her Zambian passport. This one was in the name of Sharba Lengi. She was so glad that she had never mentioned her life in Zambia to Oliver, and that she had never let on that she had two passports. She also blessed her adoptive father for the trust fund he had set up for her, of which Oliver was unaware. Sharba then strode out of the ladies' looking poised and calm and went to find out when the next flight left for Lusaka, Zambia.

Sharba was disappointed to find that there were no flights going to Zambia for two days. She was desperate to get away from Nairobi because she figured that when her body was not found among the dead in the mall, Oliver would realise she was alive and had given him the slip. She had no doubt at all that he would hunt for her, so she needed to get as far away from Nairobi as possible before he did, because he would be furious and unrelenting in his search.

Feeling panicky, she looked at one of the monitors that gave information on flights departing from Nairobi during the next few hours and decided that her best bet was to go to Mombasa if she could get on the flight, because it was leaving within two hours. She was relieved to find the flight she chose was not full and she was able to buy a last-minute ticket.

'Do you have any luggage?' she was asked.

'No, just my handbag,' Sharba responded. She was soon checked in and waited with the other passengers that were about to board the same flight. She kept to herself and none of the people there took any notice of her.

During the short flight to Mombasa, Sharba thought about Oliver again. She wondered if he was still waiting for her to come out of the mall. Then her thoughts went back to the time when she and Oliver had arrived back in England after their Australian holiday.

5

England

After Sharba's holiday in Australia had ended, she had been glad that Oliver couldn't get a seat on the flight she was booked on from Perth to Heathrow. She had enjoyed his company immensely during much of her holiday; Oliver had been great company to start with and they'd had terrific fun, but things had subtly changed as the days went by.

She was aware that he was growing too attached to her and that was not something she wanted. She tried to keep things light and friendly as she really liked Oliver because he was such good fun to be with, but, for her, any sentimental attachment was out of the question. She sensed that Oliver was becoming unhealthily obsessed with her, and she had learned at a very early age how badly wrong an obsessional attachment could go and was determined that she would never fall into that trap. For that reason, she had purposefully not shared her family history with Oliver and neither had she asked him about his. He had told her he was an architect who worked from home, but other than that she knew little about him or his family. Now that her holiday was coming to an end, she felt it a good time to draw a line under their relationship. They had had great fun together but now was the time to part company with no regrets.

Oliver had other ideas, but he was aware that Sharba withdrew from him as soon as he tried to get close to her. It was incredibly frustrating because he felt he had made almost no progress in making the beautiful lady fall in love with him, yet he was determined not to give up on her. He was used to getting his own way and this challenge was not going to beat him!

'You're a secretive little witch, aren't you?' Oliver said to Sharba as they sat on the beach the day before she was due to leave. 'You've told me hardly anything about yourself, your life in England, or your family.'

'You're calling me a witch?'

'Well, you've certainly bewitched me! You do know that don't you?'

'Oliver, I've enjoyed every minute I've been with you on this holiday, but all good things come to an end. Come on, let's go and have a drink and then do something. Time's short and I don't want to waste any of it.' Sharba jumped up.

It infuriated Oliver that she always seemed to slide away when he wanted to bring her up close to him, but it was typical of her to want always to be doing something because she never wanted to waste a moment that could be used for fun and enjoyment.

That night they made love for the last time and it seemed so meaningful to Oliver. He was convinced that Sharba must love him even if she didn't realise it. But the next morning she was unwilling to talk about their relationship as she organised her packing.

'I just need to think about what I'm doing so that I don't forget anything,' she said to Oliver quite curtly when he tried to broach the subject of the future.

With a sinking feeling, Oliver realised that when they parted, the beautiful girl with whom he had fallen in love would consider it *adieu*, while he was hoping it would be *au revoir*. It made him feel wretched but, at the same time, angry. Already Sharba was emotionally distancing herself from him and he was struggling to connect with her again before it was too late.

'This can't be goodbye forever, my sweet girl,' said Oliver when they got to the airport. His eyes were swimming with emotion. 'Let's meet up when we're both back in England.'

'Oliver, my flight's being called!' Her voice cut his words off. 'I really must go.' They had already had a prolonged hug and kiss and she found his sudden neediness unwelcome and definitely unwanted.

'I'll ring you as soon as I get back to England,' Oliver shouted after her as she walked away. But even as the words left his mouth, he realised she hadn't given him a UK mobile number on which he could call her. She had been using an inexpensive Australian mobile phone while on holiday and he wouldn't be able to contact her on that once she had left the country.

He watched her lithe figure disappear in the crowd and wished she'd turn back to wave to him, or even blow him a kiss, but she just walked straight ahead with the other passengers on her flight. He felt bereft, but as he turned to walk back to the carpark, he straightened his back—there was no way he was going to give up on her. Although she hadn't told him where she was going to stay or left him a phone number to ring, she had let slip the name of the surgery in which she worked, so he would only have to look up the number to get into contact with her once he had arrived back in England.

❖

Ten days after Oliver had seen Sharba off on her flight from Perth he arrived at the reception of the doctor's surgery where she had said she worked as a receptionist, since he had decided to come in person rather than ring. His eyes swept over the two women working behind the desk, but neither of them was Sharba.

'Can I help you?' a busty blonde with a kind smile asked him.

'I was actually looking for Sharnique Wellby,' said Oliver. 'I thought she worked here.'

'Oh my goodness!' exclaimed the girl. 'I recognise you from the photos Sharnique showed me. You're the guy with which she holidayed!'

Oliver grinned at her. 'Yes, that's right. Unfortunately, I had my mobile phone stolen and I lost her number, but I remembered she said she worked here.'

'Well, yes she did,' said the blonde. 'She was expecting to get her job back when she returned from Aus, but, well...politics in the office ...' she glanced uneasily at her colleague behind the reception desk, an older woman with greying hair who was sorting out some forms. 'Anyway, as things turned out there was no job for her when she came back.'

'Oh, I'm sorry to hear that,' said Oliver. 'Could you tell me where she's living?'

'I'm afraid I don't know,' she replied. Then she added as an afterthought: 'But I could give you her mobile number.'

The blonde girl got out her mobile phone and scrolled through her list of contacts. 'Here we are; actually, it's against the rules to give out another person's phone number, but I'm sure she won't mind because I could see in the photos that you two were close.' She read out the number and Oliver entered it in his mobile phone.

'Thanks,' he said, feeling very pleased.

When Oliver had left the surgery, he went to buy himself a coffee and then dialled Sharba's number. The voice that answered him came out in a croak and he wasn't sure if it was her.

'Sharnique – is that you?' he asked.

'Oliver?'

'Yes, I got your number from the blonde that works at the surgery where you used to work, but you don't sound well.'

'I'm not at all well,' admitted Sharba. She sounded miserable.

'What's the problem?'

'I developed a cold on the flight home, then I started coughing and my throat was sore and now I think I've got a chest infection.'

'You poor baby. Look, where are you? I'll come round and cheer you up.'

There was a short pause and then she said, 'I'm staying at Central Backpackers; it's on Park End Street, not far from the station.'

'Okay, I'll see you in about ten minutes then.'

When Oliver rang off, Sharba wondered if it was wise to let him come to her. She had wanted to end their relationship, but now she felt so low and longed to see a friendly face. She had arrived in England feeling unwell and a bit depressed and things had just gone from bad to worse. The friends with whom she had hoped to stay were away on holiday in Thailand, her job had not been left open for her as promised, and she had very little money. She had booked into backpacker's accommodation hoping to find another job quickly, but her health had deteriorated and she hadn't felt well enough to face a job interview.

When Oliver turned up, she couldn't deny that she felt pleased to see his smiling face, but his expression turned to concern when he looked at her.

'You look really sick, love,' he said. 'Have you seen a doctor?'

'No. I was going to try and get an appointment, but I just couldn't get enthusiastic about going to the surgery that let me down so badly—that's where I'm registered—and I didn't have the energy to find another surgery.'

Sharba started coughing and just couldn't stop. Oliver got her a glass of water and eventually she managed to get her paroxysm of coughing under control and lay back grey-faced and exhausted.

'Come on, I'm taking you to the hospital,' said Oliver worriedly.

Sharba was reluctant to go with him, but she was really too sick to argue much and he soon had her bundled into his car. When they got to the John Radcliffe Hospital, he went straight to the Accident and Emergency Department, and as soon as she had been seen by a doctor she was admitted. The doctor on duty spoke in serious tones as he informed her that her chest infection had developed into pneumonia and she needed to be put onto intravenous antibiotics.

Oliver came to visit her every day while she was in hospital. He made sure she had everything she needed, from toiletries to a large cluster of grapes. When she started to recover a little, and other friends came in to visit her, they all said how lucky she was to have Oliver caring for her. Sharba knew they were right; Oliver had been so kind and considerate she felt almost overwhelmed.

'What happened to my stuff that I left at the hostel?' she asked Oliver when she was feeling better.

'I explained to the manager what had happened so he had all your things packed up and I took them home for safe keeping,' Oliver reassured her. 'So there's nothing to worry your sweet head about, babe.'

Oliver didn't mention that he had gone through her stuff to see if he could find out any more about her life. It had been a futile exercise anyway, because there was nothing but clothes and the usual things a woman would have when travelling. Her passport wasn't among her things and he had to assume it was in her large handbag that she insisted on taking everywhere.

'Most of my stuff is in storage with another friend,' mused Sharba. 'I suppose I'll eventually get everything together again when I find somewhere to live.'

However, when the hospital was willing to discharge Sharba, but only if there was someone at home to take care of her, Oliver insisted that she come and stay with him.

'It makes sense, doesn't it?' he said. 'You need to convalesce, and I can keep an eye on you and make sure you don't try and do too much too soon.'

'Are you sure, Oliver? I mean you've done so much already...'

'Of course I'm sure, you silly sausage, it'll be a pleasure,' Oliver bent and kissed her on the nose.

Oliver was delighted at how things had panned out in his favour on his return to England. While Sharba had been feeling at such a low ebb, he had been able to manoeuvre himself into her life and make her dependent on him, which is exactly what he wanted. Now all he had to do was to work to make her more and more reliant on him until he had completely taken over her life. It would be at that stage when he would be able to mould her into the loving wife that he had envisioned for so long.

❖

Sharba was amazed to find that Oliver had a big house in Woodstock, an affluent area situated about eight miles north of Oxford. The picturesque house was standing in a large and beautifully manicured garden which positively shouted 'expensive' to her!

'Is this really your house?' Sharba asked Oliver doubtfully as they parked in front of it.

'Sure is! Are you impressed?'

'Yes—but surprised as well. Why were you holidaying in Australia on a shoestring when really you must be quite ... well, rich?'

'It was more fun like that,' said Oliver. 'Now, let's get you inside and settled.'

Over the next few days, Sharba lived in luxury with Oliver on hand every hour of the day or night to see to her every need. She felt very weak and tired and enjoyed being fussed over. It had been years since anyone had cosseted her in such a caring way. But as she recovered from her illness, she grew restless and didn't want to be indulged anymore.

'Today I'm going to cook you breakfast,' she told Oliver one morning.

'Are you sure you feel up to it?' Oliver looked worried.

'Of course I am. You've been so good to me and I want to at least make myself a little bit useful.'

After that, Sharba started doing more and more in the house and garden; she wanted somehow to thank Oliver for all he'd done for her and felt it was the least she could do for him. But eventually her thoughts turned to getting a job and becoming more independent.

'You shouldn't be thinking about getting another job yet,' said Oliver. 'You should take more time to repair your health first. You've been really sick, don't forget, and you don't want to have a relapse.'

But Sharba was adamant that she was well enough to get a job. Secretly she was worried about Oliver's obvious attachment to her as well. She was more than grateful for what he'd done for her, but she wasn't in love with the man and didn't plan on spending the rest of her life with him. She proceeded to annoy Oliver by starting to check online for available jobs for receptionists.

'There's quite a good job advertised for this hotel,' she told Oliver one morning.

'But that's in Oxford,' he objected.

'So? If I got the job I could easily find somewhere to live in Oxford.'

'But you have somewhere to live here,' said Oliver, sounding hurt.

'I know, but I can't go on depending on your good will; I need to become more self-reliant and stand on my own feet again.'

'It's not just good will I feel towards you, babe; you must know that. I love having you living with me and I hate the thought of you moving out so you can work in some ill-paid job in Oxford. I earn plenty for the two of us; you don't actually need a job at all.'

'I do, Oliver, for my own self-esteem. I'm not a natural scrounger, I've always had to pay my own way in this world, and it feels wrong to live off you like a bloodsucking tick when there's nothing wrong with me.'

'Don't try and throw back in my face what I've done for you,' said Oliver sounding hurt.

'Oh Oliver, I'm not! That's not what I mean at all. You've been the best and kindest person that I've come across for years and I never want you to think I haven't appreciated all that you've done for me. I just need to do something useful and fulfilling.'

'So what you've done for me in and around the house is not fulfilling?' Now Oliver sounded offended.

Sharba didn't know how to explain to Oliver what she was feeling without upsetting him. She would be eternally grateful to him for all he'd done for her and she didn't want to hurt him in any way, but she wished he would understand how she felt.

'Please don't be angry with me,' she said forlornly.

'I'm not angry with you,' protested Oliver. 'The fact is I love you, babe; you mean everything to me—surely you can understand that?'

Sharba realised with a sinking feeling that what Oliver said was true, but she definitely didn't reciprocate those feelings. She knew he was waiting for her to say that she loved him, too, but she couldn't. Instead, she came and put her arms around him and said, 'You're the kindest and sweetest man on earth and I'm so lucky to have met you.' Her words seemed to defuse the situation and they enjoyed the rest of the day together.

However, the problem didn't go away. Sharba wanted to get a job, and she wanted to have a life of her own and a measure of independence, but Oliver seemed to want to own her, body and soul, and Sharba began to find it oppressive. During the following days, they argued a lot. Sharba didn't want to hurt Oliver after he had been so good to her but didn't feel things could go on as they were.

Oliver still went to Mass from time to time and Sharba always felt, when he returned from a service, he was slightly aloof and almost seemed to resent her.

'Why're you like this after you've been to Mass?' Sharba asked him rather irritably one Sunday.

'Like what?' Oliver asked.

'You seem remote and I feel you almost resent the fact that I'm here.'

'Of course I don't resent you being here! But when I go to Mass,

I'm aware of greater beings than you and I. You couldn't possibly understand because religion means nothing to you, but I know that everything I do is monitored and judged. I love and revere the higher being that helps me mould my life; I couldn't do without his help. When I come back from Mass, I still feel his presence and I hold him in my heart with awe and reverence ...' Oliver stopped as he saw the amazed disbelief on Sharba's face. 'How can I explain it to you who are completely godless?' he added condescendingly.

It irritated Sharba to be called completely godless. As a child she had attended Sunday school and then, when she was older, she had joined the adults in their service. She felt she had got a good grounding in Christianity and just because she didn't choose to practise her religion by going to church now, she didn't think she was godless. Oliver's condescending 'holier than thou' attitude annoyed her, especially as she thought he was a bit of a hypocrite.

'Do you go to confession then and admit to this greater being that you admire so much, that you're in a relationship with a woman who is not your wife, and that on the Sundays that you go to Mass you all but ravage her during your trysts of sex?' Sharba asked him tartly.

Oliver's face turned red with anger. 'How dare you?' he snapped.

'Well, it's true, isn't it? You're committing the sin of adultery being with me!'

'You're not married to another man, so therefore it's not a sin,' said Oliver primly. 'The one thing I would never do is have sex with a married woman because that really is a sin and it would infuriate the deity so that my very life would be in jeopardy.'

Sharba opened her mouth to contradict him because she knew that what he said wasn't correct, but he cut in before she said anything.

'Anyway, it says in the Bible that love covers over a multitude of sins—and you know how much I love you!'

Sharba shut her mouth and decided to say nothing. It was obvious that Oliver had a distorted version of Christianity in his head, but she didn't feel the inclination to help him understand the true version. He wouldn't even listen to her if she tried, she decided. She also knew that he wasn't lying when he said he loved her and, although she didn't reciprocate his feelings, she didn't want to row with him or upset him in any way. She knew she had to get away from him but had to find a gentle way to do so, because he had been incredibly kind to her.

It was a couple of days later that Oliver gave her an insight into his strange beliefs. He had been attempting to probe into her past but Sharba was still unforthcoming, so Oliver decided that he would tell her a little about himself in the hope that she would reciprocate.

'You've never expressed any interest in my past, babe, but I'm going to tell you a little about my background so that you can understand why I'm obligated to the church and feel that a higher being takes an interest in my life,' Oliver said as they sat together on the sofa having a cup of tea.

'My mother was a passionate woman by the name of Olivia Naughton and she fell in love with a young priest called Father Hughes who, of course, couldn't possibly reciprocate her feelings. But the problem was, he did. They had a secret affair, and the result was she fell pregnant.'

'You're the son of a Catholic priest, then?' Sharba was surprised.

'Yes, I'm the bastard son of a Catholic priest, but there was no happy ending for my mother and Father Hughes. He was so ashamed of breaking his vows he committed suicide; it was an act that enraged my mother because she thought he was weak and if he had had any guts, he would have left the church and stood by her. She was so angry she said her priest had no part of me, she even gave me a name similar to her own to endorse that I was hers alone.

'Although she told me who had fathered me when I was old enough to understand and also explained the events that happened afterwards, she made it clear that we must never speak about the subject again. I was her child alone, as far as she was concerned; the weak Father had no part of me.'

Oliver took Sharba's hands in his own and looked into her eyes before he continued.

'But she was wrong. My father has been watching over me all my life; he's been guiding me and helping me become successful. He helps me to get everything I set my heart on; I'm so indebted to him! I feel his presence when I go to Mass, and he understands how I feel about you, my sweet.'

Sharba saw the fanatical light in Oliver's eyes as he spoke about his father and an involuntary shudder ran down her back. This revelation was way past being weird and she wondered briefly if her boyfriend wasn't psychologically damaged in some way. What he was saying sounded creepy and unnatural to her. More than ever, she wanted to get away from this man.

But getting away from Oliver wasn't that easy because, despite his apparent idiosyncrasies, Sharba felt obliged to remember how kind he had been to her, so she needed a way to disentangle herself without causing him too much hurt.

In the end she got a job as a surgery receptionist in Woodstock, so that she could continue living with Oliver until an opportunity arose whereby she could leave him without causing too much hurt. It seemed a good compromise for the time being and Sharba hoped that she would be able to let Oliver down gently in the following days.

It was just after she had started working at the surgery that she received a letter unexpectedly to say that she was to receive money that had been in a trust fund set up for her by her late parents. Sharba quietly blessed her father because the money had come at an opportune time. Until she had got the job at the surgery, she had been financially dependent on Oliver and she hated that, especially as it seemed to give him a hold over her. Now she had a considerable nest egg and could break free at any time. She purposely didn't mention her windfall to Oliver because she was aware that he liked to feel financially superior to her, and instinctively she knew he wouldn't like her having money of her own.

However, as time went past Sharba couldn't figure out a way to leave Oliver without causing a great upset, and their relationship wasn't getting any easier. The days of their Australian trip when they had laughed their way around the country without a care in the world were long gone. Oliver became evermore possessive and suspicious of her every move. He tried to impose his will on her, even to the point of trying to make her change the way she dressed. But each time they had a row and things had settled a little, he would back down, put his arms around her and declare that he loved her so much and couldn't bear the thought of her not being with him.

Sharba felt deeply troubled. She believed Oliver when he said he couldn't do without her and really didn't want to hurt him, but at the same time she felt oppressed by his neediness and knew she was going to have to do something to change her life. But the opportunity to leave Oliver amicably just didn't present itself and Sharba began to feel completely swamped by the cloying attention she received from him every day.

It happened one day that Oliver was driving past the surgery when Sharba had just emerged and was about to walk home. He saw a young man stop her, so he pulled up to watch them covertly. The young man was blond and had an open face and smiling blue eyes. Oliver couldn't hear the conversation that ensued, but if he had been able to, he would have heard the young man ask Sharba if there was any chance of seeing a doctor that evening, and he would have heard her reply that there wasn't.

Then the young man went on to explain he had come out in a rash and was wondering if it was dangerous. He lifted his shirt up so that Sharba could see the eruption of red spots on his chest and he asked her if she thought it was the Bubonic plague. Sharba had laughed and, looking closely at the spots, said that she didn't think it was, that it looked more like a heat rash to her, but that he should go to the hospital to have it checked out if he was really worried.

Oliver couldn't hear a word that was said. He just saw them talking and laughing together and then he saw his girlfriend looking closely at the young man's chest. The scene infuriated him, and he immediately thought they must be having an affair. He drove off before Sharba could see him, but all the way home he was burning with anger.

Sharba, meanwhile, walked into town and did some shopping. She was delayed for a while when she met a friend in the shop and they stopped to chat for ten minutes. When she eventually got home, she found Oliver looking like a thunder cloud and he immediately accused her of having an affair.

Sharba was amazed at his fury. 'Who am I supposed to be

having an affair with?' She was incredulous.

'As if you don't know who! Your boyfriend that you were talking to when you came out of the surgery this afternoon, that's who! I saw you with my own eyes!'

Sharba frowned as she tried to figure out what he was talking about, then she remembered the lad with the rash who had accosted her when she was leaving work.

'Surely you're not talking about the young man who asked me, as I left work, if there was any chance of him seeing a doctor? He had a rash on his body and thought it might be something serious.'

'You were flirting with him! Don't make up some rubbish story that he wanted to see a doctor—I know what I saw!'

'You're talking absolute nonsense, Oliver. I wasn't flirting with that man. I never flirt with men, but I do try and reassure patients when I have to!'

Oliver wasn't having any of it. He ranted and raved, and eventually Sharba had had enough.

'Look, I don't know what's got into you lately, but things are not the same as they were before. I've never flirted with another man or cheated on you, but you seem to have become more and more suspicious of me for some unknown reason. Well, to be honest, I'm not happy anymore. I think the time has come to end our relationship, Oliver.'

Sharba was completely unprepared for Oliver's reaction to her blunt words. She thought he would back down as usual and declare that it was because he loved her so much that he sometimes overreacted. She was already composing in her head some gentle but uncompromising words to let him know that this really was the end of their relationship, so she was amazed when his face suddenly twisted into a mask of fury.

'No,' he screamed in her face and grabbed her around the neck. 'You're my woman and I'll never let you go! Never! If you try and leave, I won't let you! I'll hunt you down and I'll never let another man lay a finger on you!'

His hands were like steel as they locked around her throat and Sharba frantically tried to prise them away because she was being throttled. His face was very close to hers and as he intensified his grip, Sharba could see a feverish expression in his glittering eyes that were twitching and manic. His breath hissed between his gritted teeth and even in her panic she remembered the exact same scenario being played out on another occasion—although at that time the malice had not been directed at her but at her mother.

'You're hurting me,' she managed to croak, while bright lights seemed to dance in front of her eyes before darkness started to close in around her.

6

Childhood in Zambia

Sharba's mother, Eve Lengi, had been the most important person in Sharba's life when she was a child and she had loved her mum with all her heart. Eve was a handsome woman who had the same oriental eyes as Sharba, but her skin was much darker and her hair was quite frizzy. They lived together in a little house that stood next to the big house in which her mother worked as a maid. It was situated just outside Lusaka in Zambia.

Sharba was completely happy because at that time her life seemed perfect. She didn't have a father, but that didn't matter because her mother was all she needed. Eve was a larger-than-life character who was always jolly and never let life get her down. She adored her little daughter and only missed having a husband because she had a sensual dimension to her personality that needed physical expression—and this was easily rectified as she was an attractive woman and finding a man to satisfy her needs wasn't difficult.

Sharba learned that there were times when she couldn't be with her mother. She had to stay in their little house when Eve went off to work in the big house each morning, as the big house was strictly out of bounds at all times for Sharba. At other times, she had to play in the garden when her mother was visited by an 'uncle'. But Sharba knew that her mother loved her more than anything else in the world, so these men were no threat to her.

Dick and Honor lived in the big house. They had two children, Tom and Sally, who were a few years older than Sharba, but most of the time the children were far away in England attending a boarding school. Dick was a veterinary surgeon who had to travel for miles to all the surrounding farms to treat their sick animals. He was a big, strong man with a ready smile, and he always wore a red cloth hat to prevent his balding head from getting sunburned. Sharba loved him because he always had a kind word to say to her and often he gave her a chocolate bar when he had gone into Lusaka. It was a luxury Eve couldn't afford to give her daughter, so it was greatly appreciated and Sharba always shared the chocolate with her mother.

Honor was a tall, thin woman with a rather severe face who liked her house to be immaculate at all times. She didn't have a job, but spent much of her time attending charity meetings and organising fund raisers and the like, so she relied on Eve to keep her house spotless. Eve did a sterling job and even the pernickety Honor couldn't find fault with a thing. Sharba didn't like Honor as much as she liked Dick because Honor didn't seem so friendly, but she knew she was kind because she gave Eve all Sally's outgrown clothes for Sharba, and also many of her children's unwanted toys.

Eve explained to Sharba that Dick and Honor were very good people. 'Every Sunday they go to church,' she told her daughter. 'They care for the people in Zambia and pray for them. They even donate money for some of the poor folk. We're very lucky to be working for such good people because they are always fair and considerate.'

Sharba nodded her head. She believed what Eve had told her, but the only person she really needed was her mother; nothing else really mattered.

Eve was never expected to work at the weekend and this was when she occasionally had male friends to visit her. They were all 'uncles' as far as Sharba was concerned, and when they were with Eve, Sharba felt slightly resentful, because she was told to go and play outside—when it was time, she thought, that she could have been enjoying with her mother.

'I have lots of different uncles,' Sharba remarked to Eve one day. 'But I don't have a father. Why is that?'

'You're old enough now to understand a bit about men,' her mother replied. 'Most of them can't be trusted; they just want one thing and then they leave. They don't want any responsibilities, so you have to learn how to use them to your own advantage.'

'I don't understand,' said Sharba.

'Well, take your grandmother, my mummy, for example. Back in the days when Zambia was the land of plenty but Tanzania had very little, she would travel by bus to Tanzania every couple of weeks with a box full of stuff to sell in that country. It was quite a lucrative business and she made a nice profit, even after taking the bus fare into consideration. Well, on one of her trips she met a Chinese man. He was working on the road there and he liked her very much. She would meet him every time she went to Tanzania, but when one day she told him that she was expecting his baby, things changed. The next time she went to Tanzania he wasn't there. He'd gone back to China because he didn't want the responsibility of a family! I was that man's baby.'

'So your daddy was a Chinese man?'

'That's right; that's why we both have funny eyes and look a bit different from most Africans.'

'So was my daddy a Chinese man as well?'

'No, he was a white man—a European—so that's why your skin is so pale. But he had the same morals and principles as the Chinese man. When he found out I was expecting his baby, he quickly married a white woman and refused to admit that I had been his girlfriend. After that I decided that I'd only have a man on my own terms.'

Eve gazed lovingly at her daughter. 'Although I was upset at the time,' she continued, 'things worked out very well. I had you, my lovely daughter, and I wouldn't change that for anything because you're the best and most precious gift I could ever have been given. You're so beautiful and clever,' Eve ran her fingers through Sharba's soft ringlets. 'You're of mixed-race, but you've inherited the best from each of the races in you and that's why you're so lovely. In a few years, every man on earth will want you, but you must be very careful and not let any of them get too close to you until you're absolutely sure that he deserves to be with you.'

For a long while, Sharba had been very happy with her lot but then Isaac had come into their lives. He seemed different from all the other uncles and Eve told Sharba that he was from the Ngoni tribe and came from Malawi. There was no doubt that he was bigger and definitely more handsome than any of the others had been, but Sharba didn't like him because he didn't just come and then disappear like most of the uncles. He always seemed to be on the periphery of their lives and her mother never saw another man while he was around. Sharba noticed that his dark eyes seemed to glow with passion when he looked at Eve, but when they fell on Sharba they became mean and resentful, and she knew he didn't like the place of affection she had in her mother's heart. Instinctively, she knew that Isaac wanted Eve all for himself and she worried she was going to lose her mother.

'I think Isaac wants you all for himself,' Sharba informed her mother one day. 'He doesn't want you to love me; he thinks all your love should be for him.'

'I don't love Isaac at all,' her mother responded with a short laugh. 'You don't have anything to worry about my darling sweetie; all my love is only for you.' But she looked worried when she said the words. Sharba wondered why.

During the next few weeks, Sharba was aware that her mother was trying to tell Isaac that she didn't want to see him anymore, but he wasn't having any of it. He seemed obsessed with Eve and came around more and more often, his glowing eyes following Eve wherever she went. It seemed to the little girl that Isaac had transformed himself into an octopus and his big strong tentacle arms held her mother in a powerful grip. Often, she could hear them arguing in hushed voices and she no longer saw him as handsome. Now she perceived him as very black, evil and arrogant—and she hated him!

When Sharba heard raised voices coming from her mother's bedroom one day, she tiptoed to the door to listen to what was going on, because she feared for her mother. Never before had they had such a loud argument, but now she could hear things were getting very heated and Isaac's voice rumbled like thunder, while Eve's voice was high and shook with angry passion. When Sharba put her ear to the crack of the door she could hear them clearly.

'No!' Isaac's voice roared. 'I don't accept what you're saying! You're my woman now; no-one else is going to have you!'

'I'm not your woman,' screamed Eve. 'I never was, and I never will be! Just go, Isaac!'

'I'm not going anywhere! You belong to me now.'

'If you don't leave, I'll go to Bwana Dick and tell him that you're harassing me. I'll tell him I don't want you here and he'll make you leave because this is his property.'

'Don't you dare threaten me, woman!'

Sharba heard the crack of his hand as he slapped Eve's face and she pressed her eye to the keyhole to see what was happening. Isaac had her mother pinned to the bed but now Eve started to fight him, screaming obscenities at him as she did. Sharba watched in horror as her mother and Isaac brawled on the bed. Isaac was so much stronger than Eve, but she scratched at his eyes and kicked and bit him while he landed heavy blows on her head and body.

'Get out,' Eve shrieked. 'Get out of my house, get out of my life; I never want to see you again!'

Isaac roared like a lion. 'If I can't have you, no-one else will have you either!'

Sharba pushed the door open but hesitated in fear before she ran to help her mother. She could see Isaac's face clearly now, and it was contorted into an ugly mask of hatred. His hot eyes seemed to stand out in a manic way and his lips were drawn back, revealing his clenched teeth. Then, to her horror, a knife appeared in his hand and, before she could get to them, he had plunged it into her mother's neck. Eve's screeches died in a gurgle as bright red blood gushed out from the knife wound.

Sharba screamed the loudest scream she had ever made, but Isaac just pulled his knife out of Eve, wiped it quickly on the bedclothes and then left, barging past Sharba as he ran through the door, knocking her to the ground. Sharba jumped up and ran to her mother who was already dead. The blood still welled from the knife wound and saturated the bed. It ran over the side and formed in a pool at her feet while Sharba tried to revive her mother.

The metallic stench of blood was strong in her nose as she came to the realisation that her mother was dead. Bursts of white-hot lights seemed to explode behind Sharba's eyes and she screamed again. She jumped up and ran out of the house and across the garden. She didn't think twice about entering the big house where she was forbidden to go, and she leaped up the steps and raced inside following the sound of voices that came from within. Honor and Dick were entertaining lunchtime guests and four pairs of eyes swivelled towards the little girl when she burst in.

'He killed my mother,' she screamed. 'He killed my mother.' On and on she shouted the same words and was hardly aware of what happened next. She wasn't conscious of the arms that encircled her and held her gently, nor did she see the two men run out to the little house. She just kept on screaming the words until she collapsed, sobbing in Honor's arms.

Sharba was so traumatised that she was never able to remember the days after her mother's murder. She was aware only that Dick and Honor were looking after her and that they were kind and compassionate. Her mother's funeral remained a blur; all she could remember of it was clinging on to Dick's hand for dear life while the entire, depressing process dragged on.

It was as though her whole life had caved in. All the time she had horrific flashbacks and saw Isaac's manic face before he stabbed her mother—and then the blood. The police never found Isaac and it was concluded that he had fled to Malawi, but Sharba was scared that he would come back and murder her as well. Honor took her to the doctor and he gave her some pills that made her feel sleepy and not so scared, but the shock of what she'd witnessed was so severe, Honor wondered if she would ever get over it.

'She has no other relatives,' Honor told Dick. 'Eve told me it was always just her and Sharba, so what're we going to do with the poor little thing?'

'I've been thinking about that as well,' answered Dick thoughtfully. 'I don't know what you'll think about this, my dear, but I was considering the idea of adoption. My contract in Zambia will be coming to an end in a few months and then we're going to go home to England. We can't leave the poor little girl to fend for herself here, and we can only take her back to England permanently if we adopt her.'

Honor was silent for a few moments. As a Christian, she knew it would be the right thing to do, but she baulked at the thought of having another child to bring up. Her own two were growing up fast and she had been looking forward to the time when she and Dick could enjoy a quiet retirement together. But at last, she nodded her head, albeit a bit reluctantly.

'Yes, it would be the right thing to do.'

A few months after the tragedy, the Wellbys adopted Sharba before leaving Zambia and returning to England.

Arriving in England was a turning point for Sharba. Getting away from the place where the horrific events had taken place and learning about new pastures injected fresh life into her. Everything that had happened in the past was left behind in Zambia and now she embraced her new life that led to the future. She even had a new name.

'Sharba, my dear, we're going to change your name to Sharnique,' Honor told her shortly after they arrived in England.

'Why?'

'Well, Sharba isn't really a name, and Sharnique is so pretty, isn't it? It suites you.'

Sharba thought about it for a few moments and then nodded her head. She did like the name Sharnique. 'So now I'm Sharnique Lengi?'

'No, you're Sharnique Wellby, because we've adopted you, so now you have the same name as us.'

It seemed somewhat strange to have a new name and Sharba wondered if it was a bit disloyal to Eve to change the name she had picked out for her daughter, but she soon got used to it. 'I'll always be Sharba Lengi when I think of you,' she promised her mother faithfully.

Dick and Honor had a house in Dorset. It was in a beautiful country setting, so different from what Sharba was used to. Dick fell into the role of father to the little girl very easily. He had always been fond of her and he admired the way she had managed to pick herself up after such a horrendous event in her life and continue with determined vigour to adjust to such a different lifestyle.

Honor, on the other, hand struggled in her role as a parent to Sharba. She didn't dislike the little girl, but, unlike her husband, she found she couldn't love her. She did her best to be motherly but knew that she was failing because there was a subtle restraint between her and Sharba which made it awkward for both of them. Sharba was well aware that there was a problem. She instinctively knew that Honor wanted to be a good mother to her but was failing, and she didn't blame her at all. After all, she knew in her own heart that Honor could never take the place of her own mother no matter how much she tried, so she didn't resent her at all. But it did make things awkward at home.

When her adoptive parents suggested that she go to boarding school, she jumped at the idea. She would be living among girls of her own age which sounded fun, and Dick promised that he would come and visit her often. She did feel a bit apprehensive on the first day she arrived at the school, but she soon settled in and loved every minute of it. She became popular with the teachers and pupils alike because of her bubbly personality and her determination to achieve. Dick kept his promise and popped in to see her when he could. He would always bring her chocolate, reminding her of when he gave her chocolate bars in Zambia, and sometimes he took her to the cinema or for little picnics in the countryside if the weather was good.

'What would you like to do for the holidays?' Dick asked her towards the end of her first term. He noticed her face fall at the mention of the holidays and knew she was thinking about the awkwardness between her and his wife. 'You don't have to spend the entire time at home; there are alternatives,' he told her. 'There's Summer Club where you can go away with other kids and camp somewhere, or there's Activity Club where you choose an activity—say dancing for example—and spend most of the holidays learning the activity.'

This sounded far more fun to Sharba than being at home with Honor. Being a lively, energetic child, she relished the idea of having an active holiday, so every school holiday Dick would organise excursions for her and she learned a number of different skills and disciplines, while becoming a very independent and self-reliant young lady. She did go home for short periods, of course, and as she grew older she found it easier to get on with Honor. She loved Dick deeply; he was the father she had never had, and she appreciated every opportunity he had made possible for her. When she had finished her education, she knew that he had given her the very best start in life and turned the tragic event of her mother's death into something positive.

It was when she was working in her first job that Sharba heard that Dick and Honor had been killed in a motor accident on the M40 near London, and the news of their deaths devastated her. Dick had been her mainstay since the day of her own mother's death and Honor had also been kind to her, but now they were both gone. Sharba was completely devastated. She felt she was all alone in the world because she had had very little to do with Tom and Sally, and never really thought of them as a brother and sister. They were both married now and had families of their own.

At their funeral she sobbed and sobbed in a way very uncharacteristic of the British people, but she couldn't help it. Their deaths had also brought back the memory of her own mother's horrific death and she once again replayed in her mind the awful last moments before Eve died. She could see the blood as the knife struck Eve, and the memory of the malevolent evil expression on Isaac's face was etched into her memory. Now Dick and Honor were gone, she felt vulnerable again. It took all her resolve to accept that, although tragedy had struck twice in her life, she must be strong and go on. It was what Eve would have wanted, and Dick had given her the education to be successful in her life without having to rely on others.

7

The Kenyan Coast

As Sharba hovered on the brink of unconsciousness when Oliver attacked her, she saw the same expression on his face that she had seen on Isaac's face all those years ago. She was convinced he was going to kill her. But her terrified croak that he was hurting her seemed to suddenly snap Oliver out of the passion of fury that had gripped him, and he immediately released his hands from around her neck.

'Oh my darling, I'm so sorry, I didn't mean to hurt you.' Oliver was suddenly remorseful, and his expression changed to one of regret and concern. 'It's just that I love you so much and I can't bear to hear you saying you want to end our relationship.'

'It's okay, I'm not going anywhere,' said Sharba shakily. Her terrifying ordeal had left her trembling like a jelly and she felt she had to reassure Oliver, because otherwise it was very possible that he would kill her like Isaac had killed her mother. She had seen the same expression reflected in his face and she was convinced that he had Isaac's inherent evil within him that could erupt at any time into violence or even murder. She didn't want to end up like Eve, so she knew she would have to play a very clever game if she was to get away from this man unscathed.

'I know things have been a bit rough lately,' said Oliver. 'I'm sorry; it was all my fault, but you mean the world to me—you know that, don't you?' His tone was conciliatory and he seemed to be doing his best to reassure Sharba, but it took all her willpower not to draw away from him. 'Look, why don't we go away on holiday again?' Oliver continued. 'Things were so good for us in Australia, weren't they? Let's plan a trip somewhere and capture the magic in our relationship again. How about going to Africa? You said you wanted to travel, and we could start off by going there.'

Sharba didn't want to go away anywhere with Oliver and she knew that there would be no more magic in their relationship, but she felt she had to play along with him for the time being and wait for a chance when she could escape the tentacles that seemed to be gripping her ever more securely in his life. The thought of going travelling with him again horrified her.

'What about my job?' Sharba was desperately trying to think of reasons not to travel anywhere with Oliver. 'I haven't worked there long and I'm not due any leave yet.'

'Well, hand in your notice!' Oliver said cheerfully. 'I've got enough money for the both of us, babe, so you never have to work again if you don't want to.'

Sharba felt the palms of her hands growing moist with sweat. She didn't need to be with Oliver; she didn't want to be with Oliver; but she felt trapped. She didn't want to end up like Eve and she was convinced Oliver was more than capable of ending her life if he thought he wasn't going to get his way. It was a horrible situation in which to be.

Oliver was completely unaware of Sharba's turmoil. Since she hadn't pulled away from him, he thought his angry words and actions had just brought her to her senses and she was now ready to comply with his wishes. Taking his smartphone from his pocket, he immediately went on the Internet and started planning their holiday with great enthusiasm. They would fly to Nairobi in Kenya, spend a night there and then fly to the Masai Mara for a week in the game park. Then they would fly to Mombasa for a two-week beach holiday before travelling on to South Africa.

Oliver rang the surgery himself to tell them that Sharba had resigned from her job and wouldn't be coming back, then he told her to get packing because they were leaving in two days' time. It was all organised so quickly and Sharba was desperate to get away from Oliver before they left, but she knew that he would never accept her departure. He would hunt her down angrily and if she didn't agree to be his woman, she was sure that he would kill her.

Sharba then speculated if she would have a better chance of

escaping from Oliver in Africa. She had only been a child when she left Zambia, but she was pretty sure that the infrastructure of that country would not be as developed as it was in Britain when it came to tracking down a missing person. If the rest of Africa was like Zambia, then surely making a break from Oliver in Kenya or South Africa would make more sense than doing so in England. She had the advantage of money in the bank of which Oliver knew nothing—and she also had kept renewing her Zambian passport, another matter of which her boyfriend was unaware. So Sharba decided that she would pretend to go along with Oliver's plans and then try and make a break for it if the opportunity arose.

❖

When the chance to get away from Oliver had unexpectedly presented itself during the time of the attack on the mall, Sharba had acted on impulse. She had been traumatised by witnessing the shocking deaths of so many people and had made her choice instinctively without giving it any conscious thought. Now as she sat in the aeroplane heading for the coast, she felt herself start to shake. The tension of the past few hours and then the momentous decision to give Oliver the slip all seemed to be catching up with her.

Had she made the right decision to leave Oliver and fly to Mombasa? Was Mombasa the right destination? Wouldn't it be the very first place Oliver would look for her as soon as he realised she wasn't among the dead, since they had booked a holiday at Nyali Beach, a little distance north of Mombasa? Maybe she had been in too much of a hurry to leave Nairobi. She had wanted to put as much distance between herself and Oliver as quickly as possible, but maybe it had been the wrong decision. Doubts and worries assailed her, and she knew she had to stop her thoughts running riot or she wouldn't be able to pull off her escape.

With an effort she steadied herself by taking slow deep breaths. When she felt more in control, she decided that she would move on from Mombasa and make her way to Zambia as quickly as she possibly could. She had never told Oliver about her life in Zambia; as far as he was concerned she had always lived in England, so he wouldn't think of looking for her there if he thought she had got out of the mall alive. Meanwhile, she would try and stay at a hotel on the south coast of Mombasa, because Oliver had booked them into Nyali Beach Hotel on the north coast so if he followed her to the coastal area, it was there he would be most likely to go.

Sharba was roused from her thoughts as the flight attendant's crackly voice announced that they would shortly be landing at Moi International Airport. She could see the sea as they descended, and there were little houses among the palm trees that grew in profusion on the sandy terrain below. When they had touched down and taxied to the airport buildings, the doors of the aeroplane were opened and a blast of moist, overheated air blew in.

Sharba followed the other passengers out, but when they went to the carousel to collect their luggage, she made for the front entrance where there were taxi drivers touting for business. As she walked out, she felt her nerves settling. Somehow she felt at home here; it wasn't unlike Zambia, and the doubts that had squirmed in her stomach earlier now disappeared.

'Taxi, Memsahib?' The man who asked was a small African with a pleasant, open face.

'Could you take me to a hotel on the south coast?' Sharba asked him.

'Yes, of course; which hotel Memsahib?'

'I haven't booked into one yet, but it's got to be on the south coast.'

'There are many good ones there.'

'Could you recommend one?'

'You could try Papillon Reef hotel; it's very good. If it's full there are many others to try.'

'Okay, let's go and try that one,' replied Sharba decisively.

'Where is your luggage, Memsahib?'

'I don't have any, just my handbag.'

The taxi driver thought it very strange that this young woman, travelling alone, had no luggage and didn't even know in which hotel she wanted to stay, but so long as she could provide the taxi fare, he decided it wasn't any of his business and he was happy to drive her to the Papillon.

It was already getting dark as they left the airport, but they found the city of Mombasa still very busy, with many people thronging the dusty pavements walking leisurely along as the the hot, humid evening air surrounded them. Sharba was amazed at the shambolic way the heavy traffic lurched about on the roads. She was very glad she wasn't driving as it looked to her as if only the bravest motorists would actually reach their destination! It took a while to get across the island of Mombasa because of the congestion and Sharba could feel the perspiration on her face and body even as she sat relaxing in the taxi. It brought back memories of Lusaka as she remembered how hot and steamy the weather had felt there in November, just before the rainy season broke.

Eventually they arrived at Kilindini harbour where they took a short five-minute ferry trip to the mainland, landing at Likoni. People, bicycles, dogs, goats, chickens and handcarts had to be avoided as they drove through Likoni on the road towards Diani, but at last the congestion thinned and the taxi driver was able to drive at a faster pace. A breeze blew in through the open window, bringing with it the fragrance of the coast while cooling Sharba's sweaty face as she looked upwards into the starry night sky. She felt more at peace now; she was definitely on the first stage of her trip home to Zambia and it was a nice feeling. Eventually they arrived at Diani and the taxi driver drew up at the barrier outside the Papillon.

'You'll have to walk in from here,' he told Sharba. 'Find out if you can stay and then come back and pay me if there is a room for you. Otherwise, we can go to another hotel.'

Sharba had her two passports in her handbag, a British one in the name of Sharnique Wellby and a Zambian one in the name of Sharba Lengi. Since she had decided to use her Zambian passport, she presented it to the receptionist as identification as he booked her into the hotel. The British passport would remain out of sight in a little-used compartment in her handbag because she didn't want to leave a paper trail for Oliver to follow. She was very glad that she had never told him about her past.

Sharba was pleased to find that the Papillon was a lovely hotel and that they did have space for her. When the question of her luggage arose, she had thought of an answer that she hoped wouldn't arouse any suspicion.

'My luggage was missing when I flew into Nairobi,' she told them. 'Hopefully it'll catch up with me at some stage! Do you have a shop where I can buy some essentials?'

'We do have a shop where you can buy toiletries and souvenirs, but we have very few clothes,' she was told by the receptionist.

'Well, I'll have a look when I've paid off the taxi,' Sharba decided.

When Sharba returned to the hotel after paying the taxi driver, she went straight to the shop because she was told that it would be shutting up for the night very soon. She was able to buy some toiletries, but as the receptionist had said, there wasn't a big choice when it came to clothes. There were some bikinis, so Sharba bought two, thinking they would do in lieu of underwear for the time being. She also managed to get a short beach dress, two kikoys and two tee-shirts, one of which had a lion on it and the other a giraffe under a thorn tree. They were what she would call 'tourist clothes', but for now they had to do.

When guided to her room, Sharba found it was on ground level and had an expanse of lawn and rustling palm trees in front of it. A little further on, the white beach glittered in the moonlight which also sparkled on the little waves that splashed along the shoreline. It was magical and Sharba found herself looking forward to her short stay.

Dinner was being served, so Sharba went to have a quick shower before she proceeded to the dining area. She tore off her sweaty, bloodstained clothes and stepped under the cascading drops of the shower. The tepid water felt divine as it trickled over her overheated body. After washing herself and her hair thoroughly, she stood for what felt like ages under the streaming water before washing herself all over again. Symbolically she was trying to wash away all that she had witnessed that day, as well as the ties that she had felt fastened her to Oliver. She needed to have a clean, fresh break from her past.

Eventually she emerged and wrapped a towel around herself, placing her stained clothes in the basin to soak overnight. After that, she put on one of the bikinis in lieu of underwear, wound a kikoy around herself like a skirt, and put on the tee-shirt on which the picture of the giraffe was embroidered. She brushed out her hair that was drying quickly in the overheated atmosphere and put on a touch of makeup.

Feeling like a new woman, Sharba made her way to the dining area. It was an open space under the stars and there was a half wall around the area. She sat near the wall and during her meal she was delighted when a little bushbaby dropped on to the wall and started feasting on the insects that were attracted to the light that shone nearby. She remembered bushbabies from her childhood years in Zambia, although those ones had been much larger.

Sharba noticed some curious stares from the other diners but she ignored them all. She knew they were probably wondering why she was alone, but hoped that they would forget her quickly. She was exhausted and retired to her room as soon as she had finished her meal. The traumatic events at the mall, along with the momentous decision to take the chance to give Oliver the slip, had completely drained her. She dropped into bed feeling that she could sleep for a week.

But then she found sleep was evasive and when she did drop off, the scenes from the mall impregnated her dreams. She saw again the terrified faces, the blood, the evil men who laughed while they killed people. Her mother's face appeared among the victims, distorted with fear and horror, and Sharba moaned in distress as she slept. Her own voice woke her up and she found she was shivering with horror.

Eventually she managed to sleep again, but this time it was Oliver who appeared in her dreams. He was outraged that she had tried to evade him and was determined to kill her. He had Isaac's knife in his hand, and as he plunged it into her chest, she woke again drenched in sweat. Sharba sat up and looked out of the window. She was glad to see it was getting light as she didn't want to risk going to sleep again and having more nightmares.

She got up and had another shower and then washed her blood-stained clothes and hung them over the bath. After that, she made herself a cup of tea and went to sit on the veranda of her room. Sitting there watching the dawn breaking on such a beautiful setting gave her a sense of peace, and as she sipped her tea, she was determined that this would be a good day. She would put the past behind her, do positive things, and start to plan for her future.

8

From the East African Coast to Zambia

On the morning after Sharba's arrival at the Papillon hotel, she was very anxious to find out what had happened at the Westgate Mall after she had left, and hoped that the shop would sell newspapers so that she could catch up on the situation. As she walked up to the dining area for breakfast, she saw a group of people standing around a television inside the main hotel building. She went to see what was attracting them, hoping it was the news and that there would be an update on the Westgate situation. She wasn't disappointed; she recognised the mall in front of which the TV presenter was standing giving her report. What amazed Sharba was the fact that the situation had not been resolved and the terrorists and a number of hostages were still in the building.

'You would've thought that the security forces would've stormed the building and flushed out the jihadis by now,' said one of the men watching the report. 'How is it possible that a handful of men can kill so many people and hold others hostage—and the security forces seemingly do nothing to stop them?' He sounded outraged. Then he turned to Sharba and said, 'Can you imagine what it must be like for those poor people who are hiding from the bastards and wondering why the security forces don't act?'

Sharba didn't have to imagine because she had been there and knew what it was like, but she didn't want anyone to know that, so she just pulled a face and shook her head. She watched as the television camera panned to the right and caught the hostages' friends and relatives waiting anxiously. For a moment, she thought she spotted Oliver, but couldn't be absolutely sure. However, she was fairly sure he would be there until the drama was resolved, hoping for her to emerge, so at least the security force's inefficiency gave her a bit more time before Oliver realised she wasn't dead and had, in fact, given him the slip.

After breakfast, Sharba asked if it would be possible to use one of the hotel's computers and was taken to a cubicle where there was one for public use. She was able to book herself a bus ticket from Diani to Dar-es-Salaam and an onward flight to Lusaka for the next day. She glanced longingly out at the beach, wishing she could linger in this beautiful place for a while longer, but her head told her that she must put as much distance between herself and Oliver as quickly as possible. She had already reverted to her original name—Sharba Lengi—and she would be using her Zambian passport from now on, so if anyone checked, it would appear that Sharnique Wellby had not left Kenya.

'Would it be possible for you to call me a taxi?' Sharba asked the clerk at reception. 'I want to go to the shops in Diani.'

'Of course, madam, we have several trusted taxi drivers we use to drive our clientele around, so I can easily get one of them for you.'

Sharba was soon picked up and she asked the taxi driver to take her to a clothes shop.

'Have you just arrived?' asked the taxi driver who had told her his name was Sam.

'Yes, I arrived yesterday,' Sharba replied.

'So you are here for a nice, long, relaxing holiday?'

'Not really, I'm meeting a friend in Tanzania tomorrow, but maybe I'll come back because it's so lovely here.' Sharba had already decided that she would tell no-one of her intention of going to Zambia.

Sam took Sharba to a large shop that sold clothes along with many mementos that a tourist might wish to buy, from animal carvings to shells. The assortment of clothes was very much what tourists would buy to remind them of their holiday—most of them were advertising Kenya or Mombasa, but at least Sharba was able to get a few dresses, some shorts and tee-shirts, a pair of sandals, a hat and a long gown that would be suitable for evening wear.

'You like our clothes very much!' said the saleswoman, who was delighted to be selling so much at once.

'Yes, they're lovely. My luggage was lost on the flight over to Kenya, so I need to buy something to wear.'

'Oh, I'm sorry; that was a bad thing to happen. But now you have beautiful Kenyan clothes to wear! Would you like to buy a bag to put them in? We have some lovely canvas bags with a picture of the sea and a palm tree on them.'

'Oh yes, that would be a good idea.'

When she left the shop, she went back to Sam who was waiting in his taxi in the scanty shade of a tree that grew on the edge of the carpark.

'Did you get everything you wanted?' Sam asked.

'Yes, thanks. Now, could you take me back to the hotel?'

Sharba's bus left the following evening, so she spent the rest of the day and most of the next enjoying the beach and sea. It was so perfect there. The long white beach that stretched for miles was dazzling under the sun and felt like castor sugar between Sharba's toes as she walked along it. The sea was the most amazing aquamarine where it was shallow and darkened to a deep indigo blue as it got deeper. Far out, she could see a line of white breakers where the coral reef followed parallel to the beach.

Sharba wandered a little way into the sea to cool off and lay floating on her back looking into the cloudless blue sky. 'This is utter perfection,' she murmured to herself as she bobbed up and down on the slight undulations. 'The whole scene is completely flawless; it's unbelievable!'

When at last she decided that she had bobbed for long enough, she waded out of the water and was making her way back to her room when she was approached by an African man who asked her if she would be interested in doing some scuba diving.

'That's my boat,' he told her pointing to a little white boat bobbing on the water. 'I'm going to take a party of people out in about half an hour, so if you would like it, you could come too.'

Sharba had learned to scuba dive in Egypt on one of her school holidays and now she jumped at the opportunity to brush up on her skills, as well as to enjoy the beautiful marine life that was on offer. She spent a magical afternoon under the waves in the crystal-clear water and only got slightly sunburned. That evening, two of the other guests who had also been scuba diving invited her to join them since she was all alone, so she had an enjoyable evening hearing about the safari on which they had been before coming to the coast.

It was only when she got back to her room and tried to settle for the night that doubts and fears again tormented her. As far as she could gather, the drama at the Westgate Shopping Mall continued, but she knew that as soon as Oliver realised she was not among the dead he would do his best to track her down. She slept fitfully and Oliver invaded her dreams again. Always he had Isaac's knife in his hand, and he was murderously angry.

'Why? Why are you doing this to me?' Sharba cried out to Oliver as he leaned forward to stab her in the neck.

'I told you before,' Oliver said, his lips drawn back in a snarl. 'If I can't have you, no-one else will have you, either!'

He lunged at her and she tried to jump out of his reach and struggled madly in an endeavour to get away from him. But he seemed to be holding her somehow and the more she struggled the more securely he held her. She expected to feel the cold metal of the knife stabbing into her and she screamed out in panic. Her scream woke her up and she found she was entangled in the mosquito net that she must have inadvertently pulled down while she was having the nightmare.

Sharba sat huddled on the bed amid a tangle of sheets and net. Her teeth were chattering, and she couldn't stop shivering even though it was hot in the room. 'It was only a dream,' she told herself, but it made it no less horrifying. Again, she watched the dawn breaking and was up and walking down the beach to fill in time before breakfast.

It was lovely on the beach. The tide had swept and washed it, so it looked newly created and it gleamed in the sunshine. The tide was out, there was no wind, and everything was beautifully calm. Sharba felt herself becoming at one with nature as the terrors of the night slipped away. She decided that after breakfast she would go to the water-sports centre and hire a windsurfer. The tide would turn soon and there would be a breeze with the incoming tide. It would be a nice way to end her short break in this beautiful place.

After an enjoyable morning skimming over the little waves, Sharba had a bite to eat and then returned to her room to pack. She had managed to ascertain that still the drama went on at the mall, so she was confident that Oliver wouldn't be looking for her yet. Her bus left that evening and she was glad she didn't have to spend another night being terrified by nightmares about Oliver. But as she waited for the bus, she felt disappointed that she couldn't stay a little longer. It was a wonderful place for a holiday and there were plenty of activities in which she would have loved to participate. Her nightmares aside, she had really enjoyed her short stay and she decided that when she was sure Oliver was no longer looking for her, she would come back for another longer holiday.

Sam took her to the bus station in his taxi and he shook her hand before she climbed on the bus. 'Come back again and see us soon,' he invited.

'I will,' Sharba promised. 'I wish I could stay longer now, but I'll definitely come back.'

Although the sun had set, the inside of the bus was oppressively hot. Sharba thought it must have been standing in the sun all day, and although the passengers were all trying to open the windows as wide as possible, it didn't seem to make much difference to the temperature. Sharba found her seat, which was by the window, but she had to climb over a very large African woman who was already ensconced in the seat next to her one.

'May I squeeze past, please?' Sharba asked politely.

The African woman tried to pull in her legs and feet, but found she couldn't because her huge belly was in the way. With a sign, she mumbled something and struggled to her feet and moved into the aisle so that Sharba could slip in.

'Thank you; sorry I had to disturb you,' murmured Sharba. The African woman gave another huge sigh, settled down and closed her eyes without saying anything to her. During her movement, the large woman's sweet and sickly perfume had wafted in waves up Sharba's nostrils and left her feeling slightly queasy. As soon as she was settled in her seat, Sharba opened her window and tried to breathe in the warm outdoor air rather than the woman's perfume, but she could still smell it as the woman wriggled about trying to get comfortable. She was so large, she seemed to overflow her seat onto Sharba's and it made her feel squashed in and rather claustrophobic.

As the bus got underway, the passengers were asked to close their windows as the air conditioning would be coming on. Everyone duly complied and waited hopefully for the cold rush of air, but instead of getting cooler the interior only heated up and everyone started sweating more than ever. Sharba thought she was going to suffocate as the smell of the woman's cheap perfume intensified and mingled with the smell of everyone's perspiration, making her gag with every breath. At last, she could bear it no longer and forced her window open again. Soon everyone else did the same; it was clear that the air conditioning was not going to work, and the night air circulating in the bus seemed fresh after the fug that had hung there before. But having the windows open also allowed the dust to filter in and Sharba could feel it settling on her. It felt gritty as it stuck to her moist, sweaty skin.

The large African lady beside her seemed to be very tired and had no trouble sleeping sitting in her upright seat, but her head kept lolling on to Sharba's shoulder, while bubbling noises came out of her mouth and nose. It was most unpleasant and Sharba sighed as she thought of the many uncomfortable hours ahead as they travelled south in the bus.

They had to stop at Lunga Lunga to go through customs and immigration control before entering Tanzania, so Sharba was glad to get out and stretch her legs. But butterflies fluttered in her stomach as she presented her Zambian passport with the name Sharba Lengi emblazoned across the front. What if they noticed there was no entry stamp in the passport and queried it, Sharba wondered uneasily.

When she got to the front of the queue, she saw the man at the desk looked dishevelled and sleepy. She wasn't sure if he was at the end of a long night stint, or at the beginning of an early morning shift. He yawned widely as she approached, showing her all his teeth, and held out his hand for her passport. Without even glancing through it he opened it randomly at a blank page and stamped it; then he handed it back.

'Thank you,' murmured Sharba feeling very relived.

Once they boarded the bus again, Sharba found that the large lady had acquired some samosas for her breakfast which she consumed noisily as they drove along. She could smell the garlic in them and the woman kept wiping her greasy hands on her scarf and burping. It made Sharba feel sick again and she turned away and looked at the drab scenery out of the open window.

At last they arrived on the outskirts of Dar-es-Salaam. Her bus journey was almost over and Sharba couldn't wait to get off and away from the smells and discomfort of the last few hours. With a sigh of relief, she disembarked when at last they reached their destination. She immediatly went in search of a taxi to take her to the airport.

Unlike the bus, the taxi's air-conditioning was working perfectly so Sharba sank into the clean and comfortable back seat with pleasure. It was pure bliss to feel cool and not have a multitude of disgusting smells assailing her nostrils!

'You're not staying to go on safari in our beautiful parks?' The taxi driver seemed disappointed that she was going straight to the airport.

'Not this time, I'm afraid,' Sharba said. 'Maybe I'll come back another time, but I need to move on right now.'

'All over Africa the wildlife is good,' said the taxi driver. 'But I think our parks and animals are better! You must definitely come back and go on safari here!'

They reached the airport with plenty of time to spare before her flight departed and Sharba headed to the ladies' room to freshen up. She sighed when she saw her reflection in the mirror. 'I look just as tired and dishevelled as the immigration officer,' she thought. 'And much dirtier, too!'

When she emerged a while later, she looked much tidier. She had washed as best she could, applied deodorant, changed her tee-shirt, and fixed her hair and makeup. She really longed for a hot shower, but for now she would just have to do. Since she had not eaten since the previous day at lunch time, she was hungry and headed to a shop that sold food along with other things. She purchased a packet of biscuits and a can of Coke and then saw they sold newspapers, so she added one to her shopping. She saw one of the articles was about the attack in Nairobi, so as soon as she had sat down, she opened the paper and read with surprise that an anti-tank shell had been fired into the building in an endeavour to overcome the jihadis, and hostages had also been killed in the blast. The article mentioned that some of them were completely obliterated so that their bodies would never be found.

Sharba sat deep in thought as she munched a biscuit and sipped her Coke. Would Oliver assume she was one of those who had been obliterated when her body wasn't found? It would be the obvious thing to assume since she hadn't apparently emerged from the mall. If he did think that, she was at last free and her heart leapt at the thought. But then she remembered how suspicious Oliver was of her and realised that he may not be completely convinced that she was dead and there was a good chance he would continue looking for her. 'I just need to be very vigilant,' she thought. 'If he thinks I'm still alive he'll presume I've gone back to England. He doesn't know about my old name and my connections with Zambia. If I'm careful and never mention to another soul that I was Sharnique Wellby for a period of my life, I'll be just fine.' She made a solemn promise to herself that she would tell absolutely no-one that she had had another name for part of her life, no matter what.

❖

'You look tired, dear,' said the Asian lady who was seated next to her on the flight to Lusaka.

'I am rather,' responded Sharba. 'I travelled from the coast in Kenya to Dar last night by bus and didn't get a wink of sleep!'

'Are you going to Zambia to visit the game-parks?'

'No, not really, although I'd love to do that; I'm actually going home! I was born in Zambia but I left there to live in England when I was ten years old.'

'How lovely that you're going back! Do you plan to stay in Zambia permanently?'

'I'd like to, but I don't have any friends or relatives there anymore, so the first thing I need to do is find a job.'

'Maybe you could get work with one of the safari companies,' suggested the lady. Sharba nodded her head. 'But then there's

Huber Enterprises as well,' the lady continued after thinking for a few seconds. 'You could try them.'

'Huber Enterprises?'

'Yes, Arlo Huber of Huber Enterprises is a German who's lived in Zambia for years. When he first came out from Germany, he opened a cheese factory and it was very successful. Since then, he's expanded into all sorts of other enterprises—from German sausage making to hotels—so he may be able to give you a job. His head office is situated in Lusaka.'

Sharba wrote down the name Huber Enterprises after thanking the woman for that useful bit of information.

As they disembarked from their aeroplane at Lusaka International Airport, Sharba had a real feeling of homecoming. The dry heat, the dusty atmosphere with half-forgotten odours of wood smoke and frangipani blossom, combined with a hundred other African fragrances, wafted up her nose and impinged on her senses so that she was suddenly transported back to her childhood. She almost expected to see Eve's smiling face among those who were meeting their loved ones off the flight. It was an emotional experience and Sharba had to blink the tears off her lashes.

'Are you all right, dear?' The Asian lady had seen the tears in Sharba's eyes.

'Yes, it's just a bit overwhelming coming home after all these years.'

The Asian lady put her arm around Sharba's shoulders and gave her a squeeze, showing that she understood. Then she said, 'How're you going to get to your hotel in Lusaka? My husband will be here to meet me, so we could give you a lift there, if you like.'

After being dropped off at the Intercontinental Hotel in Lusaka by the kind Asian couple, Sharba was glad to find that she could easily book a room there. The first thing she did was head into the shower to wash off the sweat and grime of her journey, then, feeling refreshed, she lay on the bed meaning to rest only for a little while. She was surprised to wake up some hours later and realise she had been sleeping for a long time. This was the first time since she had been a hostage in the mall that she had slept peacefully, with neither the faces of the dead she had seen nor Oliver's face contorted with jealousy disturbing her with nightmares.

'I feel safe here,' Sharba thought to herself. 'If Oliver doubts that I'm dead, he'll never think to look for me in Zambia. I shall always be Sharba Lengi from now on. Sharnique Wellby no longer exists. I'll build a new life for myself here where I belong.' Then she turned over and slept peacefully again until morning.

9

Unexpected News

When Oliver arrived back in England after leaving Kenya, he felt sad, flat and empty. For months, his whole ambition had been to make Sharba his woman—body and soul—and he had been completely sure he could achieve this. Now she was apparently dead, and he felt bereft and lacked motivation to do anything.

All his life he had got what he wanted. Sometimes he had achieved his goals by devious means, but the end always justified the means as far as he was concerned. He had refused to be beaten by anything, but death was something else altogether; he couldn't compete with death as it was so final. He felt that it was unfair that life had thrown something at him that he could not control or manipulate to his advantage. It made him angry.

There was no doubt that he had loved Sharba; she had meant everything to him and he knew he would never have relinquished her. He would have done whatever it took to make her his woman for eternity and that would have required her to love and trust him unconditionally. He had envisioned a future where she totally depended on him and looked to him to decide her every move in life. He'd had an obsession to own her completely, and anything less would have been unthinkable.

In despair, Oliver made his way to the Roman Catholic church where he felt he could commune with his father whom he had never known on this earth. Crouched down on one of the pews in the attitude of prayer, he didn't pray to God but spoke brokenly to the weak Father Hughes.

'I would do anything to re-wind to the day that we decided to go to the shop in Westgate,' he sobbed. 'My darling Sharnique was just coming around to accepting my love for her and I was going to build on that during our holiday. I loved her ... I loved her so much, but that one decision to go shopping has wiped my lovely Sharnique away for ever; I feel so wretched and I don't think I'll ever be happy again.'

For a long time, Oliver pleaded with his father to make things better. And eventually when he left, he had a strange feeling that Father Hughes had heard him with compassion and maybe, just maybe, he would be able to help his son in some way that was only possible to one who was connected to deity.

❖

Just over a month after Oliver had got back from Kenya, he received an unexpected telephone call from Daly who was calling him from Nairobi.

'How're you doing, dear?' Daly asked Oliver kindly.

'Oh well, you know, getting there slowly,' replied Oliver. 'I'm still missing Sharnique like hell, but I guess it's early days. How're you and Fauji and the rest of the family?'

'We're all fine, thank you. Now listen Oliver, Fauji and I have been debating for the last couple of days whether we should ring you and tell you this bit of information. We didn't want to get your hopes up just for them to be dashed again, but one of our relatives swears that he saw Sharnique after the Westgate debacle.'

'But that would be impossible,' objected Oliver. 'I checked again and again with the police and the British High Commission in Nairobi and she was never found.'

'I know; that's why we held off ringing you to start with. But hear me out, Oliver. One of my sister's children was holidaying at the coast at the time of the attack. Sai was staying in a hotel at Diani called the Papillon Hotel, and on the second morning of the attack when a number of hotel guests were watching the news unfold on the television, he claims he saw Sharnique watching.'

'But how would he even know it was Sharnique?' Oliver demanded.

'He didn't at the time. But when he came to visit us about a week ago, the Westgate attack came up as a topic of conversation and we told him about you and how you'd lost your partner in the raid. Fauji still had one of those pictures we had printed out to show other survivors who may have had news of her; he showed it to Sai so he could see what a beautiful girl Sharnique was, and Sai is completely certain he saw her at the Papillon Hotel. Both Fauji and I told him he must be mistaken because it couldn't be possible, but he pointed out that she's a very beautiful and unique looking girl, and it would be very unlikely that she would have a double.'

'But Daly, how could that even be possible? If Sharnique had been able to get out of the mall, she would have tried to find me. If I hadn't been there at the time, she would have made enquiries and soon found out that I was staying with you. She would have spoken to the police and the High Commission; her name would appear in the records compiled of the survivors who escaped from the attack. I know her name isn't on that list. I've checked and rechecked. And why would she suddenly turn up in a hotel down at the coast? None of it makes any sense.'

'I know it doesn't; that's why Fauji and I hesitated to tell you what Sai said. But in the end, we decided you should at least be told and then it would be up to you what you did. I'm really sorry if we've inadvertently given you more grief, but please know that we're here for you and if there's anything we can do to help, just let us know.'

'Thanks Daly; you did the right thing to tell me. I need to think about what you've said and then I'll get back to you.'

After Oliver put the phone down, he found his head was spinning. Surely Sharnique couldn't still be alive, he thought. It would have been impossible for her to escape from the mall and then suddenly turn up at the coast. She would have been seen by the authorities who were helping the escaped hostages and they would have logged her name as one of the survivors. Then she would have been reunited with him. Sai must have seen a girl who looked similar to Sharnique and that was all there was to it.

But during the course of the day little niggles kept creeping into his mind. After their argument when he had lost control of his temper and frightened Sharnique, she had seemed to come to her senses and realise there was a future for their relationship.

He had thought that their little tiff had cleared the air because, afterwards, she had been far more compliant than during the previous few weeks. She appeared to readily agree that they should go for a holiday to Africa and she had put no objections in their way other than the concern about her job. But was she really as willing as she had appeared? Oliver wondered.

He thought back to the day they had arrived in Kenya. She had seemed to be happy enough as far as he could remember. On the morning before the attack on Westgate, he recalled that she had been quite excited about going on safari in the game park, but what if it had all been a front? What if she had been scheming to get away from him all the time? He knew she could be very secretive, so maybe she had planned it all out.

But that would be impossible, he decided, shaking his head. She wouldn't have known the mall was going to be attacked, or that it would afford her a chance to get away from him. It was a ludicrous idea. He tried to put the doubts out of his mind.

Oliver got on with his work, but uncertainties still danced in his mind and squirmed in his stomach and he found it hard to concentrate on what he was doing. What if she had wanted to get away from him and had suddenly seen her chance, Oliver suddenly wondered. It had been chaotic during the attack on the mall and, although there were a number or organisations trying to help the victims as they came out, there was no cohesive organised assistance that ensured every person who walked away from the mall was documented. It was possible that she could have slipped away unnoticed.

If that had happened and she had decided to give him the slip and go to the coast, it may well have been Sharnique that Sai had seen. But, on second thoughts, that didn't add up either. As far as Oliver knew, she didn't have much money, so she wouldn't have had the means to pay for a flight to the coast and a hotel once she arrived there. Her only option would have been to fly back to England and try and hide from him here. His face took on a wolfish look when he thought of that. If she was in England, there was no place she could hide where he wouldn't discover her. It would just be a matter of hunting her down and repossessing her.

Oliver looked up the Papillon Hotel on the Internet and

discovered it wasn't a cheap hotel in which to stay, so that rather proved that his girlfriend couldn't have stayed there. She had been completely dependent on him financially until she had secured a job, and she hadn't long worked at the surgery before they left for Kenya, so she couldn't have had much money in her bank account. She really didn't have the means to try and give him the slip and go it alone, he thought with some satisfaction. But then Oliver had another thought. She was a beautiful girl, so maybe she had managed to attract another man and persuaded him to pay for her flight and hotel for certain favours. The thought alone made his blood boil and his obsession for owning Sharba seared his mind and made his stomach churn uncomfortably.

If Oliver had steadied himself and allowed his brain to slow down and figure out things in a calm and composed way, he would have remembered that it would be impossible for Sharba to do something like that; it just wasn't in her character. But now the thought was in Oliver's head, it wouldn't leave. It tortured him. He imagined her naked body in the arms of another man as she laughed with him about how she'd given Oliver the slip. It was an excruciating thought, but then he suddenly wondered if this sighting of his girlfriend had not arisen by the powers of his dead father. Maybe Father Hughes was giving his son another chance to be with woman he loved.

All these thoughts swirled around in Oliver's head, and by the end of the day he knew that he would have to go back to Kenya to see if he could find out if there was any truth in his girlfriend still being alive. But first he needed to make some enquiries here at home. Being well connected, he was soon able to find out that no-one by the name of Sharnique Wellby had returned to Britain. She was on the 'missing, believed killed' list of British subjects who had apparently died in the Westgate attack. Having that knowledge afforded him the certainty that she had not been able to sneak back into the country without letting him know.

❖

'Fauji, I've decided to come back to Kenya to see it there's any truth in Sharnique's being still alive.' Oliver was talking to Fauji on the telephone. 'I really don't think there is, but there might be a possibility that she escaped from the mall and, in a traumatised state, somehow made her way to the coast. We were due to go there after going on safari, so I suppose there's a chance that she, in a very disturbed state of mind, went there anyway, expecting me to do the same.' Oliver didn't want Fauji or Daly to know what he was really thinking.

'I think you're making the right decision because it'll put your mind at rest one way or the other,' answered Fauji kindly. 'Why don't you come and stay with us again and you can meet Sai, hear what he says, and then take it from there?'

Three days later, Oliver was sitting in Fauji and Daly's sitting-room, waiting for Sai to arrive. Coming back to Kenya had filled him with emotions and now he waited uneasily, not really wanting to hear that his girlfriend was alive and living happily without him. For the last few days, his stomach had roiled with sensations that varied from hope to anger and despair, but it was anger that had the uppermost place in the end, because he still couldn't get it out of his head that she could be with another man.

When Sai arrived, Oliver saw that he was a slight young man who had a wisp of a moustache and large, soulful, brown eyes. He looked honest and Oliver decided he could trust him to give a truthful account of what he had observed at the hotel. As soon as they had been introduced, Oliver started quizzing Sai.

'Are you sure the woman you saw at the hotel was the same one as in the photo?' Oliver asked.

'Yes, I'm pretty sure.'

'But it's been a while since you saw this woman in the hotel, so how can you be so sure?'

'On the day that I saw her, the drama of the Westgate raid was being played out on the television. Everyone's eyes, including mine, were glued to the screen and then I turned for a moment and saw this woman. Had she been any other woman I don't think I would have looked at her for more than an instant, because I was so interested in what was going on at Westgate. But she was so striking and unique, I found that I couldn't take my eyes off her for a few moments. She's not someone that you could easily forget.'

'Well, what was she doing?'

'She was looking at the television like everyone else.'

'Did she look upset? Traumatised? Did she show any emotion at all?'

'No, she just stood looking at the screen. Someone said something about how dreadful it must be to be caught up in something like that, but I don't think she made any comment.'

'Was she with anyone else?'

'I don't think so; not at that time, anyway.'

'Do you know what she did after that?'

'No. I think she headed to the dining area for breakfast, but I can't be sure. I didn't see her again after that.'

Oliver showed Sai several more photos of Sharba and the more Sai saw, the more convinced he was that the woman he'd seen was Oliver's girlfriend.

'Why don't you ring up the hotel and ask them if she was staying there on that date?' suggested Sai.

Oliver thought that was an excellent idea, but when he rang, they refused to give him any information because of their confidentiality policy. Despite him pleading and then threatening, they stuck to the rules and he was unable to find out if she had stayed there.

'You could book into the hotel for a couple of days and then covertly show the staff pictures of Sharnique and ask them if they remembered her,' suggested Fauji. 'They'll have probably been told not to give out information like that, but if you wave five hundred shillings under their noses it'll definitely loosen their tongues!'

Before Oliver decided to go down to the coast, he needed to find out if Sharnique had left Kenya for another country. He thought it would be a difficult thing to find out, but Fauji told him that nothing was impossible in Kenya if you had money to pay for information. He knew people who could help Oliver if he had the necessary finances. It took far less time than Oliver anticipated and soon he knew that no-one by the name of Sharnique Wellby had departed from Kenya.

❖

When Oliver arrived at the Papillon Hotel, he was convinced that Sharba would not have been able to stay there without someone else paying the bill. As soon as he had settled in, he did as Fauji had suggested and covertly showed the photos of Sharba to various members of the staff and asked them if they'd ever seen her. They reacted with a shake of the head or a lift of the shoulders. Some said so many guests came and went they couldn't possibly remember them individually.

Oliver's next step was to say that there would be a reward for anyone who could give him information that led him to reconnect with this lovely young woman who had been his girlfriend. This caused a little more interest, but to Oliver's dismay the consensus seemed to be that a reward wouldn't be compensation enough if they were to lose their jobs, which is what would happen if the manager got to hear about their indiscretions.

Oliver was beginning to despair when suddenly he had a breakthrough. One of the waiters came to him and asked if he could have a word in private.

'I can tell you nothing because of the hotel rules,' he said. 'But I've spoken to a friend, a taxi driver who works for himself and often drives our guests to the shops. He might be able to help you. Ask at reception if Sam can come and take you shopping, then show your photos to him.'

❖

Oliver waited until Sam had driven him away from the hotel and parked at the shopping centre before he produced the photo of his girlfriend.

'Have you ever seen this lady before?' Oliver asked.

Sam took the photo and studied it. 'Yes, I do remember taking this lady to these very shops a few weeks ago,' he said, handing back the photo.

'Are you completely sure it was her? It might have been a similar looking lady.'

'I'm quite sure it was the lady in the photo, sir. She asked me to take her to a clothes shop. I waited outside and then took her back to the hotel when she had finished her shopping.'

'Can you tell me the name of the lady that you drove here?'

'No sir. Although most of my clients know me as Sam, I never ask them their names. Some of them do introduce themselves, but this lady did not.'

'Was she alone? Did you see if she had any friends?' Oliver asked.

'No, she was alone. I never saw anyone with her. A day later—or it might have been two days later—I drove her to catch a bus that was going to Tanzania, and she was still alone.'

'Tanzania?' Oliver was surprised. 'But she would've needed to pass through passport control if she were to enter Tanzania.'

'Yes, of course.'

'Did she say why she was going to Tanzania?'

'Umm...well, all she said to me was that she was meeting a friend in Tanzania, but she would like to come back and have a holiday here.'

'Did she say who the friend was? A man? A woman?'

'She didn't say, sir.'

Oliver told the taxi driver to wait for him and he made his way to the clothes shop. Producing the photo, he showed it to the sales attendant and asked her if she had ever seen the woman in the picture.

'No,' said the girl after looking at it. 'I've never seen her.'

'I believe she came into this shop and bought some clothes a few weeks ago,' Oliver persisted. The girl looked at the photo again and shook her head.

'Wait a minute,' the girl left through a side door. A few minutes later she reappeared with another older woman. 'This lady might be able to help you,' she said.

Oliver showed the photo to the older woman and asked her if she recognised the girl in the picture. A big smile spread over the woman's face.

'Yes, I do remember her. She bought a lot of clothes when she came here.'

'Are you sure it was the same woman?'

'Oh yes. She was so pretty and she spent a lot of money here, so I remember her very well.'

After thanking the woman, Oliver went back to the taxi deep in thought. None of Sharba's clothes had been removed from the hotel in Nairobi, so she would have needed to buy some more. But where did she get the money to buy them? He knew nothing about the inheritance she had received and believed her to be short of money, so now he was convinced she wouldn't have been able to pay for the flight, the hotel and the clothes without help from someone.

And why did she travel to Tanzania, he wondered? It would have been more expense and when she got to the border, she would have had to produce a passport and it would be recorded that she'd left Kenya. And the information he had obtained indicated that no-one by the name of Sharnique Wellby had left Kenya.

Oliver felt sure that Sharba couldn't have planned an escape from him without help. As far as he knew, she hadn't know anyone in Kenya before they left, so she must have hitched up with someone after she had escaped from the mall and persuaded that person to help her. In his mind he was convinced it was a man and anger roiled in his stomach. He was looking like a thundercloud when he got back to the taxi.

'Is everything okay, sir?' Sam asked, noticing Oliver's angry face.

'Yes, but are you quite sure that this woman was never with a man?' Oliver asked again.

'Whenever I saw her, she was alone,' Sam replied. 'I never saw her with a man or a woman.'

On the way back to the hotel, Oliver thought that Sharba must have arranged to meet the person who was helping her at the Tanzania border. Perhaps they had met in Nairobi and made a plan. It was likely he had given her money so that she could fly to the coast and then go further south on the bus. Perhaps he knew of a way of getting her illegally into Tanzania, or maybe he lived somewhere in the border area and that was where she was heading.

Once they had arrived back at the hotel, Oliver rewarded Sam generously for the information he had given him. He also left money with the taxi driver for the waiter who had suggested he ask Sam about the girl in the picture.

'I'm going to leave you my email address,' Oliver told Sam. 'If you ever see the lady again, I'd be grateful if you'd let me know.'

'Of course, sir.' Sam was delighted with the money Oliver had given to him and hoped that the beautiful girl would turn up again so he could earn some more easy cash.

When Oliver had left Sam and returned to his room in the

hotel, he wondered what to do. He was completely focused on finding his girlfriend and nothing was going to entice him away from his mission, but he was unsure how to proceed.

The facts he had gathered so far were that his girlfriend was still alive and had briefly been at the coast. She had caught a bus that was heading for the Tanzania border at Lunga Lunga, but she had definitely not left Kenya as there were no records of her departure. So where could she be now? He had enquired about what could be found in the Lunga Lunga area and was told there was very little of interest there. There was a border control point where everyone who was departing the country had to produce a passport, but that was about it.

After some thought, Oliver decided that it would be pointless to go to Lunga Lunga. If there was very little there, his girlfriend would have gone on to somewhere else—and Kenya was a very big place to hunt for one missing woman! He knew she must still be in the country at the moment because no exit had been recorded, but her holiday visa stipulated that she could only remain in Kenya for three months. After that, she would have to leave.

If he paid Fauji's contacts to tip him off when she left Kenya, he would have a better idea of where to look for her and the chances were that she would fly back to England anyway, and that would make things a lot easier for him. All he had to do was be patient. If she did go to another country, he would go there and find her. One way or another, he was going to locate her and make her his woman again. Meanwhile, he would go back to England himself and try and find out a bit about her background; she had told him very little, but if he dug around somewhat, he may find something interesting that could lead him to her.

10

Seeking Employment

It wasn't difficult to find the offices of Huber Enterprises. Everyone knew where they were located and Sharba decided to go along straightaway and see if there was any chance of getting a job with them. She didn't want to waste the inheritance money she had received from Dick by living in the hotel for an extended time, so, feeling rather apprehensive, she dressed as smartly as she could with the limited wardrobe she had and found her way to the office with the words 'Huber Enterprises' emblazoned on a big board above the door.

Sharba found her way to reception and saw there was a stunningly beautiful Indian woman behind the desk. She had a mane of shiny black hair that framed her delicate face, and her huge brown eyes regarded Sharba rather sceptically when she stated the reason she was there. It was quite obvious that it was not a normal procedure for someone to barge into the building and ask if there were any jobs going!

'Wait here a minute,' said the Indian woman, and, with a rustle of her brightly coloured sari, she disappeared into an office to consult with another member of staff. After a few minutes, she appeared again and beckoned Sharba to come through.

The Indian receptionist left as soon as Sharba entered the office and she found herself now in the presence of an African lady. She must have been in her early fifties, but she was still a handsome woman and was impeccably dressed. She introduced herself as Mrs Phiri.

'I understand that you're looking for a job as a receptionist?'

Mrs Phiri said.

'Yes, that's correct.'

'What made you apply to Huber Enterprises? We haven't been advertising for personnel.'

'I've recently come back to Zambia after living in England for a number of years, and I met a lady on my flight who suggested that I apply to Huber Enterprises for a job as a receptionist,' Sharba told her honestly.

'Well, do you have any qualifications or references?'

'I do, but my luggage was lost when I flew from Heathrow to Nairobi earlier this week. I'm hoping it'll catch up with me at some point, so although I do have experience and qualifications, I can't show you anything to prove it.' In her own ears Sharba thought it sounded like a rather feeble explanation and she was prepared for Mrs Phiri to dismiss her, or tell her to come back when she had the relevant paperwork.

Mrs Phiri didn't say anything for a moment; she just sat looking at Sharba and then she seemed to come to a decision. 'If you wouldn't mind, I'd like you to go and sit in the waiting room for five minutes while I make a phone call and then we'll resume this interview after that.'

Mrs Phiri didn't know if Sharba was lying about her qualifications or not, and she had been about to tell her to come back when she could prove what she said was true, but she had also noticed what an unusually beautiful girl she was, and Arlo did love to have beautiful women working on the front desks of his enterprises. She knew he was about to open a newly built hotel on the banks of the Zambezi River near Livingstone, and they had planned to advertise for staff that very day, so maybe, if what this girl said was true, she could work as a receptionist at the hotel. But Mrs Phiri needed to ring Arlo first to see what he thought.

Sharba went back to the waiting room and found a white man sitting there whom she immediately identified as a farmer. He was wearing a freshly laundered safari suit, but she could see his bare arms, face and neck had been deeply tanned. His sun-bleached hair was grey at the temples and his face was prematurely wrinkled by the hot beams of the Zambian sunshine.

'Hello there,' he said cheerily when Sharba came in and sat

down. 'Have you come for an interview of some sort?' He had a kind, open face, and a warmth to his personality to which Sharba immediately responded.

They were soon chatting like old friends and Sharba learned his name was Len Raven and that he had land near Choma where he had farmed cattle and maize for years. Recently, he had decided to go into market gardening as well and he was hoping to get a contract to sell his produce to Huber Enterprises for their hotels.

'If they'll take the lot, it'll save me from rushing around like a maniac selling a little here and a little there,' Len told her.

Sharba was called back by Mrs Phiri before Len went for his interview and he wished her good luck as she left the waiting room.

'I've been in contact with Mr Huber, the owner of Huber Enterprises, and he thinks you may be suitable to work as the receptionist in his newly built hotel near Livingstone,' Mrs Phiri informed Sharba. 'However, since you can't provide any references or qualifications, he would like you to go to Livingstone so that he can interview you himself. He said that if he thinks you're suitable, he'll put you through some tests and then offer you a trial period. How does that sound to you?'

'It sounds wonderful,' said Sharba. She had thought she was going to be dismissed and told to come back when she had the relevant paperwork, so she was more than delighted that she had a chance to prove herself.

'Good. Now, we have transport going to Livingstone tomorrow and Mr Huber says you can have accommodation in the staff quarters at the hotel, so do you think you can be here at the office tomorrow at eight in the morning so you can take advantage of the lift we're offering?'

'Absolutely, I'll be here; and thank you very much for organising this for me.'

Sharba felt very happy as she left the office. She didn't see Len Raven as she left, but hoped that he'd had as much success as she. For the rest of the day, she went around Lusaka shopping for clothes, a mobile phone, and other things she thought she might need. She also bought a backpack in which to carry them since the bag she had bought in Kenya would be too small. Then she took a taxi to Dick and Honor's old property where she had spent her childhood. She wasn't able to go in, of course, but asked the taxi driver to park outside the gate so that she could look at the place in which she had lived so many years ago.

It didn't seem that much had changed. The little house that she had shared with Eve still nestled behind some trees that were covered in a bougainvillea creeper. Emotions pulsed through her as she remembered how happy she had been there living with her mother. Then she looked towards the big house that was a short distance from Eve's residence across neatly cut lawns. It was all just as she remembered it. She had never gone back to the little house after Eve had been murdered; she had lived in the big house and, although she remembered the kindness shown to her by Honor and Dick, it had been an unhappy time. 'Maybe I shouldn't have come back,' Sharba thought as the emotions churned in her stomach. I need to be looking forward, not backwards. Coming to herself, she asked the taxi driver to take her back to the hotel.

Later that evening when she went down to the hotel dining room to have her dinner, Sharba was surprised to hear someone call her name and, turning to find out who it was, she saw Len's cheerful face.

'Come and have a drink with us,' Len said when she went over. 'This is my beautiful wife, Elizabeth, I've already told her all about you. Did you get the job you were after?'

It was nice to be able to sit with people and be sociable. Elizabeth was a motherly sort of woman who was every bit as nice as her husband. Sharba was pleased to learn that Huber Enterprises had agreed to take all Len's produce.

'We thought we'd spend the night here to celebrate,' Len told her. 'It's also Liz's birthday next week, so she deserves a bit of spoiling.'

After having a drink together, they all went to the dining room for their dinner, and after chatting about this and that, the conversation turned to Arlo Huber.

He came out to Zambia years ago with very little money,' Len told Sharba. 'Now he's got an empire and he's a millionaire.'

'That was partly due to his first wife, Anna,' said Elizabeth. 'She had a good business head on her, and she was devoted to Arlo and determined that he was going to make something of himself here.'

'Yes, and Arlo has always been a grafter,' said Len. 'He was devoted to Anna and was devastated when she died.'

'What happened to her?' Sharba asked.

'She died of cancer,' Len told her. 'But after her death, Arlo seemed to go a bit crazy and he chased after anyone who wore a skirt. We felt sorry for him at first because we felt he was on the rebound from his dear wife's premature departure, but after a while it got a bit embarrassing because you would see his van parked in obscure places—and because it was rocking around, we all knew what was going on inside! He must have had hundreds of liaisons with the most unsuitable women.' He gave a short laugh.

'Then he met and married Rosa,' said Elizabeth. 'We all thought he'd lost his mind completely when he announced he was going to marry her, because she was at least thirty years his junior and she was a troubled young woman.'

'As a young adult, Rosa lived with her father, who was a good friend of ours, and one night they had their house broken into,' Len explained. 'The thieves roughed her dad up quite badly and then they turned on Rosa and raped her before ransacking the house. It was a dreadful experience for them both, and Rosa swore that she would never let another man near her after that.'

'She was a pretty little thing,' Elizabeth said. 'We all hoped she would get over the experience and find a nice husband, but men seemed to shy away from her when they heard she had been raped by a gang of black men. It was really sad. Then she met Arlo and it was not long after that when she agreed to marry him. Perhaps he was like a father figure, and despite everyone being sceptical, the marriage did work. Arlo never looked at another woman after that, and they're still happily married and have a daughter about the same age as you.'

'Their wedding wasn't without drama, though,' said Len.

'Why, what happened?' Sharba asked curiously.

'Well, Arlo wanted it to be the perfect wedding. He spent a lot of money to ensure that there would be a flawless ceremony and reception; he even managed to get a soloist to sing Ave Maria. But when Arlo and Rosa were about to exchange their wedding vows, there was suddenly a commotion at the back of the church. To everyone's horror a very pregnant black woman had come in and was yelling at Arlo. "What about this?" she was shouting, pointing to her very pregnant stomach. "What about this baby that you made?" Well, Arlo indicated to his youngest son, Karl, to get rid of her, which he did. Then the service went on, but it did spoil it a bit!'

'What happened to the poor pregnant woman?' Sharba asked.

'Well, we didn't know at the time what happened to her,' said Elizabeth. 'I was actually quite appalled when I later learned that Karl had bundled her into a car, driven her almost all the way to Kafue, about forty kilometres away, and then kicked her out on a deserted stretch of the road and told her to walk back to Lusaka. I mean the poor woman was heavily pregnant—presumably with Arlo's child—and she shouldn't have been treated like that!'

'Well, I suppose they didn't want her to disrupt the reception, but I agree that it was a dreadfully harsh thing to do,' Len concurred.

The topic of conversation then changed to something else and, at the end of the evening, both Len and Elizabeth made Sharba promise that she would come and visit them on their farm when she got the opportunity.

'It's lovely on our farm,' Elizabeth told her. 'It's called Concord Estates and you'll love the peace and tranquillity there. Just look for the sign 'Concord Estates' on the left hand side of the road about seven miles out of Choma when heading towards Kalomo.'

Sharba promised them that she would visit them when she could.

11

Huber's Riverside Lodge

The next morning, Sharba made her way to the Huber Enterprises offices well before eight o'clock and had to wait for the transport she was promised to arrive. When the van did appear, she found it loaded to capacity with things Arlo had requested to be brought to Livingstone, but there was just room for Sharba's backpack on top of everything else. She sat next to the driver on the front seat and found him to be a chatty African called John, who told her all about his wife and six children whom he clearly idolised.

The road south passed over generally flat land and after they had crossed over the Kafue River Bridge, there wasn't any great scenery to admire. They just seemed to pass endless trees as the ribbon of road stretched out in front of them.

'Have you worked for Mr Huber for long?' Sharba inquired.

'Yes, I've worked for him for many years; he's a good bwana to work for and has given employment to many Zambian people so that they can eat, and also support their families. He has many businesses, you see, and this new hotel that he has just built has been a godsend to Kapotwe Village.'

'In what way?'

'Kapotwe Village is situated about two miles from the new hotel. It's a small village and the people there have survived for many years by being self-sufficient; they have gardens for vegetables and a few mealies, and of course they have hens and ducks. But the problem was the young people of the village didn't want to stay there because they wanted the good life! They wanted mobile phones and trainers—you know how young people are! Anyway, the village was shrinking and Luckson Malupande, the chief of the village, was worried because for the village to survive the young people must stay.

'Then Mr Huber acquired land about two miles from the village and wanted to build a hotel there. So he needed people to clear the land and then help with the building. It was very good work for the young people of Kapotwe Village and they could make money without leaving home. It saved the village from dying.'

'But they've finished building the hotel,' said Sharba. 'So surely they won't be needing the people anymore?'

'A section of the hotel is finished,' agreed John. 'But another section is still under construction, so the people involved in building are still required. And now they also need gardeners and maids—they need a lot of people to run such a big hotel, so there'll always be employment for the people of Kapotwe.'

As the journey progressed, they passed through Mazabuka, Choma and Kalomo, none of which looked very exciting, and eventually arrived in Livingstone at about lunch time. Sharba had never been there before and commented in delight on the Edwardian buildings that lined the city's main road. She thought the town was utterly charming.

'Have you never been to Livingstone before?' John asked.

'No, this is my first time.'

'So you have never seen the great Victoria Falls?'

'Never; well, only in pictures.'

'You must go and see them as soon as you can. They're magnificent! Livingstone is a very good place to live because of the falls and there are so many activities you can do when you stay here—river-boarding, white-water rafting, canoeing, boat cruises, kayaking, or if you don't like water activities you can go on horse-riding trials, elephant-back safaris, or quad-bike riding. There're other things as well. How would you like to walk with lions?' Sharba shook her head. 'Okay, well, maybe Mukuni Cultural Village would suit you better!'

Sharba laughed. 'There certainly seems to be plenty to do, so let's hope I get the job I'm after and can stay here.'

A large sign with the words 'Huber's Riverside Resort' indicated the road that they should take after leaving Livingstone. They travelled for about four miles along the dusty surface of the road and then they arrived at the newly built hotel which was situated right next to the Zambezi River. Sharba was pleased to see that it had been sympathetically built with materials native to the area so that it looked rustic and blended in with the surroundings, but at the same time she could see it was top-notch and classy. Palms dotted the expansive gardens that were perfectly manicured and contained an amazing infinity pool which looked out on the Zambezi River. The pool was surrounded by a terrace where people would be able to relax and be served food.

The perimeter of the hotel grounds followed the Zambezi River and at the rear of the hotel there was a jungle of natural vegetation that had been left untouched. Sharba could hear loud birdsong coming from the trees and noticed a number of fire finches, their scarlet feathers glowing like hot embers as they descended to drink at the edge of the river. There were also starlings shining in iridescent green plumage, and higher in the trees she spotted a troop of monkeys. Overhead, wild duck flew in their arrowhead formation, dark against the blue of the sky.

'This is absolutely magical!' she exclaimed in delight to John.

'Well, I'm glad you approve!' said a deep voice behind her. Turning, she saw a heavyset man in his early seventies who had a shock of dense, white hair and brilliant blue eyes. Although he was no longer a young man, he was still very attractive.

'Arlo Huber,' said the man, holding out his hand.

Sharba had learned quite a lot about this man, courtesy of Len and Elizabeth, but she wasn't prepared for the strong aura of authority he exuded, nor the warmth that clearly radiated from his brilliant eyes. She had imagined him to be aloof and now beyond condemnation for what had happened in the past because he was so successful, but he looked pleasantly approachable as he studied her with kindly eyes.

'Come,' he commanded. 'We will go in.'

The great A-framed thatched entrance to the lodge was impressive and was an indication of the grandeur that would be found within the hotel. Arlo took pride in showing Sharba around the entire resort. The rooms were stunning and comfortable, with four-poster beds already draped in mosquito nets. Each one had a private bathroom, a shower, and its own private balcony overlooking the river. The suits contained a hot-tub and lounge area.

Outside the main building there was a buffet dining area and a cocktail bar, while inside there were more dining areas, seating areas and bars. All the fixtures and fittings were high spec and classy, and Sharba was left in no doubt that it would be an expensive hotel in which to stay.

'The main part of the hotel is ready and will open very shortly,' Arlo told her. 'But beyond the present perimeters, out of sight, we are already extending the hotel, and the buildings are in progress.'

After the tour they sat in Arlo's office where he quizzed her on her experience and qualifications—and also on her life up to this point. Sharba tried to be as truthful as she could without letting him in on her secrets. She said she had been born in Zambia and then adopted by British people when her mother had died, after which she had been taken to England where she had gained her qualifications and experience.

'What made you come back to Zambia?' Arlo asked. 'Was it to find out more about your African background?'

'No, not really,' Sharba said truthfully. 'I was sick of the English weather and had a holiday in Australia which I really enjoyed. So then I decided that my next trip would be to Africa.'

'So this is more of a holiday than anything else?'

'No, not at all. Once I landed here and my feet touched Zambian soil, I felt I'd come home. I absolutely knew for sure that this is where I wanted to stay, if I could get a job.'

'But would you be happy working in this hotel that is away from all the bright lights and social events that a young person such as yourself might wish to participate in?'

'I'd be very happy working here. The last thing I'm looking for at the moment is bright lights!' There was no doubt about the sincerity in Sharba's voice as she stated this.

'Well, we'll give you a go and see how you get on,' said Arlo. He was a good judge of character and he already knew he wanted to employ her permanently—so long as she could do the job. She was exquisitely beautiful and had a lively intelligent face; she was exactly the sort of person he liked to have on the front desk of his enterprises. He also found her to be poised and confident; in some ways she appeared old beyond her years. He pressed a buzzer on his desk and a little African man came in.

'Yes sir?'

'Luyando, could you please ask my daughter to come to the office?'

'Yes sir.'

Luyando went off and a few minutes later there was a light tap on the door and a young woman about the same age as Sharba came in. She had a curvy figure, masses of blonde curls on her head, and a friendly smile on her lips. Arlo introduced her as Clara and asked her to show Sharba her accommodation and then organise her a sandwich and a drink.

'Come on, let's get something to eat first,' Clara suggested when the two women had left the office together. 'I'm starving and I'm sure you must be as well after your journey here!'

The hotel wasn't in operation yet, so Clara took Sharba to the Huber residence which was a large, single-story building within the hotel grounds, but set apart in its own garden, complete with a swimming pool. It was very private and wasn't overlooked by the resort. They were met by Rosa, Clara's mother, who was large, handsome woman with a youthful face. She exuded cheerfulness.

'Welcome to Huber's Riverside Lodge, dear,' she said to Sharba when they were introduced. 'Why don't you girls go and sit on the veranda and I'll have a sandwich and drink sent out to you. I'm sure Sharba has a lot of questions to ask you about the job she's hoping to secure.'

It was pleasant sitting on the veranda with the view of the Zambezi River meandering past. Clara gave Sharba a fairly comprehensive account of what she would have to do if she worked as a receptionist for them, and after asking some pertinent questions Sharba felt quite confident she would be able to do the job easily.

'Dad's a bit of a perfectionist,' Clara told her. 'So he'll expect you to be on top of your game at all times. That means always looking smart, being friendly and helpful to the guests whilst maintaining professionalism and being on top of the paperwork as well. Dad's always fair, but he hates it when people are sloppy or make too many mistakes! I'm going to be working as a receptionist as well. Dad was planning to advertise for another receptionist to work alongside me, and then you turned up! I do hope you'll take the job as I think we'll be able to work well together.' Already Clara liked Sharba and knew that they would get on and complement each other in the workplace.

Sharba also hoped that she would get the job. She liked the Huber family; Arlo seemed like a decent employer and his wife was lovely. As for Clara, she had immediately liked her from the moment they had met. She was so friendly, there was no snobbishness because she was the boss's daughter, and she genuinely seemed to want Sharba to work with her on reception.

An African man dressed in white clothes, who Sharba correctly assumed was their cook, arrived with a plate of delicious sandwiches and two glasses of orange juice. While they were eating, Clara changed the subject and started talking about her father in a more personal way.

'Dad's a really good sort,' she said. 'I expect you'll hear all sorts of adverse things said about him, and some may be true, but most are greatly exaggerated. The truth is he was married to his first wife for twenty-five years and was never unfaithful to her, but when she died he went bonkers for a bit; it was probably due to his grief. It was during that time that he had a string of affairs but found no happiness. It was only when he met Mum that things changed for him and, after he married her, he remained completely faithful to her. So if you do hear things about him, bear that in mind.'

Sharba nodded her head. She didn't like to say that she had already heard some of the gossip about Clara's father.

'There's another thing I should mention: my half-brother, Karl, is also here working at the hotel.' Clara's expression now changed and it was obvious that there was no love lost between Clara and her half-brother.

'Karl's involved with the building of this hotel and is busy at present on the extension. When it's all finished, he'll stay on as head of maintenance. He and his brother, Albert, were both living in Germany. Albert is a model citizen who works in a bank in Berlin, but Karl seemed to be a restless soul and was in all sorts of trouble. Dad has a bit of a heart problem and he said he'd decided to bring Karl out to Zambia to help him, but in reality he brought Karl over here to try and sort him out!' Clara shook her head as if it were a task that even her father would not be able to accomplish.

'Everyone here says Karl is a chip off the old block. That's because he has a roving eye and likes women, but I actually think he's not a very nice person at all. Anyway, he has settled down a bit now; he has a permanent partner, Amanda, and they've got a little boy, George, but I still wouldn't trust him too much. Anyway, I'm just warning you because you're very pretty and it's entirely possible that he'll hit on you.'

'Well, I'm sure I'll be able to manage the situation now that you've warned me,' answered Sharba.

When they had finished eating, Clara took Sharba to her accommodation. It was in a thatched rondavel that stood at the end of a row of identical buildings that had obviously been built for accommodating the senior staff who would work at the hotel. They were situated at the rear of the property out of sight of the hotel and Sharba was delighted to see that they backed onto a jungle of flora and trees that were teeming with wildlife.

Right outside the veranda, there was a tangle of vegetation in which the weaver birds had built their intricate nests. They hung down from the branches of the trees like untidy fruits, and the bright yellow birds could be seen coming and going, flashing like streaks of gold against the junglelike background. There were also monkeys in the trees. When Sharba looked up, she could see the little black face and bright eyes of a vervet monkey looking back at her.

'You have to watch the monkeys,' Clara warned her with a laugh. 'They can be thieving little nuisances and are bold enough to go right into your house and look for food to steal!'

Inside there was a bedsit, a shower and toilet room, a tiny kitchen, and a veranda that encircled the entire rondavel. The bed had already been made up and a brand-new net hung above it. It was a pretty little place and Sharba loved it the minute she walked in.

'This is absolutely perfect!' she exclaimed, smiling in delight at Clara.

'I'm glad you like it,' said Clara, looking pleased. 'Now, the hotel isn't open yet, so you can come and eat with us at mealtimes for the time being. Once the hotel is up and running, you'll be able to get your meals from the kitchen. I'll leave you to get settled in now, and tomorrow we can go over what you need to know about being a receptionist here, and we'll work together and see how it goes.'

Someone had already put Sharba's backpack in the rondavel, so after Clara had left her alone, Sharba unpacked and then took a shower because it was so hot and she felt grubby and sticky from the trip to Livingston. She felt very happy because everything seemed so positive and she was sure she would be able to cope with the job and work happily with Clara.

That evening she was called by one of the servants and told that she should go to the Huber's house for the evening meal. When she got there, she found that Karl, Amanda, and George were already there. They had their own house, which was built further along from Arlo's, but had come to eat with the family that evening.

Karl was large, muscular and extremely handsome. He looked a lot like his father although he was much slimmer, but his bright blue eyes had a mean predatory glint in them that made Sharba shudder. Amanda was pretty in a delicate sort of way and she seemed to be a very shy and timid person. She said hardly anything at all and busied herself with George most of the time. He was a bonny three-year-old who had dark curls like his mother. When Amanda did speak, it was with a strong Afrikaans accent and she continually glanced at Karl in a rather apprehensive manner, which indicated to Sharba that she was scared of him.

During the meal, Sharba was aware of Karl's bright eyes boring into her more often than necessary and it made her feel uncomfortable. She had already decided that Clara was right, and Karl wasn't a very nice person, but on the whole the time around the meal went well. Arlo and Rosa were good hosts and ensured that the conversation flowed easily. They made sure they included Sharba so that she didn't feel left out. Things only got a little uncomfortable when the subject of hunting came up.

Both Arlo and Karl liked to go hunting and, although Rosa and Clara disapproved of the pastime, they obviously accepted that it was the right of the menfolk to indulge their hunting instincts in a blood sport, so they didn't judge them. But hurting any animal was dreadfully wrong in Amanda's view, and her tortured expression said it all when the men spoke about shooting wildlife.

Karl noticed her discomfort and said unkindly, 'You can come with us next time we go, doll. Bring George as well; it's about time the boy started to learn about the pursuits of men.'

Amanda just shook her head, but she looked as though she was about to burst into tears. Karl was about to make another jibe, but Clara cut him off sharply.

'Shut up Karl. You know Amanda hates hunting and George is far too small to appreciate it, so stop being a smart aleck.'

Karl gave his half-sister a poisonous look, but Rosa skilfully steered the conversation on to another topic and defused the situation.

After they had finished their meal, Arlo and Carl went off to Arlo's office to discuss some business matters, and the woman sat on the veranda drinking coffee. The sunset over the river was spectacular and the orange sky reflected on the ripples of the river making it a peaceful, romantic scene.

Rosa and Clara had to go and sort out a problem in the kitchen, so they excused themselves for a few minutes, leaving Amanda and Sharba alone.

'You must love living here,' Sharba said to Amanda. 'It's so lovely, isn't it?'

'It does look lovely,' agreed Amanda gazing at the sunset. 'But you have to remember that it's dangerous as well. There're huge crocodiles in the river, and hippos as well. I have to constantly keep George away from the Zambezi because he's fascinated by the water and keeps trying to go to the river's edge.'

George was now relaxing on one of the veranda chairs, sucking his thumb and looking sleepy, but he smiled at his mother when he heard his name mentioned. 'You're a little skellum, aren't you?' Amanda said to her son fondly.

Amanda was more inclined to talk now that her husband and

the others weren't present, and she told Sharba that she was a South African and had lived in Johannesburg for most of her life.

'I came on a short break from Jo'burg to see the Victoria Falls, but I met Karl and it was love at first sight.' Amanda looked at the floor and then added quietly, 'Well, I thought it was at the time.' She sighed and turned to Sharba again. 'When I got home, I discovered that I was pregnant. It was a disaster because my family are members of the strict Dutch Reformed Church and pregnancy out of marriage just doesn't happen in our family. I was thrown out, so I came back here. Arlo and Rosa have been so kind to me, and after Karl got over the shock of being an expectant father, he agreed that we should live together and be a family, but he says he doesn't believe in marriage. So in the eyes of my family, I'm now committing another sin by living with a man who isn't my husband and they'll never allow me back into the fold, or acknowledge George as their grandson.' Poor Amanda looked anguished and Sharba felt sorry for her.

'I'm so sorry,' said Sharba. 'But your life isn't a complete disaster—look what you've got...' she pointed at George who had now succumbed to sleep and lay curled up on the chair, the picture of childish innocence and beauty.

'I know; he's my life and I wouldn't change him for anything,' said Amanda softly, stroking his dark curls. 'The trouble is, Karl wants to make a man of him. He's only three, for goodness' sake, still a baby really, so it's far too soon to think about making a man of him! But Karl can be quite rough with him and insists that he needs to be brought up tough.

'George has been potty trained for a while now, but he had an accident in his shorts the other day and Karl took them off and then slapped him hard on his little bottom with a flip-flop three times, calling him a dirty child. I just can't bear that sort of thing, but Karl says I'm too soft on the boy and he needs input from his father if he's to grow up a man.'

Just then, Rosa and Clara returned to the veranda and the conversation turned to a more general topic. The hotel was due to open in two weeks' time and the senior members of the staff would be moving into the accommodation in the hotel grounds in the coming week, so all the rondavels and had to be prepared.

'Those who have the more lowly jobs will not live on site,' Clara told Sharba. 'They'll come from Kapotwe Village; that's situated a couple of miles from here.'

Sharba was glad that she had been the first to arrive, as her rondavel was at the end of the row and nearest to the hotel. It was also more private than the others and although it was set back in the hotel property, she could still catch a glimpse of the river from her veranda.

'We've arranged for the chef to come the day after tomorrow,' said Rosa. 'He'll be the first to come after you, Sharba, and he'll be able to familiarise himself with the hotel kitchen by cooking for the staff who will all be trickling in from now on. There'll also be an under-chef arriving at some point, and of course there will be an army of others who can help in the kitchen by the time the visitors are due.'

Later, when Sharba retired to her rondavel, she lay thinking about the events of the day. She knew she wanted to stay and work there, but was also aware that the family that owned it was not without complications. There were Rosa and Clara who seemed to be lovely, uncomplicated people; then there was Arlo who had blotted his copybook in the past and still carried the stigma, although he seemed to be a changed character and Sharba instinctively liked him. Last of the family that she had met was Karl, and she shuddered when she thought of him.

Karl was good looking, self-assured, and appeared to be focused on his work at the hotel, but Sharba could feel inherent evil in the man. She remembered that he was the person who had dropped the poor pregnant woman in the middle of nowhere on the day of his father's wedding and told her to walk home. Now it seemed as though he was cruel to his son as well. Amanda was also his sweet innocent victim who Sharba felt sure was going to get very hurt in the end. And George...well he was a guileless, vulnerable little boy at the moment, but with a father like Karl, who knew what lay in his future?

12

Good and Bad Fortune

Oliver had returned to England, expecting to hear in a few weeks that his girlfriend had exited Kenya. Her three-month visa had now expired, but she had not turned up in England nor, it appeared, had she left Kenya. Surely she couldn't be risking infringing immigration regulations and hoping to get away with it? Oliver thought she was too intelligent to do that, but where could she be? He had decided to enlist the help of a private detective to uncover her past history, and now he whistled softly when he read the report that had landed on his desk.

'What a secretive little bitch she is!' Oliver muttered to himself.

She had never mentioned to him that she had been adopted, and had actually been born in Zambia and lived there for ten years before moving to England with her adoptive family. Oliver tapped his pen against his teeth as he digested that bit of information. Could she have been making her way to Zambia via Tanzania when she left Kenya, he wondered? It seemed a distinct possibility to him, because she could easily still have relatives there, but she would have needed to use her passport to exit Kenya and seemingly she hadn't done that. Could it be possible she had a Zambian passport, maybe in another name, Oliver wondered? It seemed to him that this was a possibility because she would certainly have been entitled to hold a Zambian passport. It was time to give the private detective some more work.

❖

Sharba, meanwhile, had settled happily into her job as receptionist at Huber's Riverside Resort. The Hubers were pleased with her because she was diligent and worked very hard to make their guests feel welcome. She was a delight to work with and soon became a very popular member of the staff. Arlo and Rosa often invited her to have a meal with the family and they generously allowed her to use their swimming pool wherever she had time off and felt like having a swim.

'It's better than using the hotel pool because it's private and no one can ogle you while you're cooling off in the water,' Rosa said.

Sharba and Clara worked well together, and they soon became firm friends and often did things together when they both had time off.

'Let's invite Amanda to come with us,' Sharba suggested one day when they were planning an expedition. 'She seems such a lonely little person; usually she only has George to talk to, so I'm sure she'd like to come.' She had noticed that Amanda often looked sad and Karl seemed to take little notice of her.

Clara wasn't so keen on Amanda, but she nodded her head, albeit a bit reluctantly.

'It's not that I dislike her,' Clara explained to Sharba. 'She's nice enough, but she's such a dying swan! I find weak people incredibly irritating, and she's so weak! She allows Karl to walk all over her and she goes about with a hangdog expression on her face. Why doesn't she stand up to him? He's a bully and he'd treat her better if she let it be known that she wasn't a doormat!'

Sharba secretly agreed with Clara, but she understood that Amanda was in a difficult position. Her family had disowned her and now she was desperate to make her own little family with Karl and George, but Karl was making it challenging for her.

When asked, Amanda jumped at the chance to go out with the other two women. After the first time, she and George often accompanied them.

❖

'It's raining, it's raining!' George cried in delight as the drops of water fell on his upturned face. He jumped up and down, his feet splashing in the puddles on the ground.

Sharba, Clara, Amanda and George were standing in front of the magnificent Victoria Falls which was thundering down into the gorge and causing spray to rise up and then fall like rain on the four of them. It was an awe-inspiring sight that left Sharba feeling mesmerised and exhilarated, but George just liked the feeling of the spray falling on his face. He stopped jumping and held his face up and opened his mouth so that he could try and catch the drops of water that were raining down.

'I'm drinking the rain,' he said laughing.

Amanda held his hand tightly as she didn't want him falling down into the gorge, but she also looked happy. She was a different person when she and George were out with Sharba and Clara. Her happiness reflected in her face and completely transformed it, so she looked really pretty in a delicate kind of way, with her dark dancing curls and endearing dimples that showed when she smiled or laughed, which was often when she was out with them. She had a bubbly personality, but it only showed when Karl wasn't around. George loved their jaunts as well. He called Sharba 'Auntie Sharba', much to her dismay.

'I'm sure I'm much too young to be called "auntie",' she objected. But Amanda, giggling at Sharba's horror, assured her it was the correct way for her son to respectfully address her. Shaba thought George was the cutest little boy she had ever seen and when he was out and about in the hotel grounds, she noticed that he was a favourite with all the staff as well. They all had a kind word for him and if they had time, they would play with him for a few minutes, football being his favourite pastime. Sharba loved him as well and she spoiled him by buying him ice cream or sweets when they were out.

Sharba was glad that Amanda and George often accompanied her and Clara on their excursions, but when they got back to the hotel Sharba noticed that a shadow seemed to fall over Amanda's face, and she assumed it was because Karl treated her badly. Amanda assured Sharba she was still in love with Karl, but privately Sharba was pretty sure he bullied her badly when no one else was around. She knew for certain Karl never missed an opportunity to criticise Amanda and compare her unfavourably with Clara and herself.

'Those two chicks have to work all day, but they still look nicer than you who has nothing better to do than make herself beautiful,' Sharba overheard Karl saying to Amanda one day.

Sharba was on her way to have a swim in the Huber's swimming pool and stopped out of sight on the other side of the fence when she heard them talking by the pool.

'Look at you!' she heard Karl say. 'You look like something the cat dragged in; it makes me quite ashamed to acknowledge you as my woman!'

'I'm sorry, Karl,' Amanda responded, sounding upset. 'I've been playing with George and he's messed me up a bit.'

'Well, that's another thing. You spend all your time on that child; you won't employ a nanny, so you have no time for anything else—not even for me.'

'That's not true,' said Amanda tearfully. 'I'm always there for you, I love you.'

'You love George more, though! And you're making a complete mess of bringing him up, you know. He's a boy and you're turning him into a namby-pamby. I should really take him under my wing and toughen him up before you ruin him completely.'

'But he's little more than a baby,' she objected.

'Well, you need to get your act together if you want to stay with me. If you go on the way you are, I'll keep my son and send you back to South Africa!'

Sharba heard Amanda break down in sobs and then the heavy clump of Karl's footsteps as he walked away from her. She felt like going to comfort Amanda, but she thought that it might embarrass the poor woman to know Sharba had overheard one of their tiffs and probably she shouldn't interfere, anyway. She figured Amanda could confide in her if she wanted to, but otherwise it would be prudent to keep her nose out of their business.

❖

One day a family by the name of Greyson came to stay at the hotel. There was Charlie Grayson senior, Brigitta his wife, and their son, Charles, who had flown them in a helicopter to Livingstone from Botswana for a short holiday to celebrate his parents' twenty-fifth wedding anniversary. They were wealthy landowners who owned a huge cattle ranch in Botswana and several other business enterprises in that country. Apart from their sprawling ranch house in Botswana, they also had a luxury residence in Cape Town and a house in Germany. Although they had the natural self-assurance of wealthy people, they were not arrogant or self-important in any way, and they very soon became friendly with the Hubers, because Brigitta was German and had lived very near the village in which Huber had been brought up. When they had first walked into reception and Clara had gone to welcome them, the air between her and Charles immediately seemed to sizzle.

'My God, Sharba, he's the most stunning man I've ever set eyes on!' Clara told her friend that evening. 'I've never felt such an instant attraction to a man in all my life!'

Sharba could understand why Clara had found Charles so attractive. He was six foot of solid muscle, tanned to perfection and topped with a mop of fair hair that had almost been bleached white by the sun. His pale blue eyes were direct and penetrating, and his square jaw and firm mouth left no one in doubt that he was a self-assured and confident young man.

'Well, it was quite obvious he was attracted to you as well,' laughed Sharba. 'I could literally hear the crackle of the magnetism between the two of you!'

It was the start of a romance between Charles and Clara. Charles was completely smitten by the bubbly blonde, and after that first visit he would fly up from Botswana whenever he could in his helicopter so that he could be with her. Arlo and Rosa were delighted that their daughter had found such a suitable man with whom to fall in love, and it was obvious to all that this was not just a passing romance—it was the real thing. It was only Karl that did not like Charles.

'He's just the spoiled kid of a family who has too much money,' he said unkindly. 'He needs to stand on his own two feet and realise that this is a cruel world, and most people have to work incredibly hard before they can even imagine swanning around in a helicopter!'

'Oh yes, and you're an expert in working hard and achieving things in this cruel world!' Clara responded hotly. 'You, who couldn't make anything of your life in Germany and had to come back to your daddy before you completely crashed and burned!'

'I came out here to help the old man,' Karl blazed back. 'He needed my skills as a builder, and I forfeited everything I had in

Germany and came out here to assist him!'

'Bullshit! You were brought out here by Dad because he thought you'd end up in prison if he didn't do something! And I'll tell you another thing: Charles is a very hard worker, he helped his father to build up the ranch and their various businesses, and he learned how to fly and bought that helicopter out of his own money!'

'Pah!' Karl knew he wasn't going to win this argument with his sharp-tongued sister, so he swung on his heel and left.

Sharba was happy that her friend had found love, and she often did extra shifts so that Clara could spend time with Charles. She thought it was so romantic when he swooped down in his helicopter and whisked Clara off to Botswana for a weekend. It meant, of course, that she didn't have the pleasure of Clara's company anymore when she had time off, but she and Amanda and George still had outings together, so Sharba was very happy with the life she had carved out for herself in Zambia. She felt safe and hardly ever thought about Oliver anymore. But when she did, she was quite confident that he would never find her in this quiet corner of Zambia if, by any chance, he didn't believe she had died and had started looking for her.

There was only one fly in the ointment in Sharba's life—Karl. To start with, she was aware that he scrutinised her covertly with his heavy-lidded eyes, but she chose to ignore him and pretend she hadn't noticed his scrutiny. He obviously didn't like being ignored, so he began to seek her out and make suggestions that she didn't consider appropriate. She wanted to tell him to get lost in no uncertain terms, but also didn't want to fall out with any of the Hubers, so she bit her lip and batted him away gently with a flippant remark that would leave him in no doubt that she wasn't the slightest bit interested in him. It annoyed her that Karl was so persistent, but she didn't want to complain and cause a rift in the family. But one evening things came to a head.

Sharba had finished work for the day and, as she often did, she went for a swim in the Hubers' pool where she had privacy from the hotel guests. It had been an overpoweringly hot day and very humid, so the water felt divine as it cooled her down while she swam her normal twenty lengths. She found swimming was an excellent therapy after a hot, tiring day working at the front desk;

it seemed to reenergise her and relax her at the same time.

Although it was now evening time, it was still extremely hot and humid, so after she had heaved herself out of the pool she lay on a sun lounger and relaxed with her eyes shut as the drops of water on her body evaporated into the hot atmosphere. Suddenly she was aware that she was no longer alone and, opening her eyes, she saw Karl's leering face as he towered above her.

'What's wrong?' Sharba asked. 'Is something the matter?'

'Yes there is,' he replied. He sat down on another sun lounger and leaned towards her so that she could smell his breath was heavily laced with alcohol. 'You're a sex-bomb and I've fancied you from the moment I first saw you, so I think we should do something about it.' He leaned closer to her and tried to kiss her, but she pulled away in disgust.

'Get off me, Karl; you know very well I'm not interested.'

'Well, you should be. I'm the son of the owner and I will inherit all this one day; if you play your cards right you could be co-owner with me.' He grabbed her hands and tried to draw her towards him.

Sharba leaped to her feet while trying to jerk her hands away. 'Let go, you idiot. If you weren't drunk, I'd lay a charge of assault against you! As it is, I don't think you know what you're doing!' Sharba tried to keep her voice down as she didn't want anyone, especially Amanda, seeing Karl behaving so badly.

'Ha ha, an assault charge, hey? I do want to assault you, darling; let me show you how much I want to assault you.' He was now standing as well and he pulled her to him and held her tightly with one arm while he rubbed his lower body against her; she could feel his hard erection and fought to get free.

'Let go, you bastard,' Sharba's voice was rising. But he didn't, and it was as though she was being held in an iron vice. Then Karl, holding her securely with one arm, put his other hand on her head and, bending down to her level, he pushed it towards his face and tried to force his tongue into her mouth.

'No,' she screamed, turning her face aside. 'Let me go, let me go!' He voice was shrill and loud now, but Karl didn't seem to care. Still holding her securely with one hand, he pulled her bikini top up with the other and exposed her breasts. Then he slid his hand down inside her bikini bottoms and started feeling around.

'Just relax darling and enjoy what I'm doing to you. You know you want it just as much as me.'

By this time Sharba was screaming loudly and this attracted attention; several people came running, Arlo and Amanda among them. To Sharba's utter relief, strong arms yanked Karl off her and she scrabbled to pull her bikini top down and make herself decent again as she sank sobbing on to the sun lounger.

'What the hell do you think you're doing?' Arlo shouted at his son.

'She's been flirting with me for weeks,' Karl lied. 'Now when I offer to give her what she wants, she screams blue murder!'

'You're lying and you're drunk!' Arlo said contemptuously. 'If you ever again lay a finger on Sharba or any of the other staff, I'll send you back to Germany and you'll end up in a German prison, which is where you probably should be anyway. Now go home and sober up. When you're sober, I want you to apologise to Sharba in my presence.'

'I suppose you're hoping to keep Sharba pure for you own convenience,' sneered Karl. 'It's no good coming over all "holier than thou" Father, we all know what you like to get up to—and I have your genes in my blood!'

With a roar like a lion, Arlo lunged at his son and punched him on the nose. There was a meaty thwack as the blow landed, and Karl went down on his back. A cry of horror broke forth from Amanda and she rushed forward to help her boyfriend.

'Leave him, Amanda,' cried Clara. 'He deserved to get that, and you shouldn't give him any sympathy!'

Sharba was horrified at the turn of events. She knew she wasn't to blame, but somehow she felt partly responsible for the drama and she couldn't stop shivering. Suddenly she felt a towel being placed gently around her shoulders and looked up to see Rosa standing next to her.

'Don't let Karl's appalling behaviour upset you too much, dear,' Rosa said quietly to her. 'He's as drunk as a skunk, and when he drinks too much it always brings out the worst in him.'

Karl was now struggling to get up and Amanda attempted to help him, but he pushed her roughly aside. 'If you weren't such a pathetic excuse for a woman none of this would have happened,' he said unkindly to her. His nose was pouring with blood and there was murder in his eyes. 'This is not the end of the matter,' he said. 'And if anyone thinks an apology will be forthcoming from me, they're sadly mistaken!' He then stomped off with Amanda running behind him.

'Why is that girl so bloody stupid?' Clara was clearly disgusted that Amanda felt any sympathy for Karl at all.

'Come on Sharba,' said Rosa. 'Let me walk you to your cottage. You need to get some clothes on, and I'll make you a cup of tea. You've had a bad fright.'

Sharba allowed Rosa to walk her to her cottage and while Rosa made a pot of tea she took a shower. She felt dirty and sullied where Karl had touched her, and Rosa seemed to understand.

'Are you feeling a bit better now?' Rosa asked her when they were sitting drinking the tea.

'Yes, I'm fine. I just wish it hadn't happened, though.'

'Of course you do, and I'm so sorry you've been subjected to this sexual abuse from Karl; he can be a very nasty person when he's drunk. I hope you won't be tempted to move on due to this incident. We all value you as an employee and a friend, and we would hate you to leave.'

'I don't want to leave. I love working here, but how is it going to be possible to continue now that this has happened?'

'Arlo will speak to Karl when he's sobered up and this will all blow over. Karl knows that he's on probation and Arlo won't hesitate to send him back to Germany if he misbehaves, so I imagine Karl will soon be giving you a grovelling apology and then he'll keep his distance.'

'I do hope you're right,' said Sharba worriedly, but she had her doubts.

13

Appalling Testimonies

The next day, Sharba was dreading meeting Karl, but when she arrived for work Clara told her that he wasn't there.

'Dad decided to send him to Lusaka on an errand, so he'll be away for a few days,' Clara said. 'Dad thought it would be a good way to let everything cool down, and also, Karl's face was a bit of a mess!' Clara looked rather pleased when she divested this bit of information. 'Dad must pack a mean punch because Karl's nose looks a bit squiffy and he has a huge bruise on his face and round his eye. Dad didn't think it was a face that the hotel guests would want to look at!'

'Did Amanda and George go with him?' Sharba asked.

'No, so they'll have a breathing space as well. I think Karl tries to blame everything bad that happens on Amanda and then gives her a hard time, so I'm sure she'll be glad to see the back of him for a bit.'

Later that morning Arlo called Sharba into his office. 'I just wanted to apologise on my son's behalf for what happened yesterday. I hope you've recovered from the trauma Karl put you through?'

'Yes, I'm fine,' Sharba assured him.

'Good. It shouldn't have happened, and I'll make sure it never happens again. I hope this incident won't make you consider leaving your job here? We really do value you as a member of our staff and would hate to lose you.'

'No, I wasn't thinking of resigning,' Sharba reassured him. 'I love working here, you've all been so good to me and I don't have any family or friends in Zambia, so this is like home to me.'

'I'm pleased to hear that,' said Arlo looking relieved. 'I had hoped Karl had settled down a bit. He was a problem child and a troubled young man. As he grew older, he did not calm down as I had hoped would be the case. So I brought him out here to try and get him on the straight and narrow and I thought it was working, especially when Amanda and George came into his life. But now I see him abusing Amanda and being overly harsh with his son. Now there's this trouble he's caused for you, I just don't know how to help him.'

Arlo seemed almost to be talking to himself now, but Sharba couldn't just leave so she sat quietly and let him ramble on. 'None of us are perfect; God knows I'm not perfect and there are parts of my life about which I'm very ashamed. But I've tried to make amends, I have.' Arlo leaned back in his chair and stared out of the window almost as though he was looking back over his past. 'Despite the wrongs I've committed, I've been blessed,' he continued. 'I've made money and become influential, but that doesn't help me sort out my son.' Suddenly he seemed to notice Sharba was still there and brought himself up short. 'But I mustn't keep you from your work, my dear. Thank you for your understanding.'

Later that day when Sharba was going back to her cottage, she saw Amanda in the distance and decided to check she was okay, but as soon as Amanda saw her coming in her direction she disappeared into her house, pulling George with her. She was very obviously trying to avoid Sharba, so Sharba decided that it was possible that Amanda was embarrassed about what had happened the previous day and was not yet able to face her, so she didn't go and knock on her door.

By the next day, Sharba knew for certain that Amanda was still taking every opportunity to avoid her, and she decided that it was ridiculous and they needed to clear the air between them. She went to her house and knocked on the door. There was no answer, so she knocked harder. She knew Amanda and George were inside. Suddenly the door opened and little George stood there, a big grin stretched his face when he saw it was Sharba.

'Auntie Sharba!' George exclaimed in delight, and ran to throw his arms around her.

'George, I told you not to open the door,' Amanda arrived looking apprehensive.

'Amanda, what's going on?' Sharba asked, after giving George a hug.

'You can't come in,' said Amanda desperately. She glanced worriedly around as though she thought someone might be watching them.

'Why? You don't blame me, surely, for what happened with Karl?'

'No, of course not, but Karl has told me that I mustn't have anything more to do with you.'

'But that's just ridiculous!'

'I know, but I have to obey him.'

'Karl's not even here; please let me come in so that we can talk.'

Amanda hesitated and then nodded her head. 'I hope he doesn't find out,' she muttered, anxiously glancing around again as Sharba walked into the house. 'That big Zulu, Samson, is always spying on me.'

'What's going on, Amanda? What'll Karl do if he finds out we've been talking?'

'He'll be so angry and then he'll...' Amanda's words tailed off.

'He'll what? Does he hurt you Amanda?'

Amanda burst into tears and Sharba steered her towards the sofa and sat her down on it. George, seemingly unaware of his mother's distress, went to play with his toys.

'Tell me what Karl does to you,' Sharba said, sitting beside the sobbing woman.

'I can't; it's too humiliating.'

'If Karl's hurting you, you need to tell someone.'

'Well, you must promise not to tell anyone else if I tell you.'

Amanda wouldn't say another thing until Sharba had promised.

'He pinches my nipples really hard—sometimes with pliers—until they bleed. You can't imagine how painful it is, but he knows I'll never show anyone because it's just too embarrassing.'

'But that's terrible!' Sharba was really shocked. 'He's physically abusing you. Why do you let him do that to you?'

'He's so strong. He can easily hold me down and do it to me.'

'But what I mean is, why do you let him get away with it?'

'You don't understand the position I'm in, Sharba. I don't have any qualifications to get work and Karl doesn't want me to work anyway. My family have disowned me, so all I have are Karl and George. If I do anything to displease Karl, he'll take George and kick me out. He always threatening to do that. And if he does, I'll have nothing! I know you think I'm stupid, but I still love Karl when he's not being cruel, so I just have to put up with the pain when he gets angry.'

'But this is madness, Amanda! Things can't go on like this. You have to do something, tell somebody, or things might get worse. What if Karl turns on George?'

'He won't if I'm there for him to take his frustrations out on. He can be a bit harsh with George, but he's never hurt him badly. If I tell anyone what's going on, Karl will kick me out and keep George, then it'll be George that Karl will hurt when he's cross or frustrated.'

'But Karl won't be able to keep George if he kicks you out. You're George's mother and you're not even married to Karl, so he'll have no claim on George.'

'Yes, but if Karl sent me packing, I wouldn't have any means of providing for George. I'd have to leave him with Karl because otherwise he'd starve.'

'But surely there's someone you could turn to? Even if you own family has disowned you, I'm sure Arlo and Rosa wouldn't let you and George starve if Karl kicked you out.'

'The thing is, I don't want to leave Karl, Sharba. I don't want him to kick me out, I still love him, and I want us to be a family.'

'But surely you couldn't really love him if he's ill-treating you in the way you described? It's positively brutal!'

'I know it sounds crazy, but I do still love him, and more than anything I want our relationship to work. He has faults, like everyone else, and when things upset him he turns on me, but after he does awful things to me, he's very contrite and loving and he shows me he still loves me.'

'But he shouldn't be doing those things to you in the first place; it's sick, Amanda, and you shouldn't just forgive him because he says he's sorry. He must be psychologically messed up if he does something like that; he needs help. Why don't we both go to Arlo and Rosa right now and tell them what's been going on?'

'No! I don't want anyone to know, and you've promised not to tell either.'

'But I had no idea how bad things were...'

'Look Sharba, Karl didn't want to marry me because he doesn't believe in marriage, but we did have a little ceremony just between the two of us. It was something that I wanted, and he agreed because he knew it was important to me. I promised before God to love, honour and obey him. I promised I would acknowledge him as the head of our family, and I would always submit to him. That promise is important to me and I've always kept it, until today, that is. He told me I mustn't have anything more to do with you and now I've taken you into my confidence. He mustn't ever find out I've disobeyed him; he said he'd take the sjambok to me if I ever spoke to you again, and I believe him!'

Sharba was amazed that Amanda would want to keep her promise even when Karl was abusing her so badly. She was determined to make the girl change her mind and seek counsel from Arlo and Rosa, but she just wouldn't agree to it. Eventually Sharba left, shaking her head.

'Listen Amanda,' she said as she was leaving. 'I won't ever let on that you and I are still friends, but if things get worse for you, please, please come to me and let me help you.'

❖

Later that evening, there was a soft tap on Sharba's door. She opened it expecting it to be Amanda, but it was one of the hotel maids that stood on her threshold. Uzma lived in Kapotwe Village and walked to work every day as she didn't qualify for one of the cottages. She was a pretty little African girl of about nineteen whom Sharba had often seen diligently going about her duties. Sharba frequently chatted to her and she had discovered that the girl had had a good education and spoke perfect English. She had confided in Sharba that, although she was just working as a maid, she hoped in the future she would be promoted, because she was ambitious and wanted a career in hospitality. When Sharba mentioned this to Clara, Clara nodded. 'It's already been noted that she's a good little worker, always cheerful, and clearly well educated. Dad is looking to put her in an admin position in the near future.'

But this evening, Uzma didn't look cheerful and her usual dazzling smile was not on her face. 'Hello Uzma, how can I help you?' Sharba asked, smiling at her.

'First I wanted to tell you I'm sorry for what Mr Karl tried to do to you; he's a bad man; we all know that!'

'Well, thank you for your sympathies, but nothing happened and I'm fine.'

'I'm happy that you're fine, but I need to tell you something else,' Uzma glanced around as though she was worried someone would see her talking to Sharba.

'You'd better come in,' invited Sharba, noticing how uneasy Uzma seemed.

They went inside and Sharba poured them both a glass of orange juice while indicating that Uzma should sit down.

'Now, what exactly is the problem?' Sharba also sat down and looked expectantly at the troubled girl.

'No one wanted to say anything because Mr Karl is Mr Huber's son and we thought it would bring trouble to everyone in our village, but now that he's tried to do it to you, who are a friend of Miss Clara, I think I must speak out.' Uzma looked down at the floor.

'Are you trying to tell me that Karl has tried to molest other woman here?' Sharba guessed.

'All the time, Miss Sharba! No woman who is young and pretty is safe from his groping hands, and he has already raped some of us. He often comes to Kapotwe Village; he just strides in like he owns the village and has no respect for our chief, Luckson Malupande. Many of those who live in the village work here and we don't want any trouble, so he takes advantage of this and he insists he gets his way with the ones he likes.'

'But this is terrible!' Sharba was really shocked. 'Why don't you report him to Mr Huber?'

'How can we do that? Mr Karl is the son of the boss and we can't afford to lose our jobs! Mr Karl has told us if anyone says anything, he'll make sure we're all sacked, every single person from Kapotwe Village who works at this hotel! There're a lot of us; we depend on our jobs here and can't afford to get sacked. But many of the young women are suffering at Mr Karl's hands because there is nothing anyone can do to change anything.'

'Why don't you report him to the police then?'

'The police?' Uzma gave a bitter laugh. 'Mr Karl has made sure that the police are on his side; what he does to us is only one of his vices, and he pays the police to turn a blind eye to all his wrongdoings.'

Sharba wasn't entirely surprised to hear this as she knew many of the police in Zambia were corrupt. She knew Uzma was appealing directly to her for help, but didn't think she was in a position to be able to do anything.

'But...why are you telling me this?' Sharba asked. 'I'm also a victim and I can't afford to lose my job either.'

'I know and I'm sorry. But if at any time you can say something to help us from being preyed upon ...'

'Uzma, I want to help, but I'm in the same boat as all the other women. I wanted to leave after what Karl did to me, but I have nowhere to go and I depend on this job for my livelihood.'

'I'm sorry, I shouldn't have bothered you,' said Uzma sadly, getting up to leave. Her face that had been filled with hope now drooped with despair.

'No, I'm sorry I can't be of more help. I'm in a difficult position, but let me think about things. If I can come up with a bright idea of how to deal with the situation, I'll let you know.'

'Thank you, Miss Sharba.'

After Uzma had left, Sharba made her way to the jetty where the hotel guests could embark on the boats that took them on a sunset cruise of the river; it was lovely and peaceful there, a good place to think. The setting sun was decorating the river in her vivid colours as the water slid serenely by. Everything seemed so calm and beautiful, completely at odds with Sharba's distressing thoughts. What a despicable man Karl was! He physically abused his wife and child and also preyed upon those he felt could not stand against him. How she wanted to expose him for what he was, but could she risk losing her job? She decided to sleep on the problem and make a decision in the morning.

14

A Dreadful Shock

Oliver was feeling extremely frustrated because it seemed Hugh Fortrum, the private investigator he had hired and whom he was paying a huge amount of money, had not found out any more that he, Oliver, had on his trip to Kenya. He swept Hugh's report off his desk in irritation.

The only additional piece of information that he had given Oliver was that it was highly unlikely that Sharba would be staying in the region of Lunga-Lunga, because there was little there apart from the border crossing. There were no large towns or big estates in which she might be living, and he had to assume she had crossed over the border and entered Tanzania, probably on another passport, as Sharnique Wellby had definitely not passed through the Lunga-Lunga border crossing. The trouble was that the bus on which it was supposed she had continued her journey had first gone to Tanga before continuing on to Dar-es-Salaam, so there was a huge area in which to hunt for his girlfriend.

After thinking for a while, Oliver sat down at his computer and emailed Hugh. He told him to forget Tanzania and go to Lusaka, since they had discovered she had been born in Zambia and therefore it was likely that was where she was headed. Hugh had followed his instructions and flown into the capital of Zambia. A couple of days later, he emailed Oliver to say he thought he'd had a breakthrough and said he would send another email in a day or two when he'd had a chance to check on all his facts.

Oliver waited impatiently for the email to come, but the days went by and nothing arrived. He sent several emails to Hugh asking what was going on, but Hugh seemed to be ignoring him. Oliver then tried to ring Hugh, but every time he put a call through it went to voice mail. It was so frustrating. So, two weeks later when Oliver's phone rang and he saw it was a call from the private investigator, he snatched it up.

'What the hell's happening?' Oliver demanded angrily.

'Good morning sir,' replied a strange deep voice with an African accent.

'Hugh? That's not Hugh! Who're you?'

'I'm sorry sir, I'm a police officer and I'm using Mr Fortrum's mobile phone to try and contact one of his relatives. Are you by any chance related to him?'

'No, he works for me. What is this, anyway? I've been trying to contact him for days!'

'I'm very sorry, sir, but Mr Fortrum was killed in a motor accident near Lusaka. His car was involved in a collision with one of the minibus taxis and, unfortunately, he died at the scene of the accident. I have not been able to find out who his relatives are and hoped that by using his mobile and calling the number he seemed to have rung the most, I could contact a family member.'

'Well, I'm sorry I can't help you. I don't know who his relatives are. You should try going through the British High Commission.'

Oliver rang off feeling irritated. Surely they should have done what he suggested in the first place, rather than taking a stab in the dark and ringing someone on Fortrum's mobile phone? But in a way he was glad that they had done that, because now he knew what had happened. He didn't feel sorry for Hugh—he hardly knew the man—but he did feel exasperated that the private investigator was seemingly on the brink of finding out something about his girlfriend and subsequently was unable to tell him what he had found out. He now had to decide if he should engage another private investigator or go out to Zambia himself.

❖

The morning after Uzma had visited Sharba, Sharba had made up her mind what she was going to do. Both Uzma and Amanda had confided in her, so it would be morally reprehensible if she did nothing. Even at the cost of losing her job she would have to say something to Arlo, and, on thinking about things, she was pretty sure that it was unlikely that he would sack her for speaking up. He was a good man, in her estimation, so he would listen to all she said and make a fair judgement. Having made her decision, Sharba was anxious to get it over with so she set out for Arlo's office as soon as she knew he would be there. She had not taken half a dozen steps when her mobile rang.

'Sharba, would you mind coming to my office before you start work this morning?' It was Arlo who was ringing and Sharba replied she would come straight away. She had no idea what he wanted, but it would be her opportunity to let him know what his rotten son had been up to!

When Sharba entered Arlo's office she was shocked to see that Karl was there. She thought he was going to be away for a few days and hadn't realised he had come back. She felt her stomach recoil at the sight of him. His bruised face made her shudder because it caused him to appear more predatory than ever.

'Ah, Sharba, there you are,' said Arlo, breaking off what he was saying to his son. 'Karl asked me to summon you because he has something he wants to say to you.' Arlo sounded upbeat and looked pleased to be a participant of what was to follow as he nodded to Karl to continue.

Karl stepped forward and took one of Sharba's hands in both of his. He looked deeply into her eyes and said, 'Sharba, I just want to apologise for my gross and unforgivable conduct of the other day. I'm deeply ashamed of myself and I can only say in my defence that I was very drunk at the time it happened. I know I don't deserve your understanding or forgiveness, but I do hope you'll be able to accept my apology.' His tone was conciliatory and sincere, but it was completely at odds with the expression in his eyes. They seemed to bore into Sharba and she could see they gleamed with malice, so she was under no illusions that the apology was anything but authentic.

Sharba glanced at Arlo. Surely he could discern that his son was not genuinely apologising? But Arlo's expression was one of relief and benevolence. He was obviously pleased that his son had accepted he had made a bad mistake and was man enough to try and make amends for it. Of course, he would want to think the best of his son, Sharba realised bitterly as she pulled her hand away from Karl.

'Sharba?' Arlo was expecting her to say something.

Sharba wanted to tell Karl to get lost, but his insincere apology and Arlo's obvious willingness to believe his son had knocked her off balance. What could she now say that wouldn't be construed as a bitter woman taking revenge on someone who had wronged her? But she had to say something as both men were waiting for her to reply.

'I accept your apology,' she eventually muttered tightly. This wasn't the time or place to make more accusations against Karl, she decided. It would have to wait until another time when Karl wasn't present.

'That settles the matter then,' said Arlo, looking satisfied with the outcome of the situation. 'I'm glad you returned early to put things right, Karl; it's not good when there's discord between staff. Now, my dear,' he said turning to Sharba. 'Don't let me detain you further.'

Sharba left the office thankfully, but she was dismayed when Karl suddenly appeared at her side and fell into step with her. He didn't say a word until they were out of earshot of Arlo's office.

'I learned your dirty little secret while I was in Lusaka,' Karl sneered quietly, and his low provocative tone was spiked with malice.

Sharba stopped in her tracks and looked at Karl, completely speechless for a second.

How on earth could he have found out about her escape from the mall and subsequently her change of identity and flight to Zambia to evade Oliver?

'But how ...?'

'Yes, I know, we all have our little secrets, don't we?' Karl went on vindictively. 'I know I have mine! But I'm glad my father sent me to Lusaka. It was fortunate because by pure luck I found out all that you're trying to hide!'

'How?' Sharba whispered again, thinking Oliver must surely have tracked her to Lusaka and somehow Karl had met him and learned her secret. She felt shaken to the core.

'You know what? I'm a lucky guy because I met someone when

I was in Lusaka who knew all the facts and I figured out what you're all about! I was destined to meet him, I guess, because otherwise you would have put the boot in and exposed me. Oh yes, I have my spies everywhere and I know what's been going on in my absence. That's the real reason I came back early—to stop you opening your big mouth! But don't worry, sister, I'll keep your secret secure for you ... *but,* and this is a big *but,* only if you keep mine!'

Karl looked deeply into her eyes to make sure he was engaging with her before he went on.

'When the old man dies, Huber Enterprises will be mine! Albert's not interested in Africa; he's already made his money in Germany and doesn't want to bother about things in Zambia. Clara will marry her millionaire boyfriend and will have more than enough money, so I'm going to get what my father has built up here. Nothing, *especially not you,* is going to stop that happening. *Do you understand me?* I don't want my father having second thoughts about who will inherit when he dies!'

Sharba nodded her head.

'So, you can stay and work here; your pretty little ass is an asset to this place, but you'll remember that I can ruin your life very easily if you do anything to jeopardise my inheritance. Just do your job, keep your nose out of things and don't go telling tales. If you do as I say, I'll leave you alone and keep your secret safe. So, do we have a deal?'

Sharba could only nod. She felt completely dumbfounded; she had thought she was quite safe from Oliver, stuck out in the sticks on the banks of the Zambezi River, but somehow this horrible man must have met Oliver and learned what had happened. Now she felt very vulnerable.

'Let me hear you say it then,' demanded Karl. 'Promise me you won't run to my father and tell him anything that might endanger my inheritance.'

'I promise,' muttered Sharba.

'And keep away from Amanda as well. I don't want you dripping poison in her ear.'

'Okay.'

'Good, now we understand one another. But just remember,

I'm not a person to double cross. If you try anything, you'll be very, very sorry!'

Karl strode away and Sharba stared after him feeling sick. She was in no doubt that he had spoken the truth.

Sharba could hardly concentrate on her work that day as she kept going over things in her mind. She was sure that the only way Karl could have found out her secret was from Oliver, and it was a terrifying thought that her old boyfriend was so close on her trail. How on earth had he figured out that she wasn't dead and was in Zambia? She knew Oliver was tenacious and wouldn't give up looking for her if he was sure she hadn't died, so somehow he must have figured out she was alive and had found out which country she had come to. But what were the chances of finding someone who knew exactly where she was when he got to Lusaka?

He must have been there asking around, trying to find out where she had gone, and had bumped into Karl. People liked to talk and gossip—Sharba remembered how much she had learned about Arlo before she'd even met him—so Oliver had probably just started a conversation with Karl and explained he was looking for her. The only reason Karl hadn't given her away was because he could see it gave him a bargaining chip. But could he really be trusted to keep her secret?

Sharba remembered how Amanda had been fearful of letting her in when she had gone to see why she had been avoiding her, and also how Uzma had looked around nervously before entering her house when she came for help. They both must have been aware that Karl had a spy. Karl must have learned that people were confiding in her, and that was the reason he had come rushing back, to blackmail her before she could spill the beans and jeopardise his inheritance. She thought it more than likely that Arlo had threatened Karl that he would disinherit him if he didn't behave himself, and that was something Karl was determined not to let happen.

Sharba felt very vulnerable. She kept wondering if she could trust Karl to keep his side of the bargain. She knew that if word got out that she had changed her identity to evade an old boyfriend, it would be gossiped about for miles around. If Oliver was nosing about Zambia, the gossip would almost certainly come to his ears and he would soon track her down in Livingstone. It was a horrifying thought because she knew that Oliver was obsessively controlling and could be dangerous if he didn't get his own way.

She considered briefly whether she should resign from her job and move to South Africa, but soon decided against that. Zambia was her country and she had made her home here in Livingstone. This was where she would take a stand against Oliver if necessary. No, she was not going to run away, or she might end up running from him for the rest of her life, she decided. She would stay where she was and hope that Karl would keep his side of the bargain so Oliver wouldn't be able to find her. She knew she had to do everything to avoid meeting Oliver again. If that meant making a pact with the devil—Karl—in the meantime, so be it.

Sharba regretted that she would be unable to help Uzma and the rest of the women that Karl had molested. She had really wanted to help them, but now she had to consider her own predicament and act accordingly. She also felt sorry that she wouldn't be able to be a friend to Amanda anymore, not even on the quiet when Karl was away. From now on, her main priority would be to keep herself safe.

15

Alistair

To start with, Sharba lived in constant fear that Karl would break his promise and let Oliver know where she was, but as the weeks slid past and nothing happened, her anxiety lessened. It seemed to her that Karl was keeping his side of the bargain and she figured that if Oliver had been in Lusaka at the same time Karl was there, he must now have given up searching for her and gone home, at least for the time being. She knew without a doubt he wouldn't give up entirely; if he thought she was in Zambia, he would come back and look for her again sometime in the future, so she never allowed herself to become complacent and was determined to keep on her guard at all times.

She and Karl avoided each other and she felt sure that things would be okay if she could keep the status quo. She kept away from Amanda and George, but she was sad their friendship had been curtailed by Karl, especially since Clara was now spending more and more time with Charles. However, despite everything, Sharba soon fell into a new routine that was not unpleasant. She still enjoyed her job and she loved living near the Zambezi. She derived a lot of pleasure from watching the wildlife that was right on her doorstep and since she had always been a bit of a loner in the past, she didn't have much trouble amusing herself.

One day when Sharba had a day off, she decided to go and visit the little local museum. She loved history but hadn't been there before, because when she had been going out with the girls, Clara declared she didn't like museums. Amanda said George would be bored at the museum and would start fussing when he realised there was nothing there of interest to him. Sharba caught a ride with hotel transport that was going into Livingstone and the driver, a man called Jonas, asked her if she enjoyed living next to the Zambezi River.

'Yes I do,' she said. 'I love the river, I love the falls, and I love the area.'

'You don't miss living in a big city, then?'

'No, I'm not much of a city girl. Just give me the quiet life and I'm happy!'

Jonas dropped her off outside the museum and told her what time he would be going back to the resort. 'I'll give you a ring half an hour before I leave and you can tell me where to pick you up,' he said.

On entering the museum, Sharba decided it looked rather rundown and dusty. She was the only person who was there and once her eyes had adjusted from the bright glare of the sun outside, she saw there were some dioramas, a few rather dusty looking stuffed animals, and also handwritten display materials that described the area's natural and pre-civilisation history. None of it was very inspiring, but then she went into a room featuring the life of David Livingstone. This was of far more interest to her. The town had been named after him as he was the first European to see the Victoria Falls, known to the local Africans at the time as *Mosi-oa-Tonya*—literally, *The Smoke that Thunders*. David Livingstone had renamed it after his queen, Queen Victoria.

David Livingstone had lived an adventurous life that was full of danger in Africa, but he was generally liked and respected by the African people. He had wanted very much to convert them to Christianity, but seemingly had had little success because even the ones that did convert retained their African culture, much of which went against Livingstone's teachings. He died at the relatively young age of sixty in 1873. He was in Chief Chitambo's village, southeast of Lake Bangweulu at the time, and had died of malaria and dysentery. His heart was buried under a tree near the spot where he died, but the rest of his remains were carried by his faithful followers Chuma and Susi to the coastal town of Bagamoyo, over a thousand miles away. From there, the remains were returned by ship to Britain for burial, where a big ceremonial funeral was held.

Some of Livingstone's belongings were on display in the museum and there were copies of letters to and from him as well. Sharba completely immersed herself in his history, trying to feel the emotions he must have felt when he suddenly came across the spectacular sight of the waterfall.

He must have seen the great plumes of spray from afar and known that he was going to see something immense and outstandingly remarkable, she thought. He had been paddled along the Zambezi River to what was now called Livingstone Island, and that was where he had first glimpsed something so magnificent that the famous words, "Scenes so lovely must have been gazed upon by angels in their flight," had burst from his lips.

That scene must have been recompense for all the hardship and suffering he had endured on his journey through Africa, thought Sharba. She bent over the letters displayed and tried to read them. She was so engrossed that she felt as if she had jumped out of her skin when she sensed movement behind her.

'I'm so sorry, I didn't mean to startle you,' said a deep voice that sounded contrite.

Sharba saw the words were spoken by a young man of about her age, who had fair curly hair and thoughtful, deep-blue eyes. His face was suntanned and he had features that were both strong and beautiful. It was the face of a poet ,Sharba decided, but right now it was set in lines of remorse. Sharba also noticed he had epaulettes on the shoulders of his crisp white shirt.

'That's okay, I was miles away with Dr Livingstone on his travels and didn't hear you come into this room,' said Sharba with a small laugh.

'I'm a big fan of David Livingstone as well,' said the man. 'I often visit this little museum when I'm in Livingstone. It's a bit quirky and I'm sure it's under resourced, but it holds a certain atmosphere, don't you think?'

Sharba had to agree with him. Together they studied the letters and talked about Livingstone's travels. She could detect a slight Scottish accent when he spoke, and she wondered if the Scottish connection made him a fan of the famous explorer.

At last it was time to go and the man said, 'I'm Alastair Gordon.

I think I should introduce myself since I nearly scared you to death earlier!'

Sharba laughed. 'I'm Sharba Lengi,' she told him.

'You wouldn't like to come and have a coffee with me, would you? I think I owe you a coffee after giving you that scare.' Now Alastair looked embarrassed and yet hopeful at the same time.

Sharba had sworn she wouldn't have any more to do with men after her experience with Oliver, but Alastair looked so open and uncomplicated as he gazed at her, his face a mask of innocent hope. Sharba nodded her head. A coffee was a coffee, she decided, and she was just being polite, not agreeing to enter into a relationship with this guileless young man.

'Actually, I'm starving,' said Alistair as they walked out of the museum. 'How about a pizza at Olga's instead of a coffee? I've had one there before and I know they're delicious.'

Since Sharba could detect a soft Scottish accent when Alistair spoke and his name was Scottish as well, she thought he must come from Scotland.

'Have you been in Zambia for long?' she asked him as they tucked into pizza.

'I was born here,' Alistair told her. 'My parents come from Scotland and I was sent to Scotland for my secondary education, but I'm a bona fide Zambian, born in Lusaka. How about you?'

'I'm a Zambian as well. I was born in Lusaka like you, but at the age of ten I left Zambia with my parents and went to live in England. I've only recently returned to Zambia.'

Sharba found that Alistair was easy to talk to. He was interested in all she had to say and was quite open about his own life. She learned that he was a pilot who had flown down to Livingstone from Lusaka early that morning with a group of American tourists.

'I'm not one of those clever chaps who can do anything,' Alistair admitted. 'But the one thing I'm good at is flying, so I decided that I'd set up a charter business and fly tourists around Zambia in my little Cessna 206. People told me that it wouldn't work because tourists could fly to most destinations in Zambia on a commercial flight which would be cheaper for them. But I went ahead anyway, and I find that my business is booming! Loads of tourists prefer to charter a small aeroplane and I can get them to places where commercial flights can't go, so it's working really well. I have contacts at most of the places tourists want to go to, so I fly them to the destination of their choice and then my contact takes them around the area and brings them back to me when they're ready to fly to their next destination.'

'Will you be flying your Americans back to Lusaka today, then?' Sharba asked him.

'Yes. I actually suggested to them that they would need more than a day to sample all that this area has to offer, but they seemed to think that the Victoria Falls was all that's worth seeing and they dismissed my suggestion. Apparently, they have some sort of "do" that they need to attend in Lusaka tomorrow, then the following day they've booked to fly to the Luangwa Game Park for a few days. It makes no difference to me; I'll fly them wherever they want, whenever they want.'

When Alistair asked Sharba about herself, she told him she had decided to return to Zambia when her parents had been killed, and she was now working at Huber's Riverside Lodge as a receptionist. Since Alistair had been so open and forthcoming about his own life, she felt she should be the same, but then she remembered that she had promised herself never to mention that she had been Sharnique Wellby for a good part of her life. If she could keep that secret from everyone without exception, she had a better chance of evading Oliver if he ever came back to Zambia to look for her.

'Is the hotel you work in a nice hotel?' Alistair enquired.

'It's lovely, but not cheap to stay in!'

'What's it like working there?'

'I love it. It's a good job, I have my own little cottage that goes with the job, and I like the owner and most of his family.'

'*Most* of the family?'

'Yes, well, let's just say the owner's son is a bit of a prat, but he's the only one I don't like.'

Just then Alistair's mobile phone rang. 'Excuse me, it's my Americans ringing, I'll have to answer it,' he said. He spoke into the receiver and listened to what was said and then nodded his head. 'Yes, I think we can arrange that. Let me just look at my diary.' He scrabbled in his pocket and pulled out a small diary and flicked through the pages. 'Yes, that's actually two weeks today,' he said. 'That's absolutely fine.' Then he listened again and his eyes swivelled towards Sharba. 'Hold on,' he said into the receiver. Then to Sharba he said, 'Can you tell me again the name of the hotel in which you work?'

'Huber's Riverside Lodge,' Sharba replied.

'Huber's Riverside Lodge is a highly recommended hotel,' Alistair said into the receiver. 'You should try them.'

When Alistair had finished the phone call, he grinned at Sharba. 'My Americans found that I wasn't talking rubbish when I told them that they'd need more than a day in Livingstone, so they've booked me to fly them down here again in a couple of weeks. They'll most probably be booking into your hotel since I've recommended it to them, so hopefully I'll be able to see you again.' The words were no sooner out of his mouth when he realised that Sharba might not wish to see him again. He blushed to the roots of his hair. 'Well, that's if you want to see me again,' he added lamely.

Sharba felt sorry for him, but she also found him very attractive so she hastened to put him at ease. 'Yes, it would be nice to meet up again,' she said, forgetting she was sworn off men. 'If you're here on my day off we could perhaps do something together?'

After they had swopped mobile numbers, Alistair had to head off to the airport and Sharba gave Jonas a ring to see if he was nearly ready to go back to the resort. She thought about Alistair as they bumped over the dusty road on the way back. He appeared to be transparent and easy going, the total opposite to Oliver who had been so intense and persuasive. She hoped they could be good friends, or maybe even something more.

❖

Sharba found herself looking forward to seeing Alastair again. They had spoken several times on the phone and the Americans had duly booked into Huber's Riverside Resort for a night.

'I won't be staying there,' Alistair told Sharba. 'It would be cheaper for me to fly home! But I was wondering, if I did stay down there for a night—in cheaper accommodation of course— would you like to come out with me in the evening?' He sounded flustered and unsure of himself when he made the suggestion.

'I'd love to,' Sharba responded. 'Actually, I was rather hoping we could spend a day together as well. I could get a day off and I thought we could do the Livingstone Island tour and swim in Devil's Pool. I've been longing to do that but didn't want to do it alone.'

'That sounds like a fantastic idea!' Alistair exclaimed. He could hardly get his head around how this beautiful, sexy girl wanted to spend time with him. Although he was an attractive man, his shyness had always hampered him, and he hadn't had much luck with girls.

Sharba decided to meet Alistair at the airport, so she was there to greet him when he flew in with his group of Americans. She had caught an early ride in with the hotel transport and now she waited for him to arrive, feeling full of excited anticipation. It was a hot, clear August day and already she could feel the heat stoking up as their short winter had come to an end. Everywhere was dry and dusty, there hadn't been a drop of rain since March, and the ground was crying out for moisture. In contrast to the shrivelled grey to yellow grass that was awaiting the first rain to regenerate it again, the flowering trees were in full bloom. The jacaranda trees were a swirl of blue and mauve blossom, while the flamboyant trees were covered in their bold, red flowers. They gave the town a carnival feel with their bright colours, Sharba thought.

After a while, Sharba spotted the little aeroplane coming in to land. It was painted red and silver and seemed to float over the runway before touching down like thistledown. She watched as it taxied to the airport buildings and then she saw Alistair jumping out and helping his passengers to disembark and collect their luggage. He had already organised someone to pick them up from the airport and take them to the hotel and any other place they wished to see, so Sharba watched as he helped them into the minibus, chatting easily to them as they settled themselves. At last, they were ready to go and the driver, after having a quick word with Alistair, climbed into the driver's seat and drove away.

It was only then that Sharba approached Alistair and a big grin stretched across his face as he saw her. When she reached him, he gave her a hug and then stepped back looking embarrassed, because he didn't know if she had expected a hug, a kiss or a handshake.

'It's so lovely to see you again,' said Sharba, putting him at his ease. 'Shall we call for a taxi to take us to where the boat departs for Livingstone Island?'

'No need for that,' said Alistair. 'I arranged for Marcus, one of my mates, to leave a car for me here, and the minibus driver has just given me the keys—so we have wheels!'

It didn't take them long to reach the river from where the boat left for Livingstone Island. They climbed aboard with a handful of other thrill seekers and then the boat captain skilfully manoeuvred the boat down the swiftly flowing Zambezi, twisting and turning as he navigated his way through the rocky channels.

'This wouldn't be a good place to have an engine failure,' murmured Alistair as they headed towards the column of spray rising up like a beacon where the river was hurled into the gorge below.

It only took about five minutes to reach the island, where they were greeted with a drink and then led to the very edge of the Falls on the east of the island overlooking Horseshoe and Rainbow Falls. After that, the guides led them to the west of the island overlooking the Main Falls.

'Wow, this is awesome!' Sharba exclaimed as she gazed at the magnificent view of the main torrent of the great Zambezi River gushing over the basalt precipice in a foam of effervescent bubbles. They could hear the water thunder as it hit the bottom of the gorge and they could feel the vibrations of energy that were pushed right back up to the top of the waterfall together with the dense spray.

'It certainly gives a completely different perspective to the views one gets of the waterfalls from the path through the rainforest on the other side of the canyon,' observed Alistair.

Suddenly the sun caused an exquisite rainbow to shimmer in the rising spray, making Sharba feel almost emotional with the beauty of it.

'Let me take a picture of you with the rainbow in the background,' Alistair said.

Then it was time for them to wade into the river and swim slightly upstream. They found the water was refreshing and not at all cold. 'Do you think there're crocks about?' Alistair teased.

'No, we're too close to the edge,' replied Sharba. 'Crocodiles prefer to stay further up the river where there're fish for them to eat.'

Soon they got to a rocky outcrop close to the edge of the falls and Devil's Pool. The pool had been created by thousands of years of erosion, but there was a rock ledge on the lip of the falls where the water was only a few centimetres deep, forming a natural barrier.

'Come on, let's jump into the pool,' said Sharba, her eyes shining with excitement. Holding hands, she and Alistair jumped together into the deep pool. They moved to the ledge right on the lip of the falls and eased themselves forward so that they could look right into the 103-metre chasm down to the gorge, while huge torrents of water flowed over the edge just meters away. It was an adrenaline-charged experience that left them breathless with exhilaration. Alistair had given his camera to one of the guides who took a picture of them as they gazed in awe at the spectacle.

Once they got back to Livingstone Island, Sharba and Alistair talked animatedly about their recent activity as they were served lunch. They had both thoroughly enjoyed the experience and, having shared it, they found it brought them closer together.

'What would you like to do this afternoon?' Alistair asked Sharba once they had been delivered back to the side of the river where they had left their car.

'How about bungee jumping,' suggested Sharba?

'My God, girl, are you an adrenalin junkie or what?' Alistair laughed. 'Listen, I'm not opposed to bungee jumping, but I wouldn't want to do it after having just eaten a meal!'

'No, you're probably right,' conceded Sharba. 'Bungee jumping will have to wait for another time.'

Instead they decided to go on a drive around the Mosi-oa-Tunya national Park. It was only sixty-six square kilometres and afforded a wonderfully relaxing drive alongside the river for much of the circular route. They were delighted to see a wide variety of species—antelope, zebra, giraffe, warthog and an assortment of birds.

'The animals all seem so relaxed,' Sharba commented as they watched a giraffe delicately pluck some leaves from the top of an acacia tree. He was obviously savouring them as he chewed with a dreamy expression on his face. Nearby there were some zebra, looking fat and contented, while a herd of impala wandered by.

'That's because they have no predators in this park,' Alistair told her.

They were delighted to see elephants crossing the river further on, their huge bodies slick with water as they pushed their way up the bank on the Zambian side.

'How nice to be able to wander wherever you want without having to worry about a passport or the right currency for the country,' observed Sharba.

Later that evening they went to the Avanti where there was a poolside bar and grill.

'Where're you staying tonight?' Sharba asked Alistair. They had just finished eating a delicious pizza and were enjoying the fantastic sunset over the river as they sipped their drinks.

'I'm staying with a Marcus, the owner of the vehicle we've been using. He lives about five miles down the main road that heads north.'

'When do you have to fly your Americans back to Lusaka?'

'Tomorrow evening. I think they're flying back to the States the day after tomorrow otherwise they may have been tempted on staying in Livingstone for a bit longer.'

'Do you have any plans for tomorrow?'

'No, not really; I'll just hang about until they're ready to go.'

'Well, I have to work tomorrow, but I'd love it if you joined me for my lunch break. We could have a sandwich and you'd get to see where I work.'

'Great, I'll be there.'

❖

'You look like the cat that got the cream!' Clara remarked to Sharba the next morning. 'What's making you so happy?'

'I'm always happy! I'm a naturally happy person!'

'I know that, but you're extra happy today, I can see it shining out of you!'

'I've met someone I like—a lot.'

'Really? Do tell all!'

'I met him a couple of weeks ago at the museum and yesterday I spent the day with him.'

'Okay, go on! What's his name, what does he look like, what does he do...?'

'His name's Alistair Gordon, he's a pilot and you'll be able to see what he looks like later because he's coming to see me when I have my lunch break.'

'Wow, you must be serious if he's joining you on your lunch break,' teased Clara.

❖

Alistair was duly impressed when he came to the resort.

'This is the most recently built hotel down here, isn't it?' Alistair remarked. 'Well, they've certainly got it right; there's nothing more horrible than a concrete structure stuck in a beautiful location, but here they've managed to blend the buildings into the surroundings in a very complementary way. Who designed it?'

'I'm not sure but I think it was Arlo Huber, the owner.'

'Arlo Huber has more than one business in Zambia, hasn't he?'

'Yes, he's got several, I believe.'

'I seem to remember a few years ago there was quite a bit of scandal about the man. What's he like to work for?'

'He's a good boss. I like him and his wife Rosa, and I am very friendly with Clara, their daughter, who works in reception with me. I don't know what happened with Arlo before, but it's all in the past now and I don't think we should judge him.'

'You're right; it seems by what you say that they're a nice family.'

'They are, all except Karl, the son, who isn't nice at all.'

'Why do you say that?'

'One day in the future I might tell you, but for now suffice to say that he's a horrible person I do my best to avoid.'

Sharba obviously didn't want to talk about Karl, so Alistair asked her if she would like to fly up to Lusaka some time when she had a weekend off.

'You could have a bird's eye view of the Victoria Falls when we took off, and a weekend of city living.'

'I'd like that,' said Sharba. 'Let's keep in contact and we can arrange it sometime.'

❖

'I took a peek at you and your new boyfriend and I think he's gorgeous,' Clara told Sharba when she went back to work that afternoon. 'Are you really serious about him?'

'I don't know yet; it's early days,' Sharba responded.

'You did say a few months ago that you didn't want anything more to do with men when it came to relationships,' Clara reminded her.

'I know I did, but Alistair has kind of taken me by surprise. I've never been opposed to being friendly with a man and having a good time, but the last man I was with suddenly became very possessive and jealous, and it was a nightmare. I really felt I would rather be on my own than have something like that happen again.'

'But now you feel different?'

'Well, Alistair is the total opposite to my old boyfriend. He's gentle and trusting and a complete gentleman.'

'Well then, you shouldn't let him slip through your fingers!'

'I know, but I must admit I'm a bit worried he might change. My last boyfriend did. To start with he was good fun and we had such a laugh. I was quite unprepared when he changed so dramatically.'

'Well, just take things slowly with Alistair,' advised Clara. 'If he's putting on an act, he won't be able to keep it up indefinitely.' Their conversation had to end there as one of the hotel visitors was approaching the desk with a query.

❖

That evening Sharba couldn't stop thinking about Alistair. She had promised herself that she wouldn't get emotionally involved in a man, but she just couldn't help her feelings when it came to Alistair. It was too soon to say she loved him, but she felt she was on a precipice and about to be washed over it by her emotions. Alistair was different from any other man she had met. He was definitely not one of the self-assured, beer-swilling, bullshitting, alpha males that usually hit on her. Alistair almost appeared to be diffident when you first met him, but as she had got to know him, she sensed he had a depth to his character that was hidden by his shyness. But she decided that Clara was right; she should take things very slowly and make sure that Alistair was what he appeared to be.

16

A Great Party

'A re you comfortable?' Alistair asked Sharba. He had got her settled into the right-hand seat of his Cessna 206 and made sure she was securely strapped in.

'Yes thanks,' Sharba responded. She was excited to be flying with Alistair to Lusaka for the weekend. Over the past weeks, she had unintentionally fallen in love with her handsome pilot and all her resolutions never to trust another man and live a single life had been blown away by the passion of her desire to be with Alistair.

Soon they were airborne and Sharba could get a bird's eye view of the falls. Alistair made several passes so that she could take some photos, and then he turned and flew up the Zambezi so that she could also photograph Huber's Riverside Resort from the air before they headed north.

It didn't take them long to fly to Lusaka and in about an hour Alistair touched the aircraft lightly down on the runway.

'We used to be able to use the city airport,' he told Sharba. 'Now it's only for use by the military. But as far as I'm concerned, using the international airport is very convenient because I rent a farm cottage very close by.'

When they left the aerodrome, Alistair only drove down the road leading to the Great East Road for about half a mile before turning off onto an untarred road. It was very dusty and corrugated, but they didn't stay on it for long. Just after going over the Chongwe River bridge, Alistair turned right down a farm track.

'The house I rent was probably originally built for the farm manager,' he told Sharba. 'Paul Cole, who owns the farm now, doesn't have a manager so he rents out the cottage. He doesn't charge a lot as he says his main objective is to have the cottage occupied, so it suits me down to the ground. I'm not someone who likes the bright lights, so living on the farm is ideal for me.'

'Do you see a lot of your landlord, then?' Sharba asked.

'Oh yes, we're very friendly. I socialise with him and his son, Rick, quite often. Paul's away this weekend so you won't be able to meet him, but maybe Rick will come around.'

'Does Paul have a wife?'

'No, he's a widower. Pam died after being bitten by a mamba. She was in the henhouse looking for eggs when it happened, and she didn't even make it back to the house before she died; it was a terrible thing to happen.'

'That's really awful!' Sharba agreed.

'Yes, Rick was only little at the time, so Paul had bring him up on his own.'

'So how old is Rick now?'

'Um, I think he's about nineteen. He's a nice lad and helps his father on the farm; that's why Paul doesn't need a manager.'

Alistair told Sharba about the other people living and farming in the area. It seemed that he knew everyone, and there was a good community spirit.

'Actually, I've lived in this area for most of my life,' Alistair explained. My father is a doctor and worked in a surgery in Lusaka and my mother taught in the International School, but we had a smallholding about four miles west of here. We had a few cows and some sheep and poultry—of course, ducks, hens and turkeys. We also had a couple of horses, one of which often seemed to get into trouble. He managed to gash himself on a regular basis for some reason, so we'd have to call out the vet, a really nice chap called Dick Wellby, to come and stitch him up.'

Sharba had to stop herself from blurting out that Dick Wellby had been her adoptive father. Instead she asked Alistair where his parents were now.

'After they had both retired, they went back to Scotland from where they originated. They sent me to Scotland for a good deal of my education with the hope that when I graduated, I'd stay and work there, but Zambia has always been home to me. I love it here and wouldn't want to live in wet, drab little Scotland—or anywhere else for that matter!'

When they arrived at the cottage a few minutes later, Sharba saw that it was a pretty little dwelling surrounded by bougainvillea bushes and half covered in a golden-shower creeper. A German Shepherd and a Jack Russel bounced down the lawn to meet the vehicle, their eyes bright and their tails wagging.

'Meet Peg and Fifi,' said Alistair as he greeted the dogs enthusiastically. 'They're the other women in my life!'

After they had both made a fuss of the dogs, they went to the house where there was an African man waiting to greet them; he looked almost as pleased as the dogs to see Alistair. Alistair introduced him to Sharba as Dixon, his cook and right-hand man. He was a small man with grizzled grey curls and a merry smile.

'I don't know what I'd do without him,' Alistair told Sharba. 'He organises everything at home, and I don't have to worry about a thing when I have to go away for a few days because he stays and looks after the dogs.'

Sharba felt instantly at home in the cottage. It was quite small, but it had a good homely feel to it. She could understand why Alistair liked living on the farm because it was peaceful, and the magic of the place was already draining the stress of hotel living out of her system.

'It's really lovely here,' she said as they sat on the veranda drinking a cup of tea. The hum of the bees on the golden shower blossoms and the birdsong in the trees made a wonderfully relaxing background sound.

'I'm glad you like it,' said Alistair looking pleased. 'Now, we've been invited to a braai—a barbeque—tonight. Tom and Mary Hale are putting on a bit of a "do" to celebrate Tom's birthday. They live on a farm about five miles from here and I've accepted the invitation, but we can cancel if you don't want to go.'

'No, it sounds lovely,' said Sharba.

'Good. Everyone will be there, so you'll be able to meet all my friends.'

Later that evening they headed for Tom's farm.

'Would you mind holding this?' Alistair asked, giving Sharba a bottle of brandy. 'I bought it for Tom since it's his birthday; I know he likes a drop now and then.'

Alistair had told Sharba that she needn't dress up, but she still looked stunning in her skinny jeans and a floaty aquamarine blouse. It seemed as if Tom's eyes would pop out of his head when he went out to greet them on their arrival. Alistair had mentioned that he wanted to bring someone with him, but Tom had assumed that it would be one of his colleagues from the flying world, because Alistair was notoriously shy with women and never seemed to have any luck with getting a girlfriend.

'Welcome,' Tom said heartily when they had been introduced. 'Come on in and meet the wife.'

The party was set around the pool in the garden, and already the braziers had been lit and the flames caused dancing shadows around the tables and chairs that were already in place. On a nearby table, large platters of meat, sausages and boerewors were piled up, waiting for the flames to die down before they were put on to cook. There was also a trestle table holding numerous dishes of salad and bread, all covered by a net.

Slowly all the guests arrived and settled in the chairs with their drinks, chatting to one another and teasing Tom about his advancing age. It seemed that all the farmers for miles around had been invited; some of the couples were quite old, others were younger and had their children with them, and then there were yet others like Sharba and Alistair who had not yet tied the knot. Everyone seemed friendly and Sharba was beginning to feel accepted when she suddenly sensed a hostile presence. She glanced in the direction from which she had detected antagonistic vibes and saw a young woman a few years her junior staring at her. The woman immediately looked away when Sharba met her eyes.

Lyn Yates had felt outraged when she saw Sharba with Alistair, because she had earmarked the lad for herself. The previous year when Lyn had flown out from England to stay with her aunt and uncle on a nearby farm, she had met Alistair and immediately decided that he was the man that she would marry. But unfortunately, she had been due to fly back to England a couple of days after their first meeting and there had been no time for her to cultivate a friendship with him. However, she had already thought out a strategy and had planned to follow it through on her next visit a year later. But now it seemed that Alistair had found someone else. When she had first met him, Lyn still had a year to go before finishing her degree, but she had felt at the time that Alistair was bound to still be free when she returned to Zambia the following year, because he was known to be painfully shy with women.

Now when Lyn saw Alistair's hand touch Sharba's arm affectionately for a second, she wished she had never bothered to go back and finish her degree. Her parents had been keen for her to earn a paper degree, as they thought having one would be her golden ticket and opportunities would roll in. Lyn wasn't so bothered about opportunities, because she planned to meet and marry a man of means so that she wouldn't have to work. But she did like the idea of going to university, because it meant getting away from her parents and living with people of her own age with whom she could party.

Lyn had decided on getting a degree in advertising as it sounded quite glamorous to her and she imagined advertising agencies clamouring for her services when she had finished— all of which she would turn down, of course! In reality, things had been very different. She found that it would take a combination of creativity, enthusiasm, reliability and lots of hard work to be successful in advertising, and her heart really wasn't in it. However, she had completed the degree and got the treasured piece of paper. Also, she had, in many ways, enjoyed her three years of university; she had liked the freedom and the social side of being a student. When she had finished her degree, she found her bar bill had added to her debt quite considerably!

Last year when Lyn had met Alistair, she had decided he was the perfect man for her. She knew he was a pilot and assumed he flew for a big airline company which meant, in her eyes, that they would be able to travel all over the world at no expense. She loved travelling, so that would be ideal. While she had been at university, she had had several liaisons with her male colleagues, but she decided it would be better to get involved with someone who was already established in a good job, because she had no intention of working herself.

Alistair had met all the criteria. He was handsome, he had a good job working as a pilot, and, judging by his benevolent demeanour, she was pretty sure she would be able to get her own way once she was married to him. Now, as she looked at Sharba, all her plans seemed to have gone up in smoke. Although Lyn considered herself a good-looking and desirable young woman, she had to admit she couldn't compete with Sharba, and she hated her for it. With a sigh she decided to go and talk to Alistair, just on the slight off chance that the woman was his sister or another relative.

'Hi Alistair,' she said in a husky voice, as she sidled up to him and Sharba.

'Oh, hi...um...Linda.' Alistair was obviously having difficulty in recalling who she was, and it annoyed Lyn that he hadn't even remembered her name correctly.

'It's Lyn, not Linda,' Lyn corrected him.

'Oh yes, of course. Sorry. You came out from England to visit your uncle and aunt, Tony and Fi Nell, last year, didn't you? Have you come for another holiday?'

'Yes, well, that was sort of the plan.' Lyn looked pointedly at Sharba.

'Can I introduce you to my girlfriend?' Alistair said, taking her hint. 'Lyn this is Sharba, Sharba this is Lyn.'

'Hi,' Sharba said, smiling at her.

'Hi,' said Lyn grimly. 'Are you having a holiday in Zambia as well?'

'No, I'm a Zambian,' said Sharba.

Just then Paul Cole's son, Rick, arrived. After helping himself to a drink he looked around and saw Alistair, so he made his way towards him. Moodily, Lyn watched the effect Sharba had on Paul when they were introduced. Rick was literally gawping at her.

'My God, Alistair, where've you been hiding her?' Rick asked in delight after Alistair had introduced him to Sharba.

'I haven't been hiding her anywhere,' said Alistair laughing.

'Now take your covetous eyes off my girlfriend and go and play somewhere else!'

Rick burst out laughing and, punching Alistair on the arm lightly, he moved on. Lyn followed him. She knew he was the son of a landowner and thought it might be worth getting to know him better, because she rather liked the idea of becoming one of the landed gentry.

'I've had trouble with lion on my farm,' said a man called Chris Martin who had wandered over to talk to Alistair. 'Had one of my heifers taken last night—it's a bloody nuisance.'

Sharba looked surprised as she hadn't realised that there were lion in these parts.

'They occasionally walk up the Luano Valley to this area,' Alistair explained to her. 'Paul had problems with them last year. A lioness and her cubs arrived on his farm and he had several of his calves killed. It seemed that the lioness was teaching her cubs to hunt, because they didn't even eat all that they killed. Paul tried to hunt them, but they were elusive and then they suddenly disappeared, presumably back to the Luano Valley, so he had no more trouble.'

'Well, as far as I can tell there was only one lion that killed my heifer,' Chris told them. 'One of the men that work for me claims he's seen it. He says it's a big old male who looks like he's struggling to hunt because of age and old injuries.'

'Well, let's hope he goes back to where he came from,' said someone else, but Chris shook his head.

'He won't go anywhere else now that he's found easy meat to hunt,' he said. 'You mark my words; we're going to have more trouble in this area with him around.'

The conversation then turned to more cheerful topics and soon everyone was laughing again.

'Tom, it's your birthday! Surely you shouldn't be cooking the meat?' someone shouted to Tom as he started putting the meat on the barbeque.

'The thing is, I'm the master when it comes to cooking meat on the braai,' laughed Tom. 'No one is better than me!'

'Aren't you getting a bit long in the tooth to be doing something so strenuous at this time of the night?' teased someone else.

'Let me tell you, my friend, I'm more than capable of doing strenuous things at night,' retorted Tom. 'Anyway, less of the cheek from you; you give me a few years for sure, so you can't tell me I'm old!'

Soon the aroma of cooking meat filled the air, making everyone's mouth water. Meanwhile there was plenty to drink as everyone seemed to have brought a bottle for Tom, and the laughter and chatter got louder as everyone relaxed and became more uninhibited.

Tom hadn't been kidding when he said he knew how to cook the meat. Earlier, he had carefully marinated the steak with a careful selection of spices, and once it had been cooked it was delicious. When at last everyone was satiated, Mary shooed all the children off to bed. Things were getting a bit ribald, and, knowing this would happen, Mary had made up all her spare beds for the kids. They went off rather reluctantly, but shortly after they had gone Tom put on some music and everyone started to dance around the pool to the 1960s music that he liked so much. They danced into the early hours of the morning and then someone started a conga dance and everybody snaked around the garden and pool, until the person at the head of the conga suddenly leaped into the pool. Everyone else followed suit and the pool was filled with laughing, splashing, fully-clothed people, flopping around and having a great time.

'That was fun, wasn't it?' Sharba tried to wring the water out of her hair as she and Alistair sat on the edge of the pool with their feet still in the water. 'I was so hot with all the dancing, and a dip in the pool was just what I needed to cool me down!'

'Tom, check that there's no one at the bottom of the pool,' said Mary rather worriedly. 'Well, you never know,' she went on when there was a wide ripple of laughter. 'Everyone has had a lot to drink, and accidents do happen!'

Luckily there were no bodies found at the bottom of the pool and the party went on. It was almost four in the morning before Alistair and Sharba got back to the cottage. Their clothes had almost completely dried on them by then, because they had danced again under the stars as the tepid night air swirled around them.

'That was quite some party,' Sharba murmured as they walked into the cottage.

'Did you enjoy it?' Alistair asked.

'It was wonderful; I had a really great time.'

17

Lion Hunting

The next day, Charles and Sharba didn't get up until it was almost nine o'clock. Dixon served them breakfast and then Alistair suggested that they go fishing in the dam.

'It's lovely and tranquil at the dam,' he told Sharba. 'After a full-on party like we attended last night, it'll be nice to chill by the water—even if we don't catch anything.'

They walked up to the dam; there was a track and they could have driven, but both of them wanted to walk. It was already hot as they started off through the paddocks towards the dam. The dogs had to be left at home because Alistair thought they might chase Paul's cattle, but he promised them they would get a nice long walk later that day.

'What kind of fish can we expect to catch, if we catch any?' Sharba asked.

'Paul stocks the dam with bream, so hopefully we'll catch some of them because they make good eating,' Alistair replied. 'But there're also barbell in there. They're mud-fish and taste of mud, so if we catch one of those, we'll give it to Dixon because he doesn't seem to mind that they taste of mud!'

They walked past a herd of cows standing in the shade of a clump of trees, all of which stared uninterestedly at Alistair and Sharba as they walked past.

'Those are Bramen,' Alistair told Sharba. 'They get extremely aggressive when they have calves. I've had to really run for my life on one or two occasions when I've come across them and they have babies at foot, but right now they don't so they're quite relaxed and we don't have to worry. If we'd brought the dogs with us, Peg wouldn't have been able to resist chasing them—being a Jack Russel makes her naturally naughty and mischievous. Fifi is better behaved, but when she sees Peg hurtling after the cattle, she often forgets her manners and goes along for the fun!'

'Is there any wildlife around here?' Sharba asked.

'Not a lot anymore. Sometimes you see impala or duiker, but there's no big game unless they decide to walk up from the Luano Valley.'

It was pleasant sitting next to the dam. Alistair set up their rods and they lounged on a blanket in the shade of the dam wall while waiting for the fish to bite.

'We've left it a bit late,' observed Alistair. 'If you're serious about catching fish you need to come early, or later on in the evening, because that's when they bite.'

'It doesn't matter if we don't catch anything,' said Sharba. 'This is a perfect place to chill and relax after the party we had last night.'

It was lovely. The dam stretched away reflecting the blue sky, and all around there was bird song coming from the mopani trees that grew in clumps. Dragonflies and the odd butterfly flitted around the young couple, and every now and then they could hear the haunting cry of a fish eagle who was sitting on a dead tree that was protruding out of the dam. They were lying on the blanket half asleep in the warm balmy air when they heard a shout.

'Alistair, Alistair, are you there?'

'That sounds like Rick's voice,' said Alistair sitting up. 'Over here, Rick,' he shouted.

They both stood up and Rick soon came into view. He looked worried and he was carrying a rifle. Behind him there was an African man with an anxious expression on his face, also carrying a rifle.

'That bloody lion that Chris mentioned last night has killed one of our young steers,' Rick said without preamble. 'I tried to ring you at your cottage, but Dixon answered and told me you'd gone to the dam. He said you'd left your mobile in the house so I wouldn't be able to contact you. Anyway, I wanted to ask you to come as a backup gun because I have to track that bloody lion and shoot it before it does any more damage to our stock.'

'Rick, this is really bad timing,' said Alistair glancing at Sharba.

'I know, man, and I'm sorry, but I really have to go after that lion. I can't let it take any more of Dad's cattle, especially after what happened last time.'

'But you already have a backup gun,' Alistair replied, looking at the African who was standing a respectful distance away.

'I needed to start tracking the lion ASAP so I got old Jacob to come along. He knows how to use a gun, but if the crunch comes to the crunch, he's more likely to run away than shoot—and if he did manage to keep his courage and let off a shot, he'd probably shoot my bloody head off by a mistake! When we found the lion had walked in this direction, I decided to give you a shout and get you to be my backup instead of Jacob.'

'So the lion tracks are close to here?' Alistair asked.

'Yah, man, just over the other side of the dam.'

'What about Sharba? I need to get her home safely.'

'Jacob can escort her home. We need to find the bastard as soon as possible.'

'But I don't think it wise for her to be walking unarmed in an area where there could possibly be a lion.'

Both men looked terribly worried and Sharba knew what she had to do.

'It's okay, I'll come with you,' she said.

'Are you sure?' Alistair asked doubtfully. He knew from previous conversations that Sharba didn't approve of hunting.

'Yes. I don't like hunting, but this is different. Rick needs to sort out the problem and he needs your assistance, so the least I can do is tag along if it helps.'

'It's not ideal having you along,' said Rick honestly. 'But I'll get Jacob to keep an eye on you and you'll be okay.'

Jacob willingly gave his rifle to Alistair, relief spreading over his face as he did so.

He readily promised he'd keep an eye on Sharba and tell her what to do should a crisis arise. Alistair told her to keep behind him and not to make a sound.

'If you're told to do something, do it immediately without question, okay?'

'Okay.'

They walked back to the lion tracks and Rick pointed out how the pugmarks indicated that the lion was dragging his left back leg.

'He probably has an injury to that leg and now finds it hard to hunt,' Rick explained. 'That's why the bugger is killing our cattle; they're far easier to kill than wild animals.'

They followed the tracks in single file. Rick was the first in line with Alistair following; Sharba walked behind Alistair and Jacob took up the rear. The sun shone down relentlessly on them as they walked along, and Sharba wished she had a bottle of water because the heat in the open was harsh and oppressive. She wondered how far the lion had gone, hoping that maybe it was heading back to the Luano Valley. No one talked and they proceeded as quietly as possible while they all kept a sharp lookout as they walked on and on.

When they came to a barbed wire fence, there was a tuft of the lion's mane entangled on one of the barbs. 'We're crossing onto the Nels' farm now,' Alistair told her quietly as they scrambled through the fence.

Eventually, after what felt like miles to Sharba, the pug marks entered a copse of trees and the little column came to a halt.

'He could be lying up there in the shade,' whispered Rick, peering into the growth of trees and bushes that were dappled with sun and shadows. 'We need to be very careful.'

Very slowly and in complete silence, they edged their way towards the thicket. Sharba could feel the tension rising with each step.

'He is there, I can smell him,' whispered Jacob.

Sharba could smell nothing but the sweat on the men's bodies, but Jacob's words made the hair on the back of her neck rise. Then Rick suddenly stopped moving forward and everyone else also came to a halt. Rick silently pointed to the left and Sharba followed his finger but could see nothing among the trees. But both Rick and Alistair were lifting their rifles and Jacob put his hand on her arm in a gesture that indicated she must stay completely still. The tension seemed to rise still further and then suddenly Sharba made out the lion's head in the shadows of the trees. She almost gasped aloud. She felt Jacobs's fingers squeezing a warning on her arm when he felt the tremor that had gone through her when she spotted the lion.

The lion was also completely immobile and was staring straight at the little group with tawny eyes that glinted with fury. Then suddenly without warning, he exploded out of the bushes and came straight at them, his ragged mane standing out around his face while a snarl rumbled out of his throat that increased in volume to a roar as he bounded towards them. Sharba couldn't stop herself giving a scream of fright, but it was lost in the sound of the two rifles as they thundered out in unison.

Rick's shot went through the lion's brain, while Alistair's bullet entered his heart, and the beast was dead as he hit the ground. He lay there twitching. The silence after the two shots was profound, relieved only by dust motes swirling in the shafts of sunlight that filtered in through the trees. No one said a word. Rick went forward and put another shot through the lion's brain, just to make sure.

The three men went and stood around the carcase but Sharba hung back. The shots were still ringing in her ears and she felt a little nauseous at what she perceived as violence and sudden death. She couldn't stop the unexpected tears that came into her eyes as she realised a life had been taken.

'Sharba, come and have a look at this old fellow,' called Alistair. 'You'll see we did the poor chap a favour.'

Sharba came up hesitantly and Alistair put his arm around her when he saw her tragic expression. 'You can see that this lion's back leg was broken,' he said. 'Maybe he was kicked by a zebra or buffalo when he was trying to get himself a meal. It must have been incredibly painful for the poor old boy to have to hunt with a broken leg after that—no wonder he took to killing easy prey like cattle.'

'That wasn't the end of his troubles either,' said Rick. 'Look at that septic sore on his rump. It looks like a spear wound to me. More than likely he was speared by an African when he caught the lion trying to hunt one of his cattle.'

Jacob pointed to the lion's teeth. They were exposed in a snarling rictus and it was obvious they were decayed and broken.

'No good anymore,' Jacob said simply.

'What happens now?' Sharba asked, feeling slightly better now that she could see that the lion was old, sick and decrepit and they had put him out of his misery.

'The Game Department has to be informed,' said Rick. 'You usually need a licence to kill a lion, but as farmers we're allowed to kill them if they're taking our stock. This is Tony Nel's land, so he'll have to get involved. I'll give him a call now to tell him what's happened.'

Rick pulled his mobile out of his pocket and called Tony. 'Yah Tony, hello man. Look that lion Chris Martin was having problems with killed one of our young steers last night. I tracked the bastard this morning and I've finally shot him, but he's on your land.' Rick listened for a few moments then he said, 'Nah, he's on old toppie, man. A bag of bones and full of injuries.' He paused again. 'Okay,' he said at last. 'We'll wait for you here.' Then he gave Tony detailed instructions so that he could find them. 'Oh, and Tony,' he ended, 'Please could you bring us something to drink, we're all pretty parched, thanks man.'

The flies were already gathering on the carcass, so the little group went out to the edge of the copse where they could still be in the shade but away from the lion. It wasn't long before they heard the noise of an approaching vehicle and Rick stood up and waved his arms so that Tony could see exactly where they were. When he drew up, they could see that Lyn was with her uncle and she jumped out of the Toyota, her eyes shining with excitement.

'Did you really shoot a lion?' Lyn asked breathlessly. 'Where is it?'

Jacob took her into the copse to show her the lion and it fell to Tony to bring out a basket containing bottles of orange juice and plastic mugs.

They were all drinking thirstily when she came back to them. 'I need to get a photo of you with the lion, Rick,' she said. 'How brave you must be to shoot a brute like that!'

'Well, both Alistair and I shot it at the same time,' said Rick modestly. 'And we only did it because it was killing our stock.'

'In that case I need to get a photo of you both,' said Lyn. 'Actually, I'd like a photo of all the hunting party.'

Reluctantly they allowed Lyn to take her photos. Sharba thought she was a strange girl. She didn't seem to be regretful in any way that a lion had been shot, and she hadn't taken any notice when they told her that it was a mercy killing in the end. She just seemed to be thrilled that a mighty beast had been hunted and shot, and openly stated that she wished she had been part of the hunting party.

'Since it was shot on my land, I'll have to take it from here and sort it out with the Game Department,' said Tony. 'But thanks, man, for tracking and shooting it. It was obviously heading for my cattle next, so you've saved me a heap of trouble!'

They all clambered on to the back of Tony's Toyota as he was going to give them a lift back to their respective homes.

'Would you mind going via the dam?' Alistair asked Tony before they set off. 'We left all my fishing gear there when we started tracking the lion.'

When they got back to the house, Alistair asked Dixon to make them a pot of tea.

'Well, this isn't exactly what I planned to do to impress my girlfriend on our first weekend together,' Alistair said ruefully to Sharba.

'But it was exciting, and I think we did the old boy a favour in the end by putting him out of his misery,' said Sharba.

After they had slaked their thirst with several cups of tea, Sharba said she was going to have a shower.

'I feel sticky and dusty,' she said as she made her way to the bathroom.

When she had finished her ablutions, Alistair took a shower, too, and then they decided to relax and watch a DVD. They were both quite tired after their late night and then all the exercise and excitement of hunting the lion.

❖

Oliver had spent three futile weeks in Zambia trying to find out what Hugh Fortrum had been on the brink of discovering just before he died. Oliver had decided to come himself since he had already spent a large sum of money on a private investigator who had left him with more questions than answers before he was killed, and he didn't feel inclined to spend more money on some other useless bastard. Before he left for Zambia, he had managed to contact what appeared to be Hugh Fortrum's only relative, a cousin by the name of Bobby Holland.

Bobby lived in Glasgow and Oliver immediately assessed him to be a low-class waste of space when he eventually got hold of him. Bobby confirmed that he was Hugh's only relative in an indifferent tone when Oliver put the question to him, but when Oliver asked him if he had been informed by the Zambian officials that Hugh had been killed, he perked up.

'No, I've not heard that from the Zambians, but if it's true I should be in line for the inheritance since I'm the only relative he has.'

'You need to contact the Zambians and get them to confirm that what I've said is true,' Oliver told him. 'After that, you'll be able to pursue the matter of the inheritance. But listen, when you speak to the Zambians, please ask them to send all Hugh's personal effects to you, including the notes he was making on his last job. He was working for me, you see, and I need to have those notes. I've already paid a large sum of money into Hugh's bank account for that information, so if you're the one who inherits his estate, it's only right you let me have the notes.'

'Yeah, man, yeah,' said Bobby distractedly. But Oliver could tell by the tone of his voice that his mind was on other things and he wasn't surprised when Bobby didn't get back to him. When Oliver managed to contact him some time later, Bobby told him indifferently that there had been no notes among Hugh's personal effects that had been returned to him.

Oliver had found it all very frustrating and, in the end, had decided to go to Zambia himself to see if he could get hold of the notes and, most importantly, see if he could discover a lead to the whereabouts of his girlfriend. However, when he got there, he made no headway at all. The officials who had dealt with Hugh's personal effects said they had all been sent to his next of kin and they couldn't confirm whether there had been notes among his possessions or not.

Oliver went around the hotels and showed a photo of Sharba to everyone who could be bothered to look at it, but seemingly no one had ever seen her. He then went to the records office and bribed someone there to check if she had any relatives in Lusaka or elsewhere in Zambia, but again he drew a blank. He felt very discouraged and annoyingly he knew work was piling up back in England and he would have to return without finding out a thing.

When Oliver boarded a flight back to Heathrow, he was feeling irritated and depressed. He found he had been allocated a seat in the middle of a row so that he had to endure people sitting both to his right and to his left. The man on his left, after a curt acknowledgment, had retreated behind his eyeshades and gone to sleep, which suited Oliver because he didn't want to have to make conversation with anyone.

The girl on his right was another matter. She seemed to have an abundance of hand luggage and insisted on having a large bag at her feet. This forced her to push her knees over in Oliver's direction and invade his small amount of leg space, which thoroughly annoyed him. And to make matters worse, she just didn't seem to be able to settle. Oliver was becoming progressively more irritated as she squirmed around, knocking him with her arm and bumping him with her knees as she scrabbled in her bag. When the drinks trolley came around, she started drinking heavily, brandy and coke being her favourite tipple. Oliver never drank on a flight and he disapproved of anyone else doing so, but this girl was drinking doubles and breathing her alcohol fumes all over him.

Soon the alcohol loosened her tongue and she turned to Oliver and said, 'You look about as fed up as I feel, mate.' Oliver didn't appreciate being called mate and he thought that how he looked was nothing to do with this irritating young woman, so he just grunted and turned away from her, but she wasn't deterred at all.

'Well, I'm Lyn and I can assure you that whatever is biting you on the bum isn't half as bad as what's biting me!' Oliver made no remark but glowered at the seat directly in front of him. He didn't even look at the stupid woman.

'I had it all planned out,' said Lyn taking another gulp of her drink. 'I knew exactly what sort of husband I wanted, and I had picked one out. He was perfect for me, absolutely perfect, but he lived in Zambia, so I had to make the trip all the way from England to put my plan into action.'

Oliver really didn't want to hear this woman whinging on about her life, but there was nowhere for him to hide, so he gritted his teeth and continued to stare at the seat in front of him.

'I'd met this guy before, of course, on my last trip to Zambia when I was visiting relatives here, but I only got to meet him a couple of days before I was due to leave so I didn't have time to snare him. I didn't think it was such a big disaster because he was so shy and unsure of himself and I was convinced he wouldn't be able to find himself a girlfriend before I could get back again—he just wasn't the type. Anyway, I came back this year full of plans—and guess what? He had found himself another girlfriend, but not just any old girl, this one must be the most beautiful girl in the world!' The young woman took another a gulp of her drink.

'I consider myself to be beautiful and attractive, quite a catch for any man, but I don't stand a chance against the woman he was with, and that's quite a hard thing for me to admit.' She sighed dramatically and then sniffed. 'I'll show you.' She scrabbled in her bag, knocking against Oliver again, and pulled out her mobile phone and scrolled through her photos until she found the picture she wanted. 'See?' she pushed the phone in front of Oliver's nose.

Oliver felt like slapping her hand away, but his eyes slid to the screen of her mobile and focused on a group of people standing next to what looked like a dead lion. Suddenly his eyes flew wide open and he made a grab for the phone, snatching it out of Lyn's hand.

'Hey, what're you doing?' Lyn exclaimed indignantly.

'Sorry,' Oliver apologised. 'I just wanted to have a good look at the woman in the picture.'

'Typical,' sniffed Lyn, taking another swallow of her brandy. 'Just one glance at that bloody woman turns an iceberg of a man into a raving maniac!'

Oliver studied the photo carefully. It was definitely his girlfriend and he couldn't quite believe that a chance meeting with this irritating young woman had given him the lead that he so desperately needed.

'I know this girl,' Oliver told Lyn. 'Sharnique Wellby and I were good friends and then I lost contact with her, which was really upsetting, but maybe you can tell me where she is now?

'I can, but sorry mate, her name is Sharba Lengi and she's taken!' Lyn sounded vindictively satisfied.

'So, where is she?' Oliver asked, taking note of the name Sharnique was now using.

'I met her when she was with Alistair Gordon, the man I'd earmarked for myself. She was staying with him for the weekend. I'm not sure where her home is. She did tell me but I forget now; she doesn't live with Alistair permanently, that I do know.'

'So, where does this Alistair live?'

'He lives in a little farm cottage not far from the airport. He's a pilot so it's convenient for him to live there.'

'Do you know who he works for?'

'No. I just know he's a pilot. He probably works for one of the airways, but I'm not sure which one.'

'Do you have his phone number or address?'

'No, I don't. His cottage is on Paul Cole's farm, that's all I know. You take a left turn onto a dirt road just before you get to the airport, go over the Chongwe River bridge and then take a right turn to Paul's farm.'

The young woman yawned and swallowed the last of her brandy; she didn't seem inclined to say any more and her head sagged back as she fell into an alcohol-induced sleep.

Oliver got out his notebook and wrote down all she had told him; how ironic it was that he was heading back to England at five hundred miles per hour when he had at last found a lead! Back at home there would be a huge pile of work to catch up, but, as soon as he could, he would be zooming right back to Zambia armed with information that he was sure would lead him to his girlfriend. So long as she wasn't married to this guy Alistair Gordon, Oliver was pretty sure he could get her back.

Suddenly the young woman jerked awake. 'I've just remembered where she lives,' she said. 'She works for Arlo Huber in his resort in Livingstone. Arlo Huber is a very well-known character in Zambia, for more reasons than one! Anyway, she has a cottage on the hotel site.'

'Thanks,' said Oliver, but she had gone back to sleep and didn't respond.

18

George Goes Missing

Sharba felt she had got to know Alistair a lot better on that first weekend she had spent with him. The way he interacted with his friends and his dependability when Rick had needed him endeared him to her, because she could see that he had depths to his character which she had not been aware of. He may have dreamy eyes and the face of a poet, but there was a steely, resolute core to his person that belied any weakness.

They had formed a firm friendship from the very first day they had met, but now they both had fallen inexorably in love with each other. At first Alistair hadn't dared to dream that a girl like Sharba would actually like him and want to spend time doing the things he enjoyed, but to his amazement Sharba was very much on his wavelength; they seemed to fit together as if they had been carved from the same block and only needed to find each other to make a pleasing whole.

Sharba, who had been wary of men ever since she had seen her mother murdered and then had a bad experience herself with Oliver, had had her resolve to remain single swept away by her passionate feelings for Alistair; he was not like any other man she had met, and she instinctively trusted him. He was so open and honest, and she just couldn't repel the irresistible magnetism that drew her to him, so she was happy to let their relationship take its course.

Alistair would fly down to Livingstone whenever possible when Sharba had time off and they sampled all the activities on offer in the area. If she could get away for a weekend, Alistair would whisk her up to Lusaka to spend time with him on the farm, or sometimes they flew to the Luangwa Game Park and stayed in a one of the lodges. Neither of them ever tired of viewing the beautiful and varied wildlife that could be seen there.

'This is how I imagine the Garden of Eden,' Sharba said one day when they were parked by the Luangwa River in the evening, watching the animals as they came down to drink their evening fill at the river's edge.

It was just magical to sit there as the sun went down in a blaze of colour and glory, while they observed the environment that was as natural as it had been when it was created at the beginning of time. The river was serene because the rains had not yet broken, and along the banks there were kigelia trees with their heavy sausage-shaped fruits hanging down. On the far side of the river, there were rock-encrusted kopjes and a jungle of growth that hid a myriad of small animals, birds and insects.

On the side of the river on which they were parked, the grass was cropped short, and as they watched different species of animals come down to drink in their herds or groups, Sharba noticed that they were all very wary. But those that did not prey on other animals made room for other herbivores, so there was a herd of rather noisy buffalo drinking alongside a group of zebra, while a little further up some giraffes were carefully doing the splits so that they could get their heads down to the water. Flocks of birds also flew down to the water's edge to drink, and monkeys and baboons foraged around on the grass squabbling and bickering with others of their kind like unruly children.

'Here come some elephants,' Alistair said.

A group of about twelve of the huge creatures made their way on their silent, padded feet to the water's edge, rumbling in pleasure as they slaked their thirst in the cool brown water.

'Those baby elephants are so adorable,' commented Sharba as she watched them frolicking about. 'It's like being at the theatre watching all the animals here, isn't it? Only better!'

Even though Sharba loved Alistair and trusted him completely, she didn't tell him about Oliver or her flight from him and her change of identity. It was part of her past that she wanted to eradicate completely, and she felt she could only do this if it was kept a complete secret. She could almost believe that it never happened if she locked it away in her mind and told no one. She knew she was the happiest that she had been since Eve had died, and she didn't want to say or do anything that might upset the balance. Karl was the only one who knew the truth, but Sharba was sure he wouldn't say anything just so long as she kept to her side of the bargain. She had been worried at first as she didn't feel she could really trust him, but now her fears were allayed because he had not betrayed her, and even the tangible hatred that she had sensed Karl had towards her seemed to have eased. He totally ignored her now and that was fine by her.

'I have to go to Scotland for a couple of weeks next month,' Alistair told Sharba one day. 'My parents' golden wedding anniversary is coming up and they're going to have a huge celebration with all the family. It's been arranged for ages, although I had forgotten all about it until this week when I got a letter from Dad reminding me! Anyway, I would love my parents to meet you, so I was wondering if you could wangle some leave and come with me?'

'Oh Alistair, I'd love to, but I've just taken leave and I know Arlo won't let me have any more for a while because Clara is going on holiday with Charles.'

'Well, I have to go, with or without you,' said Alistair regretfully. 'But I'd much rather be with you in sunny Zambia than with a whole bunch of my relatives in dismal Scotland!'

'Of course you must go,' said Sharba. 'I'll still be here when you get back, and maybe you'll be able to persuade your parents to come to Zambia for a holiday—and then I could meet them.'

Sharba spent the weekend before Alistair's trip to Scotland with him on the farm. He was flying out on the Monday evening and he flew Sharba back to Livingstone that Monday afternoon.

'I won't be able to see you to the hotel as I do usually,' he said apologetically after they had landed. 'I'm cutting it a bit fine as it is, since you now have to check in hours before your scheduled flight actually leaves.'

'Don't worry, I can easily get a taxi to the resort; you get yourself back safely to Lusaka and give me a ring before you fly out this evening,' Sharba said before they had their last kiss.

When Sharba arrived back at the resort earlier than she would normally have done so had Alistair not had to rush off, she immediately realised that something unusual was going on. She could palpably feel an atmosphere of tension and anxiety as she walked through the hotel grounds. Charles's helicopter clattered overhead flying quite low, which was also odd as he usually headed straight back to Botswana when he flew out, but now he seemed to be flying up the river at a low altitude.

There was no one behind the desk at reception, and Sharba went in search of someone who could tell her what was happening. Walking back outside to the garden, she spied Julius, the man who kept the swimming pool crystal clear without a fleck of dirt in it. He was staring intently into the pool and didn't see her until she was right next to him.

'What's happening Julius, what's going on?' Sharba asked, as she looked to see why he was staring into the pool. It all looked perfectly normal to her.

Julius turned to her and she could see his face looked serious and worried. His eyes seem to protrude slightly because of his anxious expression and Sharba knew something dreadful must have happened.

'Miss Sharba, George is missing...'

'George? How? When?'

'He was having his afternoon sleep on the veranda of their house and when Mrs Amanda left him to go inside for a few minutes, he disappeared. He wasn't there when she returned to the veranda. She couldn't find him anywhere, and now everyone is looking for him.'

George was a very popular little boy with the staff at the hotel, and once it had been circulated that he was missing the entire hotel staff had started searching for him, but he didn't appear to be in the hotel or in the grounds, and so the awful fact that he might have wandered down to the river and fallen in had to be considered.

'When everyone went to search near the river, I suddenly thought he might have fallen into the pool and drowned because he doesn't swim very well yet, but now I am so thankful that he is not here.' Julius may have been thankful, but he still looked extremely troubled.

'But this is terrible,' said Sharba. 'Surely someone would have seen him if he'd walked across the hotel grounds heading towards the river?'

'No one saw him. The gardeners were working in the garden, but they didn't see him. Usually he talks to them if he walks past where they're working. He likes to play a bit of football with them sometimes, but they swear he didn't go by. I, myself, was also in the garden and I didn't see him either.'

'So maybe he's still somewhere in the hotel?'

'I am hoping so. Everyone is still looking everywhere for him, but it's been a while since he was first missed.'

The helicopter clattered overhead again. 'That's Mr Charles,' said Julius. 'He came to see Miss Clara, but when he found out what had happened, he and Miss Clara have been flying up and down the river to see if they can spot George. But if he's fallen in, they won't see him. He would have been swept away and if a crocodile didn't get him, he would have been washed right over the Victoria Falls,' Julius looked as though he was going to cry.

'He could have been washed up on one of the little islands,' suggested Sharba hopefully.'

'I hope so. . . I hope so.'

Sharba left Julius and went to her cottage to put her backpack there. She had a good look around just in case the little scamp had somehow got into her home and was hiding, but he definitely wasn't there, so she left her unpacking and went to join the others in hunting for the little boy.

'Where're Karl and Amanda?' Sharba asked one of the chefs who was searching in the jungle of undergrowth behind the staff houses.

'Mr Karl is searching along the riverbank with the others, but Mrs Amanda is in the house with Mrs Rosa. She became hysterical when they couldn't find George quickly, and Mr Karl is blaming her for not looking after their son properly. Mrs Rosa is trying to keep her calm in her house because it doesn't help for them to be fighting at a time like this.'

Sharba helped the chef search through the bushes and then she looked in all the other places she could think of. She didn't join those who were hunting along the riverbank because she thought there were enough people doing that, and also she didn't want to be the one to find a drowned child.

Eventually it got dark, and the search was called off for the night. Charles and Clara landed and came back to the hotel and everyone congregated in the hotel grounds. Arlo had been in the boat cruising up and down the river looking for his grandson, but he also gave up the hunt as the night closed in. Everyone looked sombre and worried. It was obvious that hope of finding the boy alive was fading, and because he was such a popular little lad, everyone was feeling devastated. Arlo was about to address them when there was a shriek, and suddenly Amanda ran up, followed by a panting Rosa who was trying to restrain her.

'Did you find him?' Amanda screeched. 'Did you find my baby?' It looked as though she had been pulling at her hair as it stuck out around her blotched face in a tangled mess. Her red, tearful eyes glittered with anguish.

'No, we didn't,' roared Karl. 'He's probably been washed over the Victoria Falls by now and it's all your fault you effing, stupid cow! You have eff-all to do all day except look after the boy— and you can't even do that! How I ever ended up with such an incredibly lazy and stupid bitch like you, I'll never know!'

'You can't say that,' Amanda screamed back at him. 'I *was* looking after him! He was asleep on the sun lounger on the veranda where he likes to have his afternoon nap. I just popped into the toilet and when I came out again, he was gone!'

'Yeah, right! You probably went to have a sleep as well because you're one of the laziest bitches I know, and when you eventually rose from your slumbers he had wandered off.'

'That's not true! I love George more than anything in this world and I've always looked after him well, while you hardly take any notice of him at all!'

'That's because you try and keep him away from me. But George is *my* son as well, and if we don't find him alive, I'm going to take the sjambok to you and thrash you to within an inch of your life. If he is found alive, I'll thrash you anyway because that's what you deserve! One way or another, our relationship is over and I'm booting you out! George will stay with me if he hasn't died, because you're definitely not fit to be a mother!'

With a shriek of anguish, Amanda launched herself at Karl like a wounded leopard. There was a look of pure hatred on her face and her teeth were bared in what looked like a snarl. She hooked her fingernails and tried to gouge his eyes, but he fended her off easily. Immediately Charles and Arlo stepped in to separate them.

'That's enough!' Arlo shouted. 'This is not helping at all! Everyone, go back to your work; there are guests that need looking after. Or go home if you're off duty. Thank you for your help. We'll all convene here again tomorrow to resume the search.'

Karl stomped off to his house while Rosa and Arlo took Amanda back with them. They had to support the sobbing woman between them as it seemed she hardly had the strength to walk.

19

Distressing Revelations

Sharba went back to her cottage. She felt devastated by the events of that afternoon and just couldn't comprehend that little George was, in all probability, dead. She made herself a cup of tea but didn't feel like eating anything. She looked at her watch and guiltily realised that she must have missed Alistair's last call before he boarded his flight to Scotland.

Looking at her mobile, she saw he had tried to call her several times and there were two messages from him on voice mail. He said in the first one that he hoped everything was okay because she hadn't been answering his calls. His voice sounded rather worried and Sharba felt really guilty. In the second voice mail, he said he was just about to board his flight and he was missing her already. 'I can't think what's happened to you, but I'll give you a ring when I get to my destination,' he promised. 'I love you.' He sounded even more worried.

When Sharba eventually got to bed, she found sleep elusive. As she tossed and turned, she could see little George's face in her imagination. He was such a sweet, happy child and she hated to think of him being terrified as he was swept away down the river. If he had been attacked by a crocodile, he might have had to endure agonies before the croc eventually killed him. Distressing visions of a crocodile's head, black and gnarled, with ragged fangs protruding over uneven lips, invaded her mind. The beady eyes of the crocodile were on George and the long, scaly body was inching towards him. It was a horrendous thought and there were tears on her cheeks as the unwanted images kept assailing her mind.

She knew that everyone would be having the same thoughts and she wondered if the dreadful events of the day would not turn Amanda insane.

Eventually, after tossing and turning, Sharba fell into a fitful sleep. It was just after one in the morning when she heard someone knocking quietly on her door, and she felt a shiver of apprehension run down her spine as she went to see who it was. A call at this time of the night could not be good news. Opening the door a crack, she saw Uzma's frightened face.

'What is it, Uzma?'

'It's George, Miss Sharba...'

'George? Have you found him? Is he all right? Is he safe?'

'Can I come in?'

'Yes, of course.'

Uzma came in; she was shivering and looked distressed. 'I know where George is; he's all right but he's not safe.' Sharba could feel the girl trembling as she gently guided her to a chair.

'Tell me where he is,' she invited.

'We need your help,' said Uzma.

'Of course, of course I'll help you, but first tell me where George is.'

'I have to tell you ... other things first.'

'No, it's George that...'

'Listen to me, Miss Sharba,' Uzma cut her off. 'Do you know Jackson? He works in the hotel garden.'

Sharba had to think for a moment before she could place him. There was a small army of people who kept the hotel grounds immaculate, but she remembered that Jackson was a young man with a small, neat body and a friendly face who always acknowledged her as she walked past.

'Yes, I know who he is.'

'Jackson got married to a woman called Kamali two years ago. Of course, they wanted to start a family straight away but Kamali was unable to fall pregnant. They tried to get medical advice but still she did not conceive, so eventually they consulted a woman who claimed to have magic powers and said she could help them. But still nothing happened, and they despaired of ever having children. They had already spent all their savings trying to solve the problem and all seemed lost, but then a few months ago Kamali found she was expecting a baby. She had conceived quite naturally without any medical or magic help! It was like a miracle and everyone in Kapotwe Village was happy for them.'

Uzma stopped for a moment and Sharba knew something bad was coming. Uzma was looking for words by which she could relate the next part of her narration.

'Go on,' Sharba prompted her softly.

'Last Wednesday, Jackson had a message to say that his father, who lives near Lake Kariba, was very ill. He asked for a few days off so that he could go to him and was granted leave. On Friday night, Mr Karl arrived in our village. We all knew what he was after and the men hid their wives and daughters in their houses, but Mr Karl knew Jackson was away and he went to his house. Kamali was inside as she hadn't gone with Jackson to Kariba, but she had locked the door and refused to open it when she knew that Mr Karl was outside. When she didn't open the door, Mr Karl became very angry and broke it down. He told her what his intentions were and she tried to dissuade him, explaining that she was pregnant. He could see that she wasn't lying because already the pregnancy was apparent, but he didn't care. He was drunk and he was very rough with her when he took her.'

Uzma looked outraged and Sharba felt sick with guilt that she hadn't exposed Karl for what he was when Uzma had asked her before.

'Later that night, Kamali found she was bleeding,' Uzma continued. 'She got assistance from some of the older women in the village, but she miscarried her son. He was alive when he was born but died within the hour. He was too little to live.'

'Oh Uzma, I'm so sorry,' said Sharba. Both women were crying now.

'When Jackson came home later that day, he was heartbroken and angry ... so angry! He wanted to kill Mr Karl, but the others in the village convinced him it would not be a good thing to do, even if Mr Karl deserved it. Eventually Jackson calmed down and the villagers thought he had seen reason. Then George disappeared and everyone—everyone except Jackson—went to search for him. We understood why Jackson was reluctant to look for Mr Karl's son and didn't question his decision. Then this evening, when I was walking in the night because I couldn't sleep due to all the unhappy thoughts in my head, I heard a whimpering sound when I went past the little hut in which Jackson stores his maize. I thought it was a dog or a puppy that had got locked in and I opened the door to let it out, but I found it was George! He had been tied up and gagged and could only make a small noise.'

'Oh my God! Poor little George!' Sharba was horrified.

'Of course I raised the alarm. Everyone came to see what had happened and Jackson admitted to Chief Malupande and the village elders that he had decided to abduct George so that Mr Karl could feel the anguish he was feeling because he had lost his son. He told them he had worked in the garden near Mr Karl's house so he could keep it under observation. When George was asleep on the veranda and Mrs Amanda went inside the house, he knew that this was his chance. He ran to the veranda, grabbed George, and jumped over the fence into the bushes and made his way back to the village. He kept his hand over George's mouth so he couldn't cry out, and when he got to the village he tied him up, put a gag on him and locked him in the maize store.'

'Poor George must have been so frightened,' said Sharba. She was horrified by what she was hearing.

'Jackson was asked what he intended to do next,' Uzma went on. 'He said he hadn't thought about that. He wanted Mr Karl to suffer greatly, but he hadn't thought what to do with George after he had abducted him. It seemed to me that Jackson was regretting his rash decision of snatching George, because he knew the whole village would be in trouble when the Hubers realised what had happened. Jackson said it would probably be best to knock George on the head and throw him in the river, then the village could never be implicated. He reasoned that already everyone thought George had wandered down to the river and been swept away, so by disposing of the boy in this way it would not cause suspicion to fall on anyone.'

'Oh no!' Sharba was totally shocked at such a callous idea.

'The thing is, some of the village folk agreed with him,' said Uzma looking troubled. 'They said that it would be right for Mr Karl to lose his son just as Jackson has lost his, and they thought it a just punishment for what Mr Karl had done to Kamali and some of the other women.'

'George must be rescued immediately,' said Sharba jumping up. 'I'll go and tell Arlo everything and ...'

'No,' said Uzma firmly, pushing Sharba down. 'Chief Malupande and the elders have agreed the boy is not to be harmed, but only if you do as I ask of you. It is the only way to ensure there will be no reprisals on the whole village.'

'What ... what is it you want me to do?'

'I'll bring George to you and you will take him to Mr Arlo and say that you couldn't sleep and went for a walk, then you found George wandering in the bush, so you've brought him back.'

'But ... but, no, that won't work! There were people scouring the bushes all afternoon, they know George wasn't there.'

'The bush is thick and he could easily have been missed.'

'But George is a bright little boy and he'll tell them he was tied up and locked in a maize store.'

'No he won't. He's been told that he is going to be released and will soon be back with his mother, but if he says he was taken by Jackson and tied up and locked in a maize store, he'll be recaptured and this time he'll be killed. He must just say he can't remember what happened.'

'You told George he would be *killed?*' Sharba was absolutely horrified.

'No, of course I didn't! It was Bali, the magic woman who told him. She can be very persuasive—she gets into people's heads—so when she tells them things, they remember what she has said and they do as she says.'

Sharba wondered if the magic woman was a hypnotist or had the powers to brainwash a person. She felt dismayed that little George would have to deal with the trauma of being kidnapped and also the thought it could happen again, but next time he would be killed. It was a dreadful thing to put in a child's mind.

'I can't do what you're asking,' Sharba told Uzma. 'It's all wrong and Karl should be exposed for what he is. It would be better that we go to the Hubers and tell them the truth.'

'No, you don't understand,' Uzma sounded agitated. 'The village fears the wrath of Mr Karl. He has the power to destroy the livelihoods of all the people who work here. He even has the power to destroy the whole village, because he is rich and knows bad people in high places who will think of a reason to annihilate the village if they're paid enough to do so. Recently Mr Arlo has been unwell. He isn't very young anymore and he has a problem with his heart. He could die at any time and the hotel would belong to Mr Karl, so to preserve our village, we must hide the sins of Mr Karl and the sins of Jackson. The only way we can do this is with your help. *Please*, Miss Sharba; every minute we delay makes it more dangerous for little George.'

Sharba felt she was being pressurised to do the wrong thing as she really didn't want to do what Uzma asked, but she understood the villagers might kill George and throw him in the river if she refused. She didn't really have a lot of choice, so she nodded her head and told Uzma that she would help them.

'Thank you,' said Uzma, looking relieved. 'Now, stay in your house for an hour, then come to the perimeter of the hotel boundary and I'll meet you there with George. You can then take him to his mother and say you found him wandering in the bush.'

20

A Terrifying Experience

During the hour that Sharba waited for Uzma to go to her village and bring George back, she made a decision. She could not possibly go along with the deception that Uzma had suggested, although Sharba understood completely the villagers' fear of reprisals from Karl. Instead, once she had George safely with her, she would go to Arlo and tell him the whole story.

Arlo was far from his deathbed and Sharba was sure that if he knew all the facts, he would understand why Jackson had acted as he had. Arlo would also have to discipline Karl as his behaviour had been completely inexcusable, and she hoped that he would send his son back to Germany where he would be unable to do any more damage. Amanda and George would be better off without Karl in the long run, and she was sure that Rosa and Arlo would look after both of them. As for the deal she had struck with Karl, well, she just had to break it now and hope for the best.

When Sharba got to the arranged meeting place, she had to wait almost fifteen minutes before she saw a figure looming up in the dimness of the perimeter light. She had worried that something had gone wrong and the villagers had already disposed of George, so she heaved a sigh of relief when she saw Uzma emerge out of the gloom carrying George on her back. She swung him to the ground when Sharba stepped forward to meet her.

'Auntie Sharba!' George rushed to her and wound his little arms about her tightly, as though he was scared he would be whisked off again. Sharba could feel his body trembling as he held on to her.

'George, oh I'm so pleased to see you! Are you all right, sweetie?' Sharba gently unwound his arms and lifted him up and cuddled him to her. He started to sob silently and clung on to her tightly.

'Take him to Mr Arlo now, and remember what you must tell him,' said Uzma.

'Thank you, Uzma, for all you've done,' said Sharba. 'I'm sure everything will be okay now.'

'We're relying on you, Miss Sharba,' Uzma's voice was intense, and then she disappeared into the darkness leaving Sharba and George alone.

'Come on, little one, let's go and find you mummy,' said Sharba. She wondered if she should take the little boy to her house first and check him over, but decided against it as she determined that her first priory was to reunite him with his mother. He hadn't uttered a word since he had said her name when he first saw her, and since he was normally such a talkative little fellow, she thought he must be very traumatised.

George didn't seem inclined to want to let go of Sharba, so she carried him across the grounds towards the hotel and Arlo's residence. She was in the deep shadows of some trees when she was suddenly grabbed from behind and spun around.

'You!' It was Karl's rough voice that spoke. 'You had my son after all!' His torch beam swung over her and the little boy.

George cringed against Sharba when he heard the anger in his father's voice. He had calmed down a little on the walk across the grounds, but now he started to shiver violently again.

'No,' Sharba said, feeling appalled that Karl had intercepted her before she had told Arlo what had happened. 'I found George wandering in the bush and now I'm taking him to Amanda.'

'A likely story! We checked all around the hotel perimeter in the bushy area and George wasn't there. You're lying!'

'I'm not lying. I couldn't sleep so I went for a walk and found him wandering among the bushes. Maybe he was missed when we looked for him earlier. He could have been curled up asleep somewhere; the bush is like a jungle and we could easily have missed him.'

'I've always thought you were brighter than my darling Amanda, so I know you're lying. No one in their right mind would go walking in that jungle at night, not even Amanda! There're a lot of snakes there and other creatures that could sting, bite or hurt you in some way. If you had wanted to take a walk because you couldn't sleep, you would have walked in the hotel grounds where it was relatively safe!'

'Well, maybe I should have, but I wasn't thinking straight. Anyway, it's lucky I wasn't because otherwise I wouldn't have found George. Now, I really think we should get him to his mother.'

'No, you're both coming with me and we're going to get to the bottom of this.'

Karl took her by the arm and pulled her towards his house. Sharba tried to resist, but Karl was too strong for her and she didn't want to upset George further by shouting or making a fuss. Once inside the house, Karl firmly shut the door and pushed her down into a chair.

'Now, I want the truth—and I'll beat it out of you if necessary!'

'I've already told you the truth.' Already Sharba was beginning to feel very apprehensive.

'Lying bitch! George, come here!'

George was sitting on Sharba's lap and he clung onto her tightly and hid his face from his father.

'Little sod is so disobedient,' growled Karl. 'It's his mother's fault, she lets him get away with murder!'

'Just leave him be, Karl; he's traumatised and the last thing he wants is you speaking to him roughly. Please, let's just take him to Amanda. We can continue this conversation after that if you want.'

'No. You're up to something and I want to get to the bottom of things before we involve anyone else.'

Karl moved close to his son and forcibly turned his head so that the little boy was looking at him. 'What happened to you?' Karl asked George. 'Where did you go when you left the house yesterday afternoon?'

George looked terrified at his father's inquisition and didn't say a word.

'Come on son, you're going to tell me, I'll slap your bottom if you don't!'

George looked confused and very frightened, but still he didn't answer his father.

'Did you go to Auntie Sharba? Or did Auntie Sharba come over to our house and get you? Did you stay with her in her house yesterday afternoon and evening? Come on George, I'm losing patience. Do you want me to get my flip-flop? You need to tell me if you don't want your bottom slapped!'

Clearly terrified that he was going to be beaten by his father, George opened his mouth to answer. He was desperate to give Karl the answer he wanted and avoid being hit, but he didn't know what to say so he shut his mouth again.

'Oh, please stop questioning him,' Sharba interjected. 'Can't you see he's traumatised and confused?'

'Shut up!' Karl said to her rudely. 'Now, come on George, answer my question. Were you with Auntie Sharba yesterday? This is your last chance to tell me before I get my flip-flop.'

'I...I don't know,' wailed George. 'I...I...I think I was.'

'Right, that's all I need to know,' said Karl grimly. 'Now you're going to bed and I'm going to talk to Auntie Sharba.'

'I want Mummy.'

'No, you're going to bed and you'll see Mummy in the morning if you're good.'

'Can't we take him to Amanda now?' Sharba begged. 'He needs his mother, and she needs to know he's safe.'

'Bring the boy,' said Karl getting up. 'We're both going to put him to bed and then you and I are going to have a chat.'

'I don't think it's fair on George...'

'*Do as I say!*' Karl snapped, making both Sharba and George flinch. 'Even Amanda, brainless as she is, made sure George didn't see me giving her a hiding!'

'Don't you dare lay a finger on me!' Sharba said. She was beginning to feel really alarmed. Karl didn't answer, he bent forward and slapped her hard on the left side of her face with his open hand making her head jerk around, then he slapped her on the right side of her face. George screamed and jumped away from her and Karl, but his father caught him easily and, pulling Sharba with them, he marched through to George's bedroom and ordered the boy to get into bed.

'Now don't you move until morning,' Karl told his son. 'If you do, I won't let you see Mummy.'

Sharba had been stunned by the two slaps that had made her head swim, but now her head cleared and her cheeks stung with pain from the blows. She felt sick with humiliation as Karl dragged her back to the living room, leaving his son sobbing in his bed.

'Now, you're going to tell me exactly what's going on,' Karl growled.

'Nothing is going on. I told you the truth,' said Sharba. She felt very shaken and frightened.

Karl slapped her again across the face and the force of the blow made blood gush from her nose. 'We've got the rest of the night to continue this conversation,' Karl told her roughly. 'And be assured I'm not going to stop hitting you until I get a plausible explanation as to why you abducted my son!'

'I promise you, Karl, I didn't abduct George. How could I? I wasn't even here; I didn't get back until after he had disappeared.'

'So you say,' said Karl. 'But you're lying, aren't you? You got back early and went to your house and then when you knew George would be sleeping on our veranda, you grabbed him and hid him in your cottage!'

'No! Why on earth would I do that? It's ridiculous!'

Karl slapped her face again three times in quick succession. The pain and humiliation made the tears run down her face and mingle with the blood from her nose.

'I don't know what you want from me, Karl,' she gasped.

'The truth,' he said, slapping her hard across the mouth so that her lip was split as it came into contact with her teeth. 'Try the effing truth! You're playing some bloody game and I intend to find out what it is.' He slapped her again and again until she became dizzy and disorientated. She knew she had to somehow stop him.'

'Okay,' she sobbed. 'I'll tell you the truth.'

Karl stopped hitting her. 'Well?

'It was someone from the village who took George,' Sharba gasped as she fought off waves of nausea. 'They didn't like what you've been doing to their woman there, so they took George in retaliation. Then they were scared of reprisals from you and asked me to take George back to Amanda. They told me to say I'd found him wandering in the bush so that they could not be implicated.'

'So you were going to take the boy to his mother and tell them that, were you?'

'Yes.'

'Well, I don't believe you; you're a lying bitch! You were going to take George back to Amanda and tell Arlo exactly what had happened, weren't you?' You were going to make sure he knew I was the villain, and it was my fault that one of the villagers took George!'

'No.'

'You're a conniving little bitch! You've been waiting in the wings hoping for the chance to discredit me so that my father disinherits me—that's the truth of the matter, isn't it? This was a wonderful opportunity to get rid of me; you knew that my father would probably pack me off back to Germany if you told him what had happened, and that would have suited you fine! Luckily for me I saw you before you got to his house.'

'I don't know what you're talking about, Karl. Why would it have suited me fine? All I know is that you're a terrible person. You caused poor Kamali to have a miscarriage after you raped her—and she had waited over two years to have a baby! You don't care about the carnage you create; all you want is to have your pleasure and to hell with whoever gets hurt!' Sharba though Karl would hit her again after that outburst, but he just stared at her thoughtfully.

'Let's get this straight,' he said. 'The villagers wanted all that has happened in the past, including the abduction of George, to be hushed up so that they don't have to suffer reprisals at my hand?'

'Yes,' Sharba muttered. 'But you should be exposed for what you are!'

'Oh yes, and you were going to expose me when you took George to Arlo. Don't lie to me and say you weren't! But as things stand, it's only you who wants to open your big trap and let the truth out. Of course you do; you were just waiting for the chance to discredit me. It's all in your sneaky little plan. However, all the villagers are willing to be silent to ensure there are no reprisals from me. That makes things more simple!'

'I don't know what you're talking about, Karl. What sneaky little plan? I don't understand!'

'Don't come over all innocent with me,' answered Karl sharply. 'It annoys me and makes me want to give you another slapping! Anyway, your time here is up; you're going to have to leave.'

Sharba thought Karl was justifiably worried that she was going to tell Arlo about his misdemeanours, and when he said she was going to have to leave she had a panicky feeling that he was going to do something dreadful to her, so she sought to reassure him.

'Karl, we made a deal some time ago and I've always kept my side of the bargain, haven't I? I'm not going to say anything to Arlo, I promise you.'

'No, I'm not going to take any more chances,' said Karl grimly. 'This is my opportunity to get rid of you and I'm going to take it. You're a liability in more ways than one so you're going to leave this resort tonight and never come back! If you do try and come back, I'll tell my father your secret and he'll make sure your name is blackened so no one in Zambia will want to employ you. Come on, we're going to your cottage and you're going to pack.'

'But...'

'No buts; you'll do as I say, or I'll really give you a thrashing! So far, I've been very restrained. Come on.' Karl took Sharba firmly by the arm and marched her towards the back door. There was a sjambok hanging on a nail near the door and he snatched it off as they went out. 'Now, if you don't do exactly what I say, I'll give you a dammed good hiding.'

Sharba was in no doubt that Karl would do exactly that. She felt so terrified, she didn't dare utter a sound and she followed his instructions hoping that he wouldn't thrash her anyway. They walked swiftly to Sharba's cottage and, once inside, Karl instructed her to pack.

'Make sure you take all your personal possessions,' he said.

Sharba quickly started stuffing all her things into her backpack while Karl stood over her, tapping the sjambok against his leg. She could hardly understand what was happening; how had things escalated to the point that she was being thrown out of her job and her home with not even a chance of speaking to the person who had employed her?

She was dreadfully worried that Karl was going to take her somewhere away from the hotel where she couldn't be heard and then rape her and beat her. It was a terrifying thought, and she knew he was more than capable of doing it. And then she had an even more terrifying thought: what if he was going to murder her and throw her in the Zambezi to be washed over the falls? She was convinced he was capable of doing anything, and her hands trembled as she stuffed all her belongings into her backpack. She knew she should try and get away from him, but he never left her or gave her a chance to escape.

'Come on, hurry up,' he urged her.

'I'm finished,' she told him.

'Are you sure you've got everything?'

'Yes.'

'Give me that scarf, then; I need to blindfold you.'

Karl ripped the scarf in two and used half of it to blindfold Sharba. Then he pulled a handkerchief out of his pocket and stuffed it in her mouth before gagging her with the other half of the scarf.

'We can't take any chances of you screaming the place down when I take you out to the carpark,' Karl said grimly. He then picked up her backpack, guided her to the carpark, and pushed her into his Toyota, throwing her backpack into the back. Then he scrabbled about and found some thin rope which he tied around her wrists and secured her to the seat. Poor Sharba was trembling with fear. What was this madman going to do now? Was she going to be raped? Beaten? Murdered?

'Sit still and don't try anything,' Karl instructed her.

Sharba did as he commanded but she tried to figure out where they were driving. As time went on and she was sure they had reached the main road, she relaxed a little. It didn't appear that Karl was going anywhere near the river, so at least she wasn't going to be thrown in to be swept away. They drove on and on, it was difficult to know for how long they drove before Karl left the main road and they continued down a bumpy track for a considerable time, but it seemed like hours. Sharba was thrown about with the bumps and she wished Karl would slow down a bit. She had lost all sense of direction by this time and just wished the journey would end.

After a while Karl slowed down and turned left. He was now

obviously driving off-road and across country. He put the vehicle into four-wheel drive and they jolted along over very uneven territory. Sharba could sometimes hear bushes scratching along the side of the Toyota and she began to feel terrified again. Surely if Karl was taking her to such a remote spot, he must be planning on doing something really horrible to her.

Eventually they stopped and Karl got out and came around to her side of the vehicle and opened the door. He undid the ropes that secured her hands and pulled the scarf off her eyes and the gag from her mouth. It was still dark and Sharba couldn't really see where they were. Karl had left the headlights on, but they just cut a swathe of light over typically wooded Zambian countryside. There were no buildings or signs of human habitation.

Karl grabbed Sharba's backpack out of the Toyota and threw it on the ground. 'Take all your shoes out of the backpack and put them in the vehicle,' he told Sharba. 'Your slippers and flip-flops as well—and the shoes you're wearing.' He again had the sjambok in his hand so Sharba hastened to obey him although she was mystified as to why he wanted her to do this. 'Now, give me your mobile phone,' Karl commanded. Sharba handed him the phone and he dropped it on the ground and then stamped on it with his foot until is lay in a shattered pile.

'When I get back, I'll tell the family that it was you who had George all along. I'll say you admitted to hiding him so that you could, in due time, produce him and say that you found him wandering in the bush. I'll say you did it to curry favour before you discredited me and revealed your big secret—I'll tell them who you really are! I'll tell them that after I confronted you and made you tell the truth, you just wanted to get away from the hotel and I didn't stop you going. They won't want to know you after I've told them all that, so don't try and get in touch. Now, I've got to get going. It's a pity I'm in such a hurry as it would give me a great deal of pleasure to give you the hiding you deserve.' He tapped the sjambok menacingly on his leg. 'However, I've got to get back before everyone wakes up. Goodbye, and have a nice walk back to civilization. Don't worry, you'll make it, you come from a strong gene pool and you're not even pregnant!'

Karl jumped into his Toyota and drove off, leaving Sharba with a mixture of emotions swirling through her head. She felt relief that he had left without further hurting her, but she also felt panic because she appeared to be miles from anywhere and she hadn't a clue in which direction to go to find help. As for his last words, they made no sense at all and she assumed he was trying to demean her by insinuating that she had African blood in her veins, so walking for miles in the bush should be no great hardship.

She watched his tail lights receding and could hear the growl of his engine for a while after the lights disappeared, then there was utter silence as she stood alone in the darkness. Surely he couldn't just leave her in the middle of nowhere? Zambia was a huge country and not overpopulated, so she was not likely to come across anyone who could tell her where to go. She stood for a long while straining her ears for the sound of the vehicle engine, thinking that he might come back, but eventually she realised that he wasn't going to.

Sharba sank to the ground and sat next to her backpack. She felt all shaken up and couldn't gather her thoughts properly, but she knew there was no point in moving from where she was until daylight. 'Think,' she told herself. 'Try and figure out why you're in this mess and what you can do about it.' She was convinced that Karl was a psychopath, but nothing of what he had said made sense to her. What was this big sin she had seemingly committed? Why did he hate her and what made him want to get rid of her so much? She was no threat to him or his family, and she didn't think that Arlo would be too worried that she had reverted to her former name to elude a mentally disturbed ex-boyfriend. He would say it was none of his business. But Karl had insinuated that the family would be incensed when they learned her secret.

She just couldn't figure out why Karl had acted as he had, but she was aware that he had deliberately put her in a very difficult spot and, in his vindictive and twisted way, he had made sure that she would have further hardship when she had to walk for miles to civilization without any footwear. 'Bastard,' she muttered under her breath. She was beginning to lose her fear and feel angry instead. She touched her face, which still felt hot and tender, and remembered the pain and humiliation she had had to endure when he had repeatedly slapped her.

'If you think I'm going to slink off with my tail between my legs just because you've slapped my face and threatened me, you're completely deluded, Karl Huber,' she muttered. 'When I get back to civilization, the first thing I'm going to do is ring Arlo and tell him everything that's happened.'

Getting back to civilization was going to be a problem, though. When she was a child, Sharba had run barefoot and the soles of her feet had been as hard as nails. But for years she had worn shoes and the soles of her feet were now soft, so walking through the bush was going to be a painful exercise. She decided that she wouldn't do anything until it got light, and then she would follow Karl's tracks back to the road and hope that someone might come along who would help her.

It was very peaceful sitting in the bush with the velvety darkness all around her. Above, the stars twinkled and gave out just enough light to show that she was sitting in a clearing and there were trees and bushes all around. Sharba didn't feel afraid now. The terror she had felt when Karl was with her had completely disappeared and being alone in the bush held no fear for her. The African night noises soothed her, the yip of a jackal, the haunting cry of the nightjar and a soft hoot from an owl on the hunt for a meal. She felt all the strain of the last few hours drain out of her as she took long, slow, deep breaths, concentrating on her breathing and not allowing any other thoughts to fill her mind. This was her time to revive her body and mind, and prepare for the ordeal that lay before her as soon as it got light.

The dawn was just breaking when Sharba got up as she decided that now was the time to move. She had a long hot walk ahead of her. It was then she remembered Len and Elizabeth Raven telling her that years ago Karl had driven another woman miles away from civilization and told her to walk back, so no change there, she thought wryly.

She was just about to set off when Karl's last words to her floated back into her mind: *"Don't worry, you'll make it, you come from a strong gene pool and you're not even pregnant,"* and then she suddenly stiffened. Something seemed to ping in her brain, and she became rigid and motionless as the thought process in her head started to work in overdrive. Facts seemed to suddenly fall into place, forming a clear picture in her mind. She gasped and sank to the ground again as her legs all of a sudden seemed to go weak.

'That woman all those years ago was Eve,' she gasped. 'And I was the baby she was carrying!'

At last, Sharba started to understand why Karl hated her so much. Somehow, during that trip to Lusaka when Arlo had sent him away for a few days, he must have discovered that Sharba Lengi was Eve's child and the illegitimate daughter of his father. Goodness knows how, but he had admitted he was lucky to find out, so it was probably just by chance. He had immediately come to the conclusion that she had sought out the Huber family to profit from their success. He had probably surmised that she wanted part of the inheritance and had infiltrated the family business as an employee in the hope of gaining acceptance and esteem, and then she would have dropped her bombshell.

When Karl had told her that he had learned her secret, she had immediately got the wrong end of the stick and assumed he had found out that she had changed her name and was hiding from Oliver. She had agreed to say nothing about Karl's misconduct in return that he keep quiet what she thought he had found out about her, so that she could keep her change of identity secret and lessen the chances of Oliver finding her. Thinking back to that day that she had made a pact with Karl, Sharba now remembered he had actually called her sister, but she hadn't realised he was using the word in a literal way.

What Karl had actually found out was that she was Arlo's daughter and, as he perceived it, a direct threat to himself. He knew that Arlo respected and liked her immensely, and there could even be the possibility that he would be pleased if he found out she was his daughter, and that would be disastrous as far was Karl was concerned. So Karl had been waiting for a chance to discredit her to the family and so get rid of her. When he had found her bringing George back to Amanda, he had seen his chance and taken it. Once he had learned that it was Jackson who had abducted George, but the whole village wanted to hush it up so that there would be no reprisals from him, he knew he could carry out his plan and implicate Sharba in a way that would ultimately alienate her from the family and ensure that she got no share in the inheritance that he was determined to claim all for himself.

Sharba figured that Karl was going to discredit her to the family by telling them that she had admitted to him that she had taken George and hidden him in her cottage. Then after a time when everyone was in state over his disappearance, she was going to 'find' him and bring him back to Amanda. Then while emotions were still running high and she was the heroine of the hour, she had planned to tell them who she was and thus ensure that she got at least a good chunk of the inheritance. Karl would tell them that she had come to work for Arlo in the hope of manipulating the family to her own advantage and had tried to execute her plan of abducting George purely for what she could ultimately get out of Arlo.

'I would never have done anything as despicable as that, even had I known I was Arlo's daughter,' Sharba thought miserably. She had never for a moment thought she was anything more than an employee to the Huber family, and had she suspected Arlo was her father, she would never have sought employment with him in the first place. 'What will they all be thinking of me now?' Sharba wondered miserably. It made her cringe to think of the family despising her for seemingly trying to manipulate them purely for financial gain.

She knew that when Karl went back home after dumping her in the bush, he would have made sure that George told the family that it was Auntie Sharba who had held him captive for the day. It wouldn't matter what George remembered or didn't remember of his ordeal; he was terrified of Karl and would say anything his father told him to say to prevent a beating with the flip-flop.

Her hasty departure would also indicate to the family that she was guilty, and if she rang them to try and explain what had happened, they surely wouldn't believe she had had no idea that she was Arlo's daughter when she applied for a job. It would seem to them that that would be far too big a coincidence and, in reality, she was just a lying little gold digger, and nothing she said could be taken as the truth. So Karl would continue to get away with what he was doing and, when Arlo died, he would inherit his father's businesses. Why did the bad guy always have to win?

21

Oliver's Search Continues

Oliver felt a grim sense of satisfaction as he sat in the taxi he had taken from the airport. He was now heading towards Huber's Riverside Lodge and he felt he was at last coming to the end of his long search for his girlfriend. When he had got back to England after his previous abortive trip to Zambia, commitments had prevented him from turning around and going straight back despite now being aware of where she was living and working.

Like a horse chaffing at the bit, Oliver was tense and frustrated until he was free to make the return journey to Africa and his biggest fear was that Sharba would marry Alistair Gordon, as that would unquestioningly put her out of his reach. It was the only thing that would stop Oliver from pursuing her with the intent of making her his own, because his religious beliefs forbade him taking a married woman. However, Sharba had made it very clear to him on many occasions when they had been together that she wasn't the marrying type, and the last thing she wanted was a husband, so he was fairly confident that she wouldn't marry Alistair or anyone else before he could reclaim her.

Now at last he was about to close in on his quarry. He assumed that Sharba would be working at reception and he was looking forward to seeing her expression when he walked in unannounced. However, when Oliver arrived at the reception, he was greeted by a friendly blonde woman and there was no sign of Sharba.

'May I help you?' Clara smiled pleasantly at him.

'Oh, hello, yes, I hope you can,' said Oliver flashing her his most engaging smile. 'I'm actually looking for Sharba Lengi; I understand she's working at this hotel.'

The smile immediately vanished from Clara's face. 'I'm sorry; she no longer works here,' she said shortly.

'Oh dear, do you by any chance know where she is now?' Oliver felt dismayed by this unexpected information.

'No, I'm afraid I don't have a clue where she is now.' Clara's face indicated that she really didn't know where Sharba was—and she didn't want to know! 'She didn't tell us where she was going when she left.'

Oliver sensed that Sharba must have been in some sort of trouble when she departed, but he could tell by the closed look on this young woman's face that he wasn't going to get any further information. 'Thanks anyway,' he said, turning away.

When Oliver turned to go, he saw that there was a handsome man with piercing blue eyes standing a small distance behind him. He was staring suspiciously at Oliver, and when Oliver left reception to go back to his taxi the man appeared again and fell into step with him.

'Karl Huber,' said the man, holding out his hand. 'I'm the son of the owner of the hotel.'

'Oliver Naughton,' Oliver said, shaking the man's hand. 'I came here looking for Sharba Lengi, but I gather from your receptionist she doesn't work here anymore.'

'May I ask why you're looking for her?' Karl didn't like the look of this man who was seeking Sharba. He had an air of purpose that indicated he wasn't the sort that gave up easily, and his strong, confident demeanour worried Karl. He perceived that this man could be trouble.

Karl was now regretting his action of leaving Sharba stranded in the bush; he had done it because he derived a great deal of pleasure from being cruel. Imagining her stumbling through miles of bushland without shoes or water in the scorching heat amused him and gratified his passion for brutality. He had considered killing her, but that was just a step too far. He had often fantasised about murdering someone and realised that one day he may well do so, but the time had not yet come. In the meantime, he needed to frighten Sharba to the extent that she wouldn't dare ever to make contact with his family in the future, and he had felt at the time that his harsh treatment of her would achieve this objective.

Now he wished that he had killed Sharba. If she survived the long walk to civilisation, he didn't think she would dare to tell the family what he had done to her after being exposed as a gold-digger, but she might well tell this man who was looking for her, and Karl sensed he would be a dangerous enemy who would seek retribution when the extent of his own cruelty had been exposed.

'I'm a good friend of Sharba's,' Oliver replied. 'I briefly lost contact with her when she came to Zambia, but when I found out she was working in this hotel I came to surprise her with a visit.' Oliver sensed that this bull of a man might know where Sharba was, and he hoped that he might get a bit of information out of him. 'I've actually come all the way from England, so it was disappointing to find she wasn't here. You don't, by any chance, know where she might be, do you?'

'No, I'm afraid I don't,' said Karl.

Karl knew that there was a chance that Sharba wouldn't make it back to civilisation. She was a clever and determined young woman, but dehydration and sunstroke could easily make her confused and cause her to walk in circles in the bush until she dried from exhaustion. It had happened to others, and now he fervently hoped it had happened to her as it would solve all his problems.

Karl hadn't worried that she might tell Alistair what he had done to her. Alistair was just a milksop of a man as far as he was concerned—and he would be easy to deal with. Karl felt that he and Huber's Enterprises were far too big and powerful for Alistair to touch. But this man was a different story. Karl wasn't fooled by Oliver's handsome, friendly face; he recognised a steely edge to the man and sensed an inherent malevolence that indicated to him he would be a bad person to tangle with. There was a resolute, determined gleam in his eyes that implied he would get to the bottom of things and not be put off by anything.

'Look, I don't want to break confidentiality, but Sharba left under a bit of a cloud,' Karl told Oliver. 'She did something unacceptable and had to leave very abruptly. I don't know where she is now, but I'm pretty sure she was going to head for Cape Town.'

'Cape Town? Do you have an address for her or a telephone number?'

'No, I'm afraid not. As I said, it wasn't an amicable parting so she didn't leave a forwarding address, but I know she has good friends in Cape Town by the name of van der Merwe, and she would have wanted to get out of Zambia as quickly as possible as her reputation is now completely ruined here.'

'May I ask what she did that was so wrong?'

'No, I don't think it would be appropriate for me to gossip about her. I've probably told you too much already, but since you've come all the way from England, I thought you might like to fly the short hop from here to Cape Town to continue your search for her there.'

When Oliver thanked him and walked off, Karl derived a sense of malicious amusement from the lie he had told the man. He laughed aloud when he thought of Oliver searching through the numerous van der Merwes who lived in the Cape area. There must be literally thousands of them, Karl thought, and by the time Oliver had got through them all and not found Sharba, he would probably be ready to give up his search—or so Karl hoped.

Oliver had a sense of anti-climax as he climbed into his waiting taxi and told the driver to return to the airport. He had been looking forward to the moment he confronted Sharba; she would have been totally shocked to see him. But when she realised that he would never let her go or give her up, she would have had to acknowledge that she was destined to be with him and that it was futile to try and run and hide. Now it appeared she had given him the slip again, and Cape Town was a huge place in which to try and find a person, even if he did know the name of the people with whom she was supposedly staying.

Oliver decided that he would fly back to Lusaka before going to Cape Town and pursue the only other line of inquiry he had—which was to seek out Alistair Gordon. He didn't care that Alistair appeared to be in a relationship with Sharba; Oliver considered her fair game so long as she wasn't married. Alistair may have dumped her, anyway, if what she had done was enough to make her want to flee the country, Oliver thought hopefully. But if by chance Alistair had decided to stick by his girlfriend, Oliver thought a few lies would be enough to discredit Sharba to the point where Alistair would probably be glad to get rid of her.

Lyn's directions to Alistair Gordon's farm cottage were enough to get Oliver to the Coles' farm and one of the labourers explained exactly where the farm cottage was situated. When Oliver rolled up in his taxi, he was greeted by two barking dogs, followed swiftly by a little old African man with a wide smile. He surmised that he worked for Alistair.

'I'm looking for Alistair Gordon,' Oliver said without preamble.

'I'm so sorry, sir. Bwana Gordon isn't here,' said Dixon.

'Do you know what time he'll be back?'

'He went to Scotland two days ago and won't be back for two or three weeks.'

Oliver exhaled and ground his teeth in frustration; he was so near to finding his girlfriend and yet still so very far. It almost appeared that everything was conspiring to prevent him from finding Sharba.

'Do you know this woman?' Oliver asked Dixon showing him a picture of Sharba.

'Oh yes,' said Dixon happily. 'I know her. This is Bwana's woman. Wait I'll show you...' Dixon rushed off into the house and was back in a minute carrying a framed photograph. In it was the picture Alistair had taken of Sharba when they had swum in Devil's Pool at the top of the Victoria Falls. She was standing on the edge of the falls in her bikini and there was a shimmering rainbow in the mist that rose up behind her. She looked ethereal and incredibly beautiful with her long hair blowing about her face.

'This is the same woman, yes?' said Dixon.

There was no mistake it was Sharba, and Oliver nodded his head. But inside he was seething with rage. The words 'Bwana's woman' had infuriated him, and now the fact that this Alistair Gordon had such a sensual photo of Sharba in his house made him angrier than ever!

'Did the woman go with Mr Gordon to Scotland?' he asked Dixon, glaring at him.

'I don't know, but I don't think so,' Dixon replied truthfully.

Oliver questioned the African further, but when it became obvious that he wasn't going to get any more information out of him, he left and asked the taxi driver to take him to the Ridgeway Hotel in Lusaka. When he arrived and had checked in, he sat wondering what he should do. It appeared that Sharba was either in Cape Town or in Scotland. Alistair Gordon was going to be away for two or three weeks, so presumably, if Sharba was with him, she would return when he did. That meant Oliver had weeks in which to kick his heels, so he decided he would take a flight to Cape Town and see if he could locate her there while he was waiting for Alistair to return.

❖

Alistair was at that time huddled in his parents' sitting room while the rain rattled against the window. He was wondering worriedly why on earth he couldn't make contact with Sharba. Every time he rang her mobile it went to voice mail and she wasn't even returning his texts.

'Why're you sitting there with a face as long as a violin?' his mother asked him.

'I can't get through to my girlfriend,' Alistair answered. 'I haven't heard from her since dropping her at the airport in Livingstone on the day of my departure. She didn't answer my call when I rang her just prior to catching my flight to the UK, which was strange because she knew I was going to ring. Now when I try and phone her, it just goes to voicemail and she's not responding to my texts. It's so out of character for Sharba to ignore me and I can't help feeling something has happened to her.'

'I expect she's quite all right, dear,' said his mother in a placating tone. 'It sounds to me like she's either lost or broken her mobile, and that's the most likely explanation.'

'You might be right, but I'm sure she would let me know if that was the case because she'd know I would worry if I didn't hear from her.'

'Well, why don't you ring her at her place of work?'

Alistair knew that Sharba was not supposed to receive private calls when she was at work, but he thought the Hubers would understand if he called her this once to make sure she was okay. He hoped Sharba would answer the call he put through to the resort, but it was Clara's cheerful voice that he heard when the phone was picked up.

'Hello, this is Huber's Riverside Lodge, how may I help you?'

'Clara, it's Alistair. I'm sorry, I know I shouldn't be calling Sharba at work, but I haven't been able to get through to her on her mobile and she hasn't answered my texts, so I was getting worried. Would it be possible to speak to her—I'll be really quick.'

There was a short pause and then Clara said, 'I'm sorry Alistair, Sharba doesn't work here anymore.'

'*What*? What are you talking about?' Alistair sounded incredulous.

'Sharba left of her own accord, and I have to tell you she left under a cloud, Alistair. We thought she would go to you, but if she isn't with you, I don't know where she is.'

'But what happened? I'm in Scotland at the moment and she hasn't been back to my cottage because I rang my house servant earlier and he would have mentioned it if she had.'

'Look, none of us are very happy with Sharba at the moment. She's not the person you think she is, Alistair. Anyway, I can't talk right now, but if you ring my mobile after six our time, I'll try and tell you a little more.' Clara gave Alistair her mobile number and then rang off.

Poor Alistair spent a miserable day cooped up in his parents' house. Because the weather was so inclement, he didn't feel inclined to go out in the rain, and there was nothing to take his mind off worrying about Sharba. He couldn't imagine what could have happened to make her leave her job and cottage so abruptly; she had been so happy there. He spent the time telling his parents about Sharba, how they had met and eventually fallen in love.

'She's the most beautiful woman I've ever met,' Alistair said. He showed them a photo of Sharba he had on his mobile and they had to admit that she was very lovely. 'I don't know what I'll do if anything has happened to her,' Alistair ended after listing every one of Sharba's virtues and admitting he was deeply in love with her.

On the stroke of six pm Zambian time that evening, Alistair rang back to Clara.

'I've been out of my mind with worry since I last spoke to you,' he told Clara. 'Please explain what's happened.'

'George disappeared on the day you flew to Scotland,' Clara told him. 'Everyone was distraught, and we immediately commenced a major search operation, but we were worried that he'd fallen in the Zambezi and been swept away. By that night he still hadn't been found and we thought the worst, but in the early hours of the next morning, Karl found Sharba walking towards Dad and Mum's house with George in her arms. She told him at first she had found George wandering in the bush, but Karl didn't believe her because the bush had been thoroughly searched during the day, and after questioning her closely she eventually admitted she had taken George and hidden him in her cottage.'

'Why on earth would she do that?' Alistair asked. He was aghast.

'Well, it transpired that Sharba had a secret agenda of her own. She had discovered that she was the illegitimate daughter of my father and she had inveigled her way into our lives by coming to work here, with the ultimate objective of claiming an inheritance or some other gratuity from my father. The reason she took George was so that she could, in due time, return him and become the heroine of the hour. Then when we all felt obliged to her for rescuing George, she was going to drop her bombshell.'

'Hang on Clara; this is Sharba we're talking about! Anyone who would do what you're suggesting would be a manipulative, calculating scumbag, and that's not Sharba. You know it isn't!'

'I know,' said Clara sounding miserable. 'I thought that as well at first, but George is adamant he was with Sharba that afternoon and evening; he's a bright little boy and there's no reason for him to lie. Also, Dad says he remembers Sharba's mother now that all this has come to light. He says he can't remember her name, but she was the woman who made a disturbance during his marriage to Mum. Apparently she looked a lot like Sharba, but in a more African way.'

'I still can't believe that Sharba could do anything like that,' said Alistair. 'And what's happened to her now? She would have rung me and told me what was happening, but now it seems something's stopping her.'

'Maybe she's feeling ashamed of what she tried to do and is keeping a low profile,' suggested Clara. 'I don't know where she is, Alistair, but I overheard Karl say to a man from England who came here looking for her that she could have gone to Cape Town.'

'Cape Town? But she doesn't know anyone in Cape Town—in fact, she doesn't even know anyone in South Africa! And who was the man who came looking for her? Did he give you his name?'

'Yes he did, it was ... um, Oliver ...um ...Oliver Naughton. He had long hair and was incredibly attractive in a macho kind of way. Maybe he was an ex-boyfriend. He certainly seemed very disappointed not to find Sharba here.'

'Clara, I know you're feeling very disgusted with Sharba at the moment, but I'm sure it's all been a misunderstanding. I know Sharba so well and she wouldn't do what you've suggested. So please, if you hear where she is, let me know. Send me a text to this number and I'll get back to you. Please promise you'll do that?'

Clara promised and Alistair rang off feeling very disturbed. He felt like getting the next flight back to Zambia to try and find out what was going on, but thought it would be unkind to leave before his parents' anniversary party. He decided to put a call through to Dixon just in case Sharba had turned up there in the meantime. Dixon answered the phone immediately.

'Hello Dixon, is everything okay at home?'

'Yes Bwana, everything is all right—the dogs are fine.'

'Thank you. Now, you haven't seen Sharba, have you?'

'No Bwana, she hasn't been here. But there was another bwana looking for her.'

'Another bwana looking for Sharba at my house?'

'Yes sir.'

'Do you know who he was?'

'No Bwana. He didn't say and I haven't seen him before. He had long hair and looked very white—not like people who live in Zambia.'

Alistair felt perplexed when he ended the call. Who was this mystery man who was looking so persistently for Sharba? The man Dixon described must be one and the same as the man who was looking for her in Livingstone—Oliver Naughton. But who was he, why was he looking for Sharba and why was he so persistent? How did he even know where Alistair's cottage was? And was he something to do with Sharba's disappearance? All these questions and more swirled in Alistair's mind and he wished more than ever he was back in Zambia.

❖

Amanda made her way to where Arlo was resting on the veranda of his house. George had been very clingy since he had been reunited with her, but now Rosa was reading him his favourite story about the three little pigs, so Amanda decided to take the opportunity to speak to Arlo in private. Arlo hadn't been very well since George had disappeared as his heart condition had flared up due, the doctor said, to the stress of the situation. But he was feeling a lot better, and Amanda decided she could consult him now without making his condition recur. She and George had been staying with Rosa and Arlo since George had been found, and now that Amanda had accepted her relationship with Karl was definitely over, she discovered she felt more confident.

'How're you feeling?' Amanda asked Arlo, sitting down next to him.

'I'm absolutely fine now. I shouldn't be lounging about like this, but Rosa is insisting that I take things easy for a while,' he replied. 'Anyway, how are you and George? It was an awful strain on you when he disappeared.'

'I'm okay now, but I'm worried about George—and if I'm honest, I don't think his version of his disappearance is true.'

'He seemed pretty sure about it when we asked him what happened,' said Arlo.

'I know; he was word perfect when he told us of the events of that day. I thought at the time that the words tripped off his tongue far too easily. It was as though he was quoting from a script.'

'What are you implying, my dear?'

'Well, George is traumatised. I may not know a lot about these things, but even I can see that he is. He used to be an outgoing little lad, he was always chatting and playing with the African staff, but now he won't go near any of them. He's terrified even if we pass one on the path when we're going for a walk. One of his favourite friends was Uzma, but he literally fled away from her when we bumped into her this morning.

'He's also terrified of Karl and absolutely refuses to go

anywhere near his father. He's always had a healthy respect for him, but not this absolute terror. He's very clingy as well and if he drops off to sleep, he has the most awful nightmares and wakes up screaming for me.'

'Don't you think it's natural that the little fellow should be troubled after the ordeal he suffered?'

'No, not if his version of the events is true. If Sharba took him from the veranda of our house and hid him in her cottage, he would have thought it was an exciting game. He loves Sharba and hiding out with her for a few hours would have been a wonderful adventure for him.'

'So what do you think actually happened?'

'I don't know. But because he's so terrified of his father, I think Karl's version of what happened may not be true either.'

'Do you doubt that Sharba took George, then?'

'I can't believe that Sharba could do anything that Karl said she did; it's just not in her character.'

'But there's no doubt that Sharba is my illegitimate daughter. I didn't know she was when she was working here, but the recent events have jogged my memory and I remember her mother who looked a lot like Sharba. She claimed she was carrying my baby and she even tried to disrupt the wedding ceremony when I married Rosa. It was a very embarrassing moment for me, but Karl got rid of her quickly and the rest of the ceremony and the reception went smoothly. It was only later that I learned from Karl that he had driven the woman miles away and then dumped her in the middle of nowhere to walk back again. Now when I think about it, I'm ashamed, but at the time I just wanted to make Rosa happy and I wasn't at all concerned about the woman who claimed she was pregnant by me. Perhaps Sharba feels resentful towards me and the family for the way I treated her mother; maybe she thought she was entitled to some sort of compensation. It's possible.'

'Well, when it comes to it, maybe she is entitled to some compensation! And if she felt that way, surely she wouldn't have slunk off with her tail between her legs. Sharba is a strong, confident, principled woman. If she felt you owed her something, she would have come right out and said it. She wouldn't have needed to kidnap George in order to manipulate the family into thinking she should be compensated.'

Arlo looked at Amanda with new respect in his eyes. He had always thought she was a bit of a birdbrain, but now she had come to him with some valid points that certainly needed exploring.

'Okay, let's take the points you've mentioned one by one,' said Arlo. Firstly, George appears to be traumatised, which he shouldn't be if it was Sharba who took him. So, who did take him?'

'Could it have been one of the Africans, since he seems so afraid of them?' Amanda suggested.

'It's certainly a possibility,' agreed Arlo. 'Except why would one of the Africans do that? They all appeared to like little George.' Arlo looked puzzled, but then he went on, 'Now, secondly, you feel George's explanations of the events that happened that afternoon are not correct. If he's not telling the truth, why isn't he? What possible reason could a young child like him have for lying?'

'I think he's been told what to say,' said Amanda. 'And since he's so terrified of Karl, I have a suspicion it might have been him who told George exactly what to impart to us.'

'What you're implying is that Karl has threated his son; that's a big accusation!'

'I'm sorry Arlo, Karl is your son and you don't want to think badly of him, but I know what he's capable of!'

Arlo was silent for a few seconds then he said, 'If it was one of the Africans who took George, why would Karl want George to say it was Sharba? It doesn't really make sense. And I know you and Karl have fallen out, but I think that, for all his faults, Karl would have the best interests of his son at heart.'

'Karl's best interests are always only for himself!' Amanda said quite sharply. 'I don't know why he would want to protect the Africans if they took George and blame Sharba instead, but I do think he's threatened George with a good hiding if he tells us anything other than what Karl's told him to say, and that's why George is so terrified of him now. Karl has controlled me with violence for a long time; he knew how to hurt me without the damage being evident and now I think he's doing the same with George.'

'This is very troubling, Amanda. Why didn't you come to me before if Karl was knocking you around?'

'I should have, but I thought I loved Karl and I was embarrassed and ashamed and wanted to hide it from everyone.'

'Well, I'm very sorry that it happened.'

'It wasn't your fault, Arlo. But let's get back to puzzling out what happened to George.'

'Yes. So we assume George was taken by one of the Africans and then, when he was returned Karl wanted everyone to think it was Sharba, so he terrorised George into making a false statement. It just doesn't make sense. What we need is Sharba to tell her side of the story, but she's left us.'

'But did she leave of her own accord, or was it Karl that made her go?' Amanda said darkly.

'So now you're suggesting that Karl threatened Sharba as well and made her leave? She never gave me the impression that she was a timid person. She was the kind of woman who would stand up for herself and not be bullied!'

'I know, I agree, and that makes me wonder why we haven't heard from her. I can see Karl slapping her about and maybe beating her into submission for a short period of time, but she's the sort who would recover quickly and come back, all guns blazing!'

'So why hasn't she come back?'

'Clara told me that Alistair phoned her today. He's in Scotland visiting his parents and he was worried because Sharba hasn't been answering his calls or texts. He hasn't heard from her since he left Zambia on Monday, and we haven't heard from her either. Oh, Arlo, I'm so afraid Karl has killed her!'

❖

Oliver was under no illusion that hunting for Sharba in the Cape Town area was going to be like looking for a needle in a haystack. He was exasperated at the way Sharba always seemed to slide out of his reach every time he thought he was about to catch up with her. His inability to have hunted her down before now had not lessened his determination to find her; in fact, it had increased it. In his mind she was his woman. He loved her, and all he had to do was to find her and convince her that she loved him as well. It didn't appear as a delusion to him, and he was fully confident that once he had caught up with her he would have his way. He always got his way in the end!

After thinking about things overnight in his hotel, Oliver decided to go back to Alistair's house and ask the African there if he had his boss's address in Scotland. He realised, after thinking about it for a while, that rushing off to Cape Town and trawling through all the van der Merwes in the hope of finding the one with whom Sharba was friendly didn't make sense. It would take ages, and the likelihood was that she had accompanied Alistair to Scotland anyway. If she wasn't there, he could perhaps find out from Alistair where she was. That Alistair was Sharba's current boyfriend was of no account because Oliver was convinced that in the end Sharba would leave Alistair to be with him.

The next day, he took a taxi to Alistair's house and was again greeted by the ever-cheerful Dixon. When he asked the African if he had Alistair's address in Scotland, he shook his head sadly. Then he suddenly brightened up.

'He is staying with his parents and I think there are letters in the desk from them. Come inside and I'll look and see if there is an address on them.'

Oliver stood impatiently by his side while Dixon rummaged slowly through the papers on Oliver's desk, searching for letters from Scotland. He felt like pushing the little African aside and looking himself, but he contained his feelings and eventually Dixon came up with an envelope with a British stamp on it. Inside, there was a letter and written neatly at the top of the letter was an address.

'This is from Bwana's father,' said Dixon. 'He then pulled out a sheet of clean paper and a pen and invited Oliver to copy down the address.

'It's okay, I'll write it directly into my notebook,' Oliver said. 'But I will borrow the pen.'

Oliver left feeling pleased. He was fairly sure that Sharba would be with Alistair, so all he had to do now was get a flight back to the UK and then travel to Scotland.

22

Where Is Sharba?

Arlo and Amanda decided that they would question George again. They agreed not to involve anyone else at the moment, mainly because Arlo didn't want to intimate to the family that he suspected that Karl was lying about what had happened. He still loved his son and even though Amanda had admitted Karl had knocked her around, Arlo didn't believe his son was capable of killing anyone.

Arlo waited impatiently until the following day after Amanda had come to him, when it was that she decided George could be questioned without traumatising him further.

'George, would you tell us again what happened on Monday afternoon when you disappeared?' Amanda asked him.

'I've already told you,' said George, hopping from one foot to the other.

'I know, but Granddad would like to hear what happened again.'

George looked at Arlo who smiled at him and nodded encouragingly. Since George had told the family what his father had instructed him to say and there had been no repercussions, he felt more confident about repeating again the words Karl had drilled into his head.

'I was sleeping and then Auntie Sharba came and took me to her cottage,' he said. 'Auntie Sharba said I must hide there with her and then later, when it was dark, we could come out and surprise everyone because they would be wondering where I'd got to. It was just a joke.'

'Did you have fun hiding with Sharba?' Amanda asked. George

nodded his head. 'So what did you do?' Now George looked a bit confused.

'We hid,' he said after pausing for a moment.

'It must have been quite boring hiding all that time,' said Amanda. 'Didn't Auntie Sharba play any games with you?'

'No ... yes,' now George looked flustered.

'What games did she play with you?'

George was beginning to look upset. 'I ... I can't remember' he said at last.

'It's okay if you can't remember,' said Amanda giving her son a hug.

'We were all looking for you,' Arlo told him. 'You must have heard us calling your name over and over. Didn't you think it would be a good time to come out and show us where you were hiding when you heard us calling you, so that we wouldn't get worried?'

George's eyes swivelled towards where Karl's house stood, and he looked terrified. His father hadn't told him what to say if he was asked these questions and he was petrified that if he said the wrong thing, he would get a hiding. Two big tears spilled out of his eyes.Amanda immediately pulled her son into her arms and cuddled him. 'It's all right, sweetie,' she cooed. 'You can tell us what really happened; we won't let anyone hurt you.'

'I don't remember,' George said hiding his face on his mother's shoulder.

'Was it one of the Africans that really took you?' Arlo asked. George burst into sobs and clung on to his mother tightly. 'It was, wasn't it?' insisted Arlo.

'No! No, no, no, I can't say that,' screamed George. 'It was Auntie Sharba! I have to say it was Auntie Sharba!' He was now in a highly emotional state and Amanda shook her head at Arlo to stop him from questioning her son further.

'It doesn't matter,' she said to George. 'It's all over now; why don't you get your Lego bricks, and you can build a castle?'

When George had calmed down and was happily playing with his Lego, Amanda said to Arlo, 'What do you think?'

'I think you're right; George has been primed to tell us a certain version of the events. We need to get to the bottom of things, but the question is, how do we proceed? I think the first thing for me to do is question Karl.'

❖

Karl walked to the hotel reception after his interview with his father, so that he could tell Clara that he was going to go quickly into Livingstone to chase up the cement that they had on order.

'There's a shortage in the country for some reason, so when they get it in, they sell it to the person who makes the most noise,' Karl told her. 'I'm going to make sure that it comes our way as soon as they get a consignment. If anyone wants me, they'll have to ring me on my mobile.'

But in reality, Karl was not doing anything of the sort. After being summoned by his father and quizzed again on the events of Monday and Tuesday, Karl now needed some time to himself, so he used the cement-shortage story as an excuse to get away from the hotel for a while.

When Arlo had questioned him, Karl had been adamant that his version of what had happened was quite true. 'Surely you couldn't be saying you believe the account of a confused little boy over what I've told you?' Karl asked his father reproachfully. 'As God is my witness, every word I've said is true!'

'Why is George so scared of you then?' Arlo asked.

'Unfortunately, his mother and I have decided to split up,' said Karl. 'In situations like this, the children are not unaffected; they usually tend to side with one parent or the other. George is obviously siding with Amanda and, in his eyes, I'm the villain. It wouldn't surprise me if Amanda wasn't whispering poison in his ears as well.'

'Perhaps you deserve her dislike since you've been knocking her around!' Arlo's tone of voice was accusing.

'Me? Knock Amanda around? What nonsense! I've never laid a finger on her! I may, in the heat of the moment, have threatened her, but it was all words not action, I can promise you that.'

'That's not what Amanda says!'

'She lying! Have you ever seen a mark on her? Have you? No, you haven't and that's because I've never hurt her! I know we've split up now, but before, when I was supposedly knocking her around, did she ever give you the impression that she hated me because I was hurting her? She was always all over me—to the point that I felt smothered sometimes!'

Arlo had to concede that this was true, but he still had doubts about his son.

After Karl had made an excuse to go into Livingstone, he drove off and headed north up the road towards Kalomo. His father was suspicious, and Karl was very worried that he might now try to seek Sharba to find out the truth. How he wished that he had killed her when he'd had the chance. It had been a big mistake to threaten her and then set her free. He didn't think she would try and contact Arlo or anyone else at the hotel, but if his father found her and started asking questions, Karl knew he could be in for a lot of trouble.

He should have taken the opportunity to kill her and throw her body into the Zambezi; it would have been so easy. 'I must be getting soft,' he thought. 'I could have taken her to a lonely place, humiliated her by raping her, and then beaten her to a pulp before feeding her to the crocodiles.' Now all he could do was hope that she had died while trying to walk to civilization, because she was a real danger to him as things stood.

Karl had been so sure that his family wouldn't want to see her again, because now that her secret was out, she would become an embarrassment to his father and to the whole family. He had misjudged the situation and assumed that if he could ensure that Sharba was embarrassed enough not to want to face the family again, they would be happy to let her go. But now that stupid woman, Amanda, had aroused suspicions, and Arlo wanted to speak to Sharba to get her side of the story.

It was a disaster as far as he was concerned, because he was banking on inheriting Arlo's enterprises in Zambia, and so far he'd managed to convince his father that he was a changed person and his troubled past was well behind him. If his father found Sharba and spoke to her, she would tell him about Karl's forays into the village and also that he had mistreated her. It would be a disaster, so it was now important to find Sharba and, if she was still alive, he would have no other option other than to kill her.

Karl drove to the place where he had left Sharba hoping to find her or her body somewhere *en route*, but all he found was her backpack that she had discarded before she had reached the track. It was lying on the ground next to his original wheel marks. Karl picked it up and hid it in a small thicket. He wondered where Sharba had walked to. She could be anywhere. He drove for miles scouring the bush, and then up and down the track looking for a body. Eventually he drove all the way back to the main road and scanned along the verges, but she wasn't there.

Maybe she had managed to thumb a lift to Lusaka, he thought moodily. She hadn't tried to get into contact with the family, which was the only positive in the situation as it was right now, because it meant that she was too ashamed. But where was she now? And would Arlo find her and talk to her? The uncertainty of the situation gnawed at his guts. He felt angry with himself for giving her the chance to survive and possibly seek retribution. He realised his error of judgement could endanger his inheritance if she spoke to Arlo, and he castigated himself for being so stupid.

'Why did I not finish her off while I had the chance?' he muttered to himself. But deep down he knew why. Ever since she had repelled his advances and got him into trouble with the family, he had hated her with a vengeance. He had wanted to degrade and humiliate her in revenge. When he caught her with George, he had seen his chance. He had enjoyed slapping her about, the pain and fear in her face giving him an overwhelming sense of power over her that he didn't want to end quickly. After he had left her in the bush, he had had hours of enjoyment envisioning her agonies as she stumbled along on bare feet under the scorching sun. If he had just killed her, it would have been an anti-climax. But now he realised that, by indulging his passion for cruelty, it had put him in danger of losing everything he hoped to inherit from his father. How he wished he had killed her when he had the chance!

❖

Alistair's continued inability to get into contact with Sharba was driving him mad with worry. He knew he loved the girl, but what he hadn't realised was what it would mean to him if he lost her. Now his thoughts were running wild, and he kept imagining horrendous scenarios in which Sharba had been snatched away from him for ever. He decided to put another call through to Clara.

'I'm sorry to ring you again,' he said apologetically. 'I know you said you'd ring me if you heard where Sharba was, but I'm going out of my mind with worry. She would have contacted me if she could, I'm sure of that, so I have to conclude something dreadful has happened to her.'

'Alistair, we're all worried about her,' said Clara quietly. 'When you last rang, we were all still getting over the stress of thinking George had drowned in the Zambezi, and when the lad told us it was Sharba who took him and hid him in her cottage, we were all outraged. Now everything's calmed down a bit and there're some doubts about George's version of the events. Amanda is convinced that Karl primed George and told him what to say— she and Karl are definitely not an item anymore and she seems to hate him now. She managed to convince Dad that George was being made to lie under the threat of a beating, and although Dad tends to agree that George isn't telling the truth, he doesn't yet seem to want to believe that Karl is capable of doing anything as monstrous as Amanda suggested.'

'What does Amanda think Karl's done?'

'She thinks Karl is hiding something and he wants to keep Sharba from telling her side of the story.'

'And?'

'God, Alistair, it sounds so awful said out loud, but Amanda thinks Karl is capable of killing Sharba to ensure her side of the story is never heard.'

'*Clara!*'

'I know; I'm sorry. Look, I've never liked Karl, but I actually doubt he's done that. Amanda is very bitter about their breakup and I believe Karl knocked her around during their relationship, so although I believe she really thinks Karl is capable of killing someone, it's probably because she's so embittered at the moment.'

'So what do *you* think has happened to Sharba?'

'I just don't know. Dad has grilled Karl and he swears she wanted to leave because she was ashamed of what she had done, and she asked him to drive her to Livingstone. He says he dropped her outside the Mosi-o-Tunya InterContinental Hotel and imagined she would ring for a taxi to take her to the airport from there, or maybe ring you to come and collect her. He didn't know you were in Scotland.'

'Do you believe he's telling the truth, Clara?'

'Lies flow out of Karl's mouth as fast as the Zambezi River flows over the Victoria Falls! No, I don't for a moment believe he's telling the truth! I think it's much more likely he's somehow bullied her into leaving the country. Perhaps she really has gone to South Africa.'

'But wherever she went, she would have rung me to let me know what was going on.'

'I know... I just don't know what to say, Alistair.'

When Alistair had rung off, he went and told his parents the whole story.

'I just don't know what's really going on,' he ended. 'It seems to me that Karl Huber is somehow implicated in her disappearance, and then there's this guy Oliver Naughton who keeps popping up—and I can't fathom how he fits into the puzzle.'

'You need to go back and find out what's happened to her, son,' his father said.

'But what about your anniversary celebration?'

'It'll go ahead and we'll celebrate it with the rest of the family and friends. But your duty is to go and find the woman you love. We understand that and wouldn't want to prevent you from doing what's right.'

Alistair was very relieved that his parents were so understanding so he made arrangements to fly back to Zambia immediately. When he landed at Lusaka International Airport and had completed the border formalities, he walked out of the building to look for a taxi to take him home. He was pleased to find one had just drawn up and was dropping off a passenger. Alistair waited while the customer paid the taxi driver and prepared to go into the airport building. After settling up with the driver, the man pushed back his long hair, picked up his luggage and strode away without a glance at Alistair. Had he taken a closer look at him, Oliver might have recognised Alistair as the man in the photo that Lyn has shown him, but he was in a hurry to check in for his flight to Heathrow.

Dixon was very surprised to see Alistair back home early. He rushed to make him a cup of tea while Alistair took a shower to wash off the grime of his journey and change into shorts and a tee shirt.

'How were your parents? Did you have a nice party?' Dixon asked him politely when he served Alistair his tea.

'They were fine, thank you,' Alistair replied. 'But I had to leave before the party because Sharba's missing. I came back because I need to look for her.'

'I'm sorry,' said Dixon sympathetically. Then he remembered Oliver's visit and added, 'That bwana with the long hair came back again, the one who is also looking for Miss Sharba.'

'Why did he come back again?' Alistair asked with surprise.

'He wanted your address in Scotland.'

'He didn't get it, did he?'

'Oh yes,' said Dixon feeling very pleased with himself. 'I remembered the address would be on a letter your father sent you, so I found it for him.'

Alistair felt appalled that Dixon had given Oliver Naughton his father's address, but he knew the little African had just been trying to be kind and helpful.

'Tell me about that bwana,' Alistair said.

'He was very white like he didn't go in the sun,' said Dixon. 'His hair was long and he just asked questions.'

When Dixon had gone back to the kitchen, Alistair put a call through to his parents.

'Now listen,' he said after reassuring his father he had got home safely. 'Dixon, the chap who works for me, has just told me that that fellow Oliver Naughton, whom I told you about, turned up again here and asked for our address in Scotland. Unfortunately, Dixon found the address on one of the letters you sent me and gave it to him. He thought he was being helpful and didn't realise it was the last thing I would have wanted him to do. Anyway, if this guy Naughton turns up at your house, please don't tell him a thing. I don't know how he fits into this saga, but at the moment I'm not inclined to trust anyone, so just tell him you don't know anything.'

23

Disconcerting Information

Alistair felt tired after his journey from Scotland, but he wasn't going to waste a second and immediately drove back to the airport when he had finished his tea. He refuelled his aeroplane and, after doing the pre-flight checks, he took off for Livingstone. Before he left, he made a call to his friend Marcus to explain the situation, and Marcus promised to meet him at Livingstone Airport.

'Drive me home first, then the vehicle is yours for as long as you need it,' Marcus told him generously when he later met Alistair. 'And just let me know if there's anything else I can do.'

'There is something,' said Alistair. 'You're mates with a lot of the airport staff, aren't you? Well, could you try and find out if Sharba was on any of the flights flying out of Livingstone early on Tuesday morning or any time after that.'

'Sure, that should be easy enough,' agreed Marcus.

After leaving Marcus at his house, Alistair drove to the Mosi-o-Tunya Hotel. He wanted to find out if anyone had seen Sharba being dropped off in the early hours of Tuesday morning.

The Indian man who was at reception was very helpful. 'No-one can drive into our carpark at night without the night guard taking his registration number and checking his business,' he told Alistair. 'It will all be documented so I'll be able to check for you.'

It was soon established that Karl had definitely not dropped Sharba in the carpark of the hotel, but there was the possibility he had drawn up outside the carpark, Alistair realised. He was walking back to the car when he got a call from Marcus.

'Just to let you know that Sharba did not catch a flight from

Livingstone on Tuesday or any other day,' he told Alistair. 'Seems she must have left by some other means of transport.'

Alistair drove along in deep thought as he headed for Huber's Riverside Lodge. When he arrived there, he asked one of the garden workers where he might find Karl.

'He's working on the new extension of the hotel,' the gardener told Alistair. 'But only staff are allowed to go to that area. If you wait here, I'll call him for you. There's a nice garden bench you can rest on. Who shall I say is asking for him?'

Alistair let the gardener walk off and when he had gone some way he got up and followed him, keeping his distance. He had a feeling that Karl would not want to answer questions about Sharba and might disappear if he knew Alistair was there and demanding answers. He didn't go all the way to the building site but stopped a little way from it in a position where he could covertly observe what happened when the gardener spoke to Karl.

From what he could gather from that distance, Alistair could see Karl wasn't very pleased when the gardener gave him the message. In fact, Karl was horrified that Alistair was there asking for him. He had gathered from Clara that Alistair was in Scotland for two or three weeks and so he wasn't expecting to be confronted by him for at least another week or so. He hadn't even thought out what he was going to say to the man to allay any suspicion he may have. He allowed his irritation to bubble over when he answered the gardener.

'Can't you see I'm working?' Karl growled at the unfortunate messenger. 'If anyone wants to see me, they should go to reception and book an appointment to see me when I have time.' With a wave of his arm, he dismissed the man. As the gardener walked away, Karl sat down and pulled a tray containing a cup of tea and a doughnut towards him. One of the kitchen staff had just delivered his mid-morning snack and he bit into the sugary bun with relish.

The gardener was surprised to find Alistair had followed him part of the way towards the building site, but he conveyed, as politely as he could, that this wasn't a good time to speak to Mr Karl and Alistair should make an appointment to see him at reception.

'Thank you, I'll do that,' Alistair assured him. He then tipped the gardener for his trouble.

As soon as the gardener had returned to his duties, Alistair walked to the building site and ignored the Africans who were politely trying to deflect him from his course. Karl didn't see him arriving until the last moment and his face registered disbelief, because he was sure Alistair was the sort of person who would stick to the rules rather than stick his neck out. He decided that the best approach was to meet Alistair with aggression. He still thought the man was a milksop and, if he himself was pugnacious, he was sure he would be able to cower him.

'Did you not get the message the gardener took to you?' Karl demanded truculently.

'Yes I did,' said Alistair mildly. 'He said you were very busy, but now I see you've stopped for a tea break, so I thought we could use this time for me to ask you some questions.'

Although Alistair's tone was mild, there was a steely edge to his voice that surprised Karl and he put aside his doughnut almost guiltily.

'What do you want to know?' he asked rudely.

'My girlfriend has disappeared without a trace and you were the last person to see her, so I want you to tell me what happened and where she is now.'

'I can tell you what happened. Your sweet little girlfriend was attempting to manipulate my family to her own advantage and got caught out. She left of her own accord because she was ashamed, but I've no idea where she is now, and I don't actually care.'

'Well, you should care because she was working for your family and they had a duty of care for her while she was one of their employees. You've thrown a lot of accusations against her, but, from what I can gather, no one has heard her side of the story because you made sure she left the premises before she could talk to anyone else.'

'Look, I don't like what you are insinuating,' Karl growled, his tone again truculent.

'I really don't care what you like or don't like,' replied Alistair. 'What I want is an account of the last hours you spent with Sharba.'

Karl glared at Alistair. He realised he had misjudged the guy— he wasn't a milksop at all, despite his appearance. Alistair hadn't raised his voice, but his eyes were like gimlets as they bored into

Karl, and he knew he would have to give some sort of account to the man, otherwise he might appear to be guilty.

'When I confronted her and she admitted what she was up to, she was ashamed and didn't want to stay here a moment longer. She asked me to give her a lift to Livingstone when she'd packed her things, and I did because I was completely disgusted and wanted to see the back of her.'

'So where did you take her to in Livingstone?'

'I dropped her at the Mosi because I didn't think she should be roaming the streets of Livingstone at that time of the night. I may have been disgusted with her, but I didn't want to see her harmed. I knew she would be able to ring for a taxi to take her to the airport and she would be quite safe waiting for it at the Mosi.'

'So did you see her actually walking into the hotel after you dropped her?'

'I dropped her right outside reception and then left immediately. I don't know if she walked in or not.'

Alistair knew Karl was lying. If he had dropped Sharba outside reception, he would have had to drive into the carpark and Alistair had already established that he had not.

'You're lying!' Alistair's words were like a whiplash. 'I've already checked the night guard's register and you're not on it!'

'That's because the lazy bastard was sleeping and I wasn't going to wake him up to sign his poxy register,' Karl spat back, the lies flowing effortlessly off his tongue. 'Now, will you please leave so I can get on with some work?'

'I'm going nowhere until you tell me what really happened.' Alistair was seething with anger now.

'Samson,' bellowed Karl. Immediately Samson was at his side. He was a huge African, a man from the Zulu tribe in South Africa, much bigger than the average Zambian. Karl had employed him for his own protection and to act as his spy. Knowing that some of his actions would have infuriated a number of his employees, he had thought it prudent to have someone watching his back. 'Please escort this man off the premises,' he ordered Samson.

Samson took Alistair by his arm, but Alistair shook him off.

'Please, Bwana,' said Samson quietly, but this time he put his huge, muscled arm around Alistair's shoulders and propelled him away. Alistair didn't want to end up in a humiliating situation by grappling with this giant, so much stronger than he, so he nodded his head.

'Okay, I'll go, you don't have to push me,' he said to Samson. Then he turned and shouted to Karl: 'This isn't the end of it—you can be sure of that!'

Samson escorted him back to his car and waited for him to get in.

'I want to first speak to Mr Arlo before I leave,' Alistair told Samson.

'No sir,' Samson rumbled. 'Mr Arlo is not well so Mr Karl is in charge and he has said you must leave the premises.'

'Well, I'll speak to Miss Clara if Mr Arlo isn't up to it,' said Alistair.

'No. You will leave, sir.'

'If your woman had disappeared without a trace, wouldn't you want to talk to the people who may be able to shed some light on her disappearance?' Alistair appealed to Samson.

Samson's expression was inscrutable, and he merely pushed Alistair towards his car without replying to the question. It was obvious that he was going to obey the man who paid him and not let any sympathies stop him from doing what he had been commanded to do.

Alistair drove back to the Mosi-o-Tunya hotel and ordered a coffee. He knew now for sure that Karl was lying and must be involved in Sharba's disappearance. He pulled out his mobile and sent a text message to Clara. "Need to speak to you urgently. Could you call me or let me know when it's convenient for me to call you?"

A couple of minutes later, his mobile rang and he saw it was Clara. He let her know that he had been at the resort and explained what had happened when he had confronted Karl.

'He had me thrown off the premises when I proved him to be a liar,' Alistair told her. 'I wanted to speak to you as well, but his big goon, Samson, wouldn't let me.'

'Bloody Karl!' exclaimed Clara. 'Who the hell does he think he is? He acts like he's in charge while Dad's under the weather, but he's not! He had no right to have you thrown off the premises. As for Samson, I don't trust him an inch. Karl says he's employed to work on the building site, but in truth Karl has engaged him as his bodyguard. That's how unpopular my half-brother is!'

'Well, I think Karl is somehow involved in Sharba's disappearance.'

'It wouldn't surprise me at all. Amanda thinks the same as you and she's already voiced her worries to Dad. Dad did speak to Karl. He denied everything, of course, and I think Dad just wants to believe his son would not be capable of killing anyone.'

'And you—do you think Karl's capable of killing Sharba now?'

'I don't know,' said Clara worriedly. Amanda thinks he is.'

'My God, Clara, if there's the slightest possibility that Karl has killed Sharba, the police should be informed. He shouldn't be happily working on the building site, eating doughnuts and having me thrown off the premises!'

'I know, but there's no evidence that he killed her. If our suspicions are made public, it will be the end of our hotel, even if we're wrong and it turns out that Karl had nothing to do with Sharba's disappearance. If you throw mud around, it sticks! We need some substantiation to our suspicions before we get the police or anyone else involved.'

Alistair didn't really agree, although he did understand what Clara was saying. 'Do you think Amanda would speak to me?' he asked.

Amanda was more than happy to speak to Alistair, and she told Clara to tell him she would meet him at the Mosi in about half an hour. When she arrived, she had George with her as she wasn't prepared to leave her precious son with anyone else. Also, he didn't like his mother to go anywhere without him, he was clingy and tearful much of the time, and he seemed to be frightened of everyone apart from his mother, Rosa, Clara and Arlo.

'It was good of you to come,' said Alistair. 'What would you both like to drink?'

Amanda settled for a cup of tea and George had a Coke and an ice cream. He had shrunk back when Alistair had greeted him, but now was happily consuming his ice cream.

'Tell me what you think happened, Amanda,' Alistair said. 'Do you really think Karl could have killed Sharba?'

'I don't know if he killed her,' said Amanda honestly. 'But I think he's capable of killing someone, and since Sharba has seemingly disappeared without a trace, it's certainly a possibility he killed her. It would be so easy for him; he could dump her body in the river for the crocks, or to be washed over the falls so no one would ever find the evidence of his crime.'

'But why do you think he would do something as drastic as that?'

'For a long time, I thought I loved Karl; whenever he did things that I didn't think were kosher, I subconsciously made excuses for him and convinced myself that what he was doing was okay. It was stupid—I know that now I'm thinking clearly—but it's only since I've split up with Karl that I've realised how bad he really is. His main priority is himself; it always has been and it always will be. When he reached the age of forty and realised he had achieved nothing but a past full of crime and offences, he knew he would have to do something about it. But instead of getting his act together and achieving something by his own initiative, he decided to manipulate his family.

'He convinced Arlo he was a reformed character and he wanted to make amends for his past and come and help his family. Arlo's not stupid, but he did want to help his son, so he offered him a job building the resort, with the condition that Karl prove himself to be a reformed character. Karl came and started the job, but he couldn't help himself getting involved in mini scams—nothing too serious, just minor things that enabled him to line his pockets. It was in his nature to do so. Arlo picked up on one of these scams and almost sent Karl back to Germany, but he gave him one more chance. Karl knew he had to convince his father he'd changed because he had his covetous eyes set on Huber Enterprises. He wanted to inherit everything in Zambia when Arlo died.'

Amanda stopped because one of the waiters had come to take the empty ice cream dish from George and the little boy screamed when the waiter swooped in.

'It's okay, sweetie, he's just taking the dirty dish; he isn't going to take you,' Amanda reassured her son. She passed the dish to the waiter who was looking rather disconcerted at George's attitude towards him.

'He's been like this since the day of his disappearance,' Amanda explained to Alistair when she had comforted her son. 'He's scared of everyone. Anyway, as I was saying, Karl wants to inherit Huber Enterprises more than anything in the world, so he needed to convince his father he'd changed. That's where I came in. I would be his perfect camouflage, because choosing a partner proved that he had changed and wanted to settle down. When George was born, Karl felt there was even more reason for Arlo to bequeath Huber Enterprises to him. Unfortunately for George and me, we were nothing more to Karl than a means of convincing Arlo that he should leave his estate to him!'

'But surely Arlo could see what he was doing? He's not stupid!'

'No, he's not. But he wanted to believe Karl had changed. He loves all his children and although Karl has always been rebellious and a problem to his father, he didn't love him any less than the others. I didn't help either; I championed Karl and made everyone believe that he was, for the most part, a good partner and father, but that was far from the truth! So everything was going to plan for Karl. Arlo was beginning to believe in him and Clara had bagged herself a millionaire, so she wouldn't need a share of the inheritance. His brother Albert was already a very wealthy man in Germany, so he wouldn't need a share either. It was looking good for Karl—and then Sharba came along!

'I don't know how Karl found out Sharba was Arlo's illegitimate daughter, but to Karl she was a big threat. Arlo had no idea who she was, but he often said what a good girl she was, always hardworking and loyal to the company. This must have infuriated Karl and he must have been dreadfully worried that she would inherit rather than he, if he blotted his copy book. I'm sure he was just waiting for his chance to discredit her and get rid of her. I personally don't think Sharba had anything to do with George's abduction; Karl just used it to disgrace her so the family wouldn't want to find out where she had gone.'

'Then you think he killed her and disposed of her body in the Zambezi?'

'I definitely think he's capable of doing something like that.'

'So we should go to the authorities with our suspicions. I know it could be bad for the hotel to have a scandal like that hanging over it, but surely if a life has been taken it shouldn't be hushed up.'

'It wouldn't help going to the authorities. Karl has the police force in Livingstone in his pocket. The police are easily corruptible in Zambia, so right from his first day in this country Karl worked to get them on his side because he knew he wouldn't be able to go straight.'

'So what can we do?'

'The only thing to do is get Arlo to see that his son is a rotten egg. He's the only one who will be able to get any truth out of Karl, but he has to understand what his son really is before he'll do anything. Unfortunately, poor Arlo is very unwell at the moment. This whole business has upset him dreadfully and his health has taken another nosedive, so now Rosa isn't letting anyone see him for the time being.'

❖

Oliver had immediately taken a train to Aberdeen when he arrived back in England, and then hired a car so that he could drive to Alistair's parents' house. He decided that he would keep the house under observation for a while in the hope that Sharba might emerge. He needed to confirm that she was there, and if he had the chance to detain her when she was on her own, it would make matters a lot more simple. He parked on the opposite side of the road to their house and a little way past it and settled down to wait.

Nothing happened for a very long time and the front door remained tightly shut. Oliver found himself growing sleepy. He was jetlagged from his flight from Zambia and tired from his journey to Scotland and could hardly keep his eyes open. He was about to get out of the car and have a little walk around to wake himself up when the front door opened. Quickly he settled back in his seat and tried to make himself inconspicuous as he looked to see who was going to emerge.

To Oliver's disappointment, it was an elderly man, presumably Alistair's father, and he had a little Jack Russel on a lead. Obviously he was going out to take his dog for a walk. He passed the car in which Oliver was sitting without seemingly seeing there was someone in it and disappeared down the street. Oliver stayed where he was and waited an hour before the man came back with his dog.

Later that morning, the door opened once more and again Oliver watched to see who was going to come out. This time it was an elderly lady, Alistair's mother, and she pulled a shopping bag on wheels behind her. She walked off in the direction of the shops and didn't come back for half an hour. After she had returned, the front door of their house remained shut for the rest of the day.

Oliver stayed until it was getting dark and then he went to find a hotel. Since he had seen neither Alistair nor Sharba, he began to wonder if they were staying there. He wondered if maybe they had gone to visit other relatives or friends for a while. It would be very unusual for them to remain closeted in the family home all day and not go out if they were actually there. He decided that the next day he would knock on the door and ask the old folk where they were.

The following day, Oliver again parked in the same spot that he had previously used and watched the house covertly for a while. He was hoping the elderly man would go out with his dog again, because he thought it would be easier to get information out of the elderly lady. A little later than the previous day, Alistair's father emerged with the Jack Russel. Oliver waited until they had disappeared down the street before he eased himself out of the car and crossed the road to the house.

After ringing the bell and knocking smartly on the door, Oliver stood back and waited. A short while later the door opened, and Alistair's mother looked out. Oliver put on his most charming smile as he prepared to ask her if he had come to the right house to find Sharba, but as he opened his mouth to speak, he was surprised to see recognition registering in the old woman's eyes. Alistair had warned his parents that this mysterious man, Oliver Naughton, who had long hair, would most probably be paying them a visit and Mrs Gordon realised who he must be. Oliver noticed in the elderly woman's eyes that she seemed to know who he was, but there was no time to ponder how that could be, so he launched immediately into the speech he had prepared.

'I'm so sorry to bother you, but I was wondering, if by any chance, Sharba was staying here?'

'No,' said the elderly woman flatly. 'No one by that name lives here.' She made as though she was going to shut the door, but Oliver quickly added,

'Maybe I could speak to Alistair instead, then?'

'Alistair's not here,' said the elderly woman shortly. 'He's gone back home to Zambia.'

'Already?' Oliver asked aghast.

'Who are you and why're you trying to find Alistair and Sharba?' the elderly woman asked sharply.

'My name's Oliver Naughton and Sharba and I are engaged to be married,' Oliver lied smoothly. 'We had a bit of a tiff and decided a bit of space would be helpful for us both, but we're still engaged and I love her with all my heart. I need to find her so that I can tell her that and we can resume our relationship.'

Alistair's mother stared at Oliver in astonishment. She had been a schoolteacher when she was younger and always considered herself a good judge of whether a person was telling the truth or not, and she was convinced Oliver was telling the truth. The man really did love the woman that her son had declared the love of his life.

'Well, I'm sorry neither of them is here,' she said in a gentler tone. 'I've no idea where Sharba is, but Alistair returned to Zambia yesterday, so you'll have to go there if you want to find him.' With that she firmly closed the door, leaving Oliver standing on the doorstep feeling utterly nonplussed.

Oliver couldn't believe that he had come all this way only to miss Alistair, his only link with Sharba. It was infuriating! Now he had to decide what to do next, but whatever he did, it seemed that Sharba was always just out of his reach.

For the first time, Oliver wondered if he shouldn't give up on his girlfriend; he knew he still loved her and wanted her, but forces beyond his control seemed to ensure that she eluded him at every turn. He shivered superstitiously at the thought of something stronger than himself influencing his future plans and then he pulled himself together. He knew what he wanted more than anything in the world, and his father had always helped him get what he desired, so surely these negative thoughts that were invading his mind were caused by tiredness. He would put

Sharba out of his head for a bit so that he could rest, and then he would put aside the fantasies that he was being stopped, and then decide what to do next.

❖

Alistair was wondering how to proceed after Amanda had left him when his mobile rang. It was his mother and she wanted to tell him that Oliver Naughton had paid them a visit looking for Sharba. When she told her son that Oliver had claimed that he and Sharba were engaged to be married, Alistair couldn't believe what he was hearing.

'Sharba has never even mentioned the man!' Alistair told his mother. 'I'm sure he must be lying because she would have said something about him had they been close in the past. I'm sure he just said that to make you tell him where she was, but as to his real reason of wanting to see her, well, I can't even guess what it is. From what I know of Sharba's past, she was a free spirit and enjoyed being independent because it gave her the liberty to do as she liked. I don't think she even intended falling for me—it just crept up on her, well, on us both really, but I knew that if I was to nurture her love so that we could have a future together, I'd have to tread carefully and not stifle her, or she would be spooked and fly away.'

'Well, maybe this Oliver Naughton just said what he did to try and generate sympathy from me,' said his mother. 'But at the same time, I couldn't help feeling he was telling the truth when he said he loved her.'

Alistair felt troubled when he had finished speaking to his mother. Surely Sharba would have told him if she had been engaged to another man in the past? She didn't wear an engagement ring, but that meant nothing because she could have taken it off. Doubts started to assail him now, because she hadn't told him she was Arlo's illegitimate daughter either, and if she was keeping secrets, who knew what else she was keeping from him? Perhaps nothing bad had happened to her and she was just staying with other people from whom she had also kept secrets. Like Oliver, Alistair didn't know how to proceed.

24

Sharba's Ordeal

It took Sharba a while to get over the initial shock of realising she was Arlo's daughter, but eventually she pulled herself together because she knew that whether she was Arlo's daughter of not, she had to make a move. As she followed the wheel tracks that Karl had made the previous day, she tried to get the thoughts that were flying around her mind in some sort of order.

Karl had obviously thought that she wouldn't want to face Arlo and his family once he had put it to them that she was a gold-digger with an agenda of her own, and he was right! Although she was quite innocent of his condemnations, Sharba quailed now at the thought of facing them all because she was sure they would all judge her of being guilty. They would never believe that it was by sheer coincidence that she had ended up working for Huber Enterprises when she had returned to Zambia after being away for years.

It made Sharba feel completely wretched that Karl had somehow manipulated her into this quandary, but as she stumbled along, she had to consider if he hadn't left her in the middle of nowhere because he was convinced she would not be able to walk to civilisation and get help. Had he wanted her to die? Perhaps he just wanted to humiliate her and cause her pain and suffering, but if she died trying to get help, wouldn't it suit him better? Sharba shrugged her shoulders. She wasn't ready to die, so if that was Karl's intention, she was going to do her best to spoil his plan.

Before setting off, Shaba had scrabbled in her backpack and found two pairs of socks both of which she put on, one over the other. She hoped they would protect her feet to a certain degree, but she was under no illusion that it was going to be tough walking through this rough bushy area without shoes of any kind. It was still cool when she eventually set off, and, picking her way carefully around bushes and rocks, she followed Karl's wheel marks that would lead her to the road. Very soon, she felt the early morning sun was already becoming warm on her head and she realised that she was going to suffer greatly walking for miles in the scorching heat.

Every stone she walked over jarred on the soles of her feet, and the thin protection of the socks was no defence against the thorns and sharp grass that spiked straight through them into her flesh. Doggedly she kept moving, trying to figure out how far they had driven after they had left the track. They had been driving slowly and it had seemed quite a fair distance, but now she was walking, and the dry spiky bush spread endlessly ahead of her, the distance seemed to increase to infinity.

The countryside in which she was walking was typical of Zambian bushveld; there was dense spiky dry grass that hid the stones and rocks, areas of thick bush, and trees and regions of bare rock and sand. It took Sharba hours to negotiate her way through it all, and as the sun rose in the sky, the heat built up and burned her exposed skin while dehydrating her as she sweated her way along the wheel marks. It wasn't long before she threw her backpack aside as it seemed to weigh more with each passing step, and then she continued unencumbered apart from her handbag. Birds flew over her head at intervals, and she saw ants and other scurrying insects as she trudged along, but apart from that she saw no other life, neither animal nor human.

At last she came to the track where Karl had turned off the road and she sank down under the scanty shade of a tree. She felt pleased that she had reached this milestone, but the track stretched endlessly ahead, and she knew she had only completed the first and shortest leg of her journey. 'Maybe someone will drive past and give me a lift,' Sharba thought hopefully. The track didn't look as though it was used very often and was obviously poorly maintained, but surely people must use it sometimes, she found herself hoping optimistically.

No vehicle drove past as she sat resting. She took off her socks and looked at her feet. They were very painful and she could see that they didn't look good. Her soles were bruised all over and the thorns and spiky grass had scratched and punctured her feet to a bloody mess. Oh well, walking on the track will be easier, she decided. She eased the socks back on, flinching as she did so, and then heaved herself up. It was already midday and since there didn't seem to be any traffic on the track, she knew she would have to walk again.

She remembered Karl had turned left off the track, so she knew she must now turn right to head back to the main road. Walking down the sandy track was certainly easier than walking in the bush, but the heat really started to torment her. To try and take her mind off her raging thirst, she thought about George. He must have been reunited with his mother by this time, and her joy would know no bounds when she had her darling son back. But Sharba knew that Karl would prime his son to tell the family that it was Auntie Sharba who had abducted him, and they would all be hating her right now. Karl would make sure he painted a very bad picture of her and, if they believed him, they would never want to see her again. It was a depressing thought and Sharba knew she must turn her mind to more positive things. 'At least I know now that Oliver isn't about to make an appearance,' she thought. 'For months I've believed he had somehow found out I was alive and in Zambia. Now that's one worry I can discard!'

Sharba toiled along the track for hours and didn't see a single vehicle. The sun threw up heat mirages in front of her and beyond them the road appeared to wiggle and shimmer. Great wafts of hot air seemed to rise from the track and engulf Sharba, making her head spin and ache. Her feet were agony, now, and her thirst was becoming unbearable. She remembered that she had heard somewhere that if you sucked a button it would alleviate your thirst, so she wrenched a button from her blouse and popped it into her mouth. It did help a little, but what she really needed was a long draught of water.

Eventually, Sharba felt so exhausted she just wanted to stop walking and lie down at the side of the road, but to stop herself from giving up, she thought of the Huber family and of their contempt for her. It made her angry to think of what Karl was trying to do to her and her anger kept her going. She didn't think she could ever face the family again if they thought she was a gold-digger, but she was determined that, somehow, she would get even with Karl. She had managed to carve out a nice life for herself working and living alongside the Zambezi River and Karl had ruined it all for her. Once again, she was on the run with no possessions apart from the contents of her handbag.

It was getting dark when she finally came to the main tarred road. Sharba knew that if she turned left the road would lead her to Livingstone, but it was miles and miles away. She figured that there could be closer towns if she turned right. She had been blindfolded, so she didn't know if they had passed Kalomo—one of the villages *en route* to Livingstone—or not. Probably not, she decided, so, taking a gamble, she turned right in the hope that she would find Kalomo not too far down the road.

After she had been walking down the main road for a while, she heard a vehicle approaching. Her heart leaped with joy and she stood on the side of the road waiting for it to come into view. It was now dark, so the first thing she saw were the headlights, but as soon as she saw them she started waving, both hands above her head in a frantic effort to make the driver realise she needed help. But the vehicle swept past without a pause, leaving Sharba standing in its dust and diesel fumes feeling outraged. 'Why didn't you stop?' Sharba shouted after the receding red lights.

There was nothing for it but to continue walking. Sharba felt deflated, but hoped there would be another vehicle soon. There was, but even though she waved even more frantically and jumped up and down as well, the car didn't stop. 'Maybe I should stand in the middle of the road,' she muttered. 'Then they would have to stop!' But even as she thought about it, she knew it would be stupid to do that. There were a lot of really bad drivers in Zambia and standing in the middle of the road at night was a sure way to get run over and killed!

Vehicle after vehicle passed her without stopping until she

hardly bothered to wave because she knew it was a futile activity. No one was going to stop for what must look like a mad woman walking down the side of the road in the night. 'I'm not going to give up walking,' Sharba told herself. 'It's cooler now and I'm not so thirsty, so I'll walk until I get to Kalomo and get help there. I can do this!'

It was after ten o'clock when she stopped, exhausted, at a track leading off the main road. There was a concrete post on which hung a sign and Sharba rested her back against the concrete post. She knew that she couldn't rest for too long or she would never be able to get underway again. So after a short rest she envisioned the lights of Kalomo to psych herself up and lurched to her feet, wincing with pain. Her feet were in fiery agony now and every muscle in her body hurt. She had a thumping headache, a raging thirst, and her body was crying out for rest, but she knew she had to go on. There was a small moon and, as she prepared to set off, she glanced at the sign under which she had been sitting. It wasn't all that clear, but she made out the words *Concord Estates* and it rang a bell.

'Where have I heard that name before?' Sharba muttered to herself as she stood staring at the sign. Then the kind faces of Len and Elizabeth Raven floated into her mind and she remembered she had met them when she first came back to Zambia, and they had invited her to come and stay with them on their farm— Concord Estates. She had had no contact with them since then, despite promising to visit them, but she remembered that they said the turnoff to their farm was seven miles south of Choma. So that meant her calculations were way out; she had been walking towards Choma and Kalomo was way behind her, but that didn't matter now because she knew she could go to the Ravens for help.

Although Sharba knew that the turnoff to Concord Estates was seven miles south of Choma, she had no idea how far she would have to walk up the track to find the homestead. She hoped it wasn't too far because the combination of her aches and pains and her raging thirst was making her feel faint. She limped off, but her progress was getting increasingly slower. It was, in fact, two miles to the farmhouse but it seemed like two hundred miles to Sharba. Every agonised step she took squeezed a little more energy out of her and when at last she came to the homestead's perimeter fence gate, she was on the point of collapse.

Sharba could see the farmhouse through the gate at the top of a long driveway, but the gate was locked with a large brass padlock. There was a very small, thatched building a little way along the inside of the fence which Sharba rightly assumed was the night-watchman's shelter, so she tried to call out to attract his attention. Her voice came out as nothing more than a thin mew and she found she was unable to raise it to a shout.

In frustration, Sharba rattled the gate and was soon rewarded by the frantic barking of two dogs that erupted from the veranda of the farmhouse. A moment later, the shadowy outlines of the dogs appeared as they ran to the gate to see who was trying to invade their space. Alerted by the barking of the dogs, the night-watchman emerged from his shelter with a torch and hurried to the gate to see what was going on. When he arrived, he swept the beam of his torch over Sharba and then stopped in surprise when he realised it was what looked like a very distressed white woman.

'Help me,' Sharba wheezed.

Quickly, the night-watchman opened the padlock and swung the gate back. He could see that Sharba could hardly walk, so he helped her along to his shelter and gently pushed her on to the chair that stood at the entrance. The dogs ran at their heels, realising that there was nothing to endanger them or those they guarded, so now they were just mildly interested in the newcomer and sniffed with interest at her legs.

'Water ... please?'

Hastily the night-watchman picked up an enamel cup that was standing next to the chair and dipped it into a nearby bucket that was filled with water, then he handed it to Sharba. She didn't care that neither the cup nor the bucket looked too clean. She eagerly snatched the cup and put it to her mouth, spilling some of the water down her chest in her eagerness. To her, it tasted like nectar from heaven as she gulped it down.

'Slowly,' the night-watchman cautioned her. She knew he was right, and she made herself take small mouthfuls rather than guzzle it down.

'Stay here. I will call the bwana.' The night-watchman left her sipping the water and headed up to the house with the dogs at his heels.

Len and Elizabeth were in bed, but they had heard the commotion as the dogs ran barking to the gate. They didn't bother to get up as they knew their night-watchman would come and tell them if anything was wrong, so when they head him tapping on the door, they both got up.

'What is it, Chibwe?' Len asked as they walked on to the veranda.

'It's a white woman, Bwana ... and she is not all right.'

Len and Elizabeth weren't too sure what their night-watchman meant, but they could tell from his face that it was serious, so they quickly followed him as he walked back to the shelter. Neither of them recognised Sharba to start with in her bedraggled state, but they could see she was in a bad way.

Sharba was feeling slightly better after having drunk some water and she tried to smile at Len and Elizabeth. 'I'm Sharba. We met some time ago at the Intercontinental Hotel in Lusaka,' she told them.

'My God, it is you, Sharba?' Len exclaimed. 'What the hell's happened to you?'

'I... well, it's...it's a long story,' said Sharba.

'Car crash?' suggested Elizabeth.

'No, nothing like that.'

'You look in a bad way, dear. Is there anyone else we should be worrying about as well? Or would you like us to call someone?' Elizabeth was trying to gather the basic facts as quickly as possible because she thought Sharba looked as though she might pass out at any moment.

Sharba shook her head. 'There's only me and it's not necessary to call anyone.'

'Come on Len, we need to get the lass to the house. She's in a bad way and needs medical attention,' said Elizabeth. 'We can find out what happened later when she's feeling better.'

But Sharba found she was unable to even stand, so Len and Chibwe carried her between them to the house and put her on the bed in the spare bedroom.

'I think she needs a doctor,' Elizabeth told Len.

'No, I'm all right.' Sharba felt a lot better now that she had some fluid in her and she was resting. 'I'm just exhausted, dehydrated, and my feet are damaged. I've been walking since early this morning and part of my journey was through thick bush which wasn't ideal since I had no shoes.'

'Well, we need to get fluids into you to start with,' decided Elizabeth, as she wondered what on earth had happed to Sharba. She sent Len off to get a glass of orange juice and then turned her attention to Sharba's feet. The socks were in shreds and they were soaked in blood. 'Doesn't look good,' she said. Your feet are a complete mess, and you may need antibiotics to prevent them from becoming infected. I'll have to wash them now and then smear them with disinfectant cream and bandage them.'

'Do you think I could have a shower, rather?' Sharba asked. 'That would take care of washing my feet—and I feel absolutely filthy all over.'

'Do you think you could manage a shower?' Elizabeth asked doubtfully. 'I think it would be better if I ran you a bath. I could help you in and out.'

Sharba drank the glass of orange juice that Len brought her while Elizabeth ran the water in the bath, then she allowed the older woman to help her into the bath and assist with her ablutions. When she was out and dry, Elizabeth gave her one of her own nighties to wear and ministered to her damaged feet, while Sharba drank another glass of juice and took some painkillers.

'I'm going to warm up some soup for you, now, and after that maybe you'd like to tell us what happened,' suggested Elizabeth when she had got Sharba comfortable in bed.

Sharba managed to drink most of the soup, but by then the strong painkillers Elizabeth had given her were making her drowsy and that, together with the fatigue of the past twenty-four hours, made Sharba fight to keep her eyes open. Elizabeth went to make her a cup of tea, but when she came back she found Sharba was fast asleep so she quietly removed the tea and replaced it with a glass of water in case the young woman awoke and felt thirsty.

'We're not going to find out what happened to her until tomorrow,' Elizabeth told Len. 'She's dead to the world now and not likely to wake up for hours.'

'I wonder what did happen to the poor girl?' Len mused. 'No one walks for miles through the bush without shoes. Something very serious must have occurred to make her do that.'

'Yes. I thought at first she must have crashed her car and lost her shoes and mobile phone before walking to find help. But now I sense some kind of skulduggery landed her in this mess.'

'Do you think she'll be all right?'

'Yes, but she might need antibiotics if those cuts on her feet become infected. I think we should ask Dr Hodgson to come and check her over anyway. She was terribly dehydrated when she arrived here, and I don't know if that causes any damage internally.'

'Well, let's get some sleep ourselves now. It's been an eventful evening!'

25

Conclusion

When Elizabeth went into their guest bedroom early the next morning to see how Sharba was, she was distressed to find the young woman bathed in sweat, muttering deliriously, and very confused.

'We need to call the doctor immediately,' Elizabeth told Len as she rushed for the phone. 'I don't know what's brought it on, but Sharba is obviously running a high fever and doesn't seem to know where she is.'

'She's suffering from blood poisoning and malaria,' Dr Hodgson told them a little later when he had come and examined Sharba. 'The wounds on her feet have become very infected and caused blood poisoning, and malaria often occurs when the body is suddenly put under a huge strain. There is also bruising on her face that would indicate that someone has slapped her about. Can you tell me what happened to her?'

'Unfortunately not,' said Len. 'We met Sharba in Lusaka some time ago but didn't see her again until she arrived here on foot last night in a very distressed state. She didn't tell us what happened, but she did say that no one else was involved and when we offered to call someone for her, she refused.'

'Well, she should be in hospital, but we can't move her in this state,' said Doctor Hodgson. 'We'll have to nurse her here. I'm not going to lie to you; her condition is serious and although she's young and strong and I'm hoping she will make a full recovery, there are no guarantees. Her family should be informed that she's ill.'

'Did she mention anything about her family when we met her in Lusaka?' Len asked Elizabeth.

'I think she said her parents had been killed in a car crash in England,' said Elizabeth. 'That's why she came back to Zambia where she'd been born. But she didn't mention any other relations.'

'Friends then? Boyfriend?' Doctor Hodgson suggested.

'No. She had only recently arrived in Zambia when we met her. She had just secured a job with Huber Enterprises.'

'Why don't you ring Huber Enterprises then and ask them if they know the address of any of her relatives. They should have a record of her next of kin, surely,' said the doctor.

After the doctor had left, Elizabeth got on the phone to Huber Enterprises and found herself talking to Mrs Phiri who had not long put the phone down after talking to Karl Huber. He had told her that Sharba Lengi no longer worked for them and her details should be destroyed forthwith. Mrs Phiri understood that the young woman had left under a cloud and she obeyed Karl's directive with alacrity.

'I'm sorry,' Mrs Phiri said to Elizabeth. 'Miss Lengi's contract with us has been terminated and we no longer have her details.'

'I do hope the girl pulls through,' said Elizabeth worriedly to Len when she put the phone down. 'Until she's able to speak to us, we don't have a clue who to contact for her.'

❖

Oliver returned to his home in Woodstock after his trip to Scotland. He was tired and dispirited, and he glowered at the pile of work that had built up and stood waiting for his attention. He decided he would catch up on his sleep overnight and in the morning he would decide what his next move would be. He couldn't believe how elusive Sharba was proving to be. But in his heart, he knew he would never give up looking for her and ultimately he was determined to bring her back and make her his woman.

❖

Alistair flew back to Lusaka and went home. He felt exhausted and didn't want to think about things anymore because everything seemed to swirl about in his head and there were no conclusions to his dilemma. He was still desperately worried about Sharba, but he knew he would have to rest before he made any more plans, because he was too fatigued to think straight. He went to bed early and slept uninterruptedly until he was awakened just before six the next morning by the ringing of his mobile phone. He picked it up sleepily and saw that it was an unknown number calling him, so he didn't bother to answer it. He rolled over hoping to catch another half hour of sleep, but a couple of minutes later the phone rang again and it was the same number calling.

'Alistair Gordon.' Alistair muttered. Thinking that it might be someone wanting to charter his aeroplane, he decided he had better reply.

'I'm sorry to call you so early,' said a soft female voice rather hesitantly. 'I'm not exactly sure what time it is in Scotland, but I hope I didn't wake you up. My name's Elizabeth Raven and Sharba Lengi asked me to put this call through.'

'Sharba Lengi?' Alistair cut in. He was suddenly wide awake. 'Is she with you?'

'She is, but she isn't at all well; she's obviously been through a dreadful ordeal, but my husband and I aren't sure what happened to her. She arrived on foot at our farm in a state of dehydration and exhaustion on Monday night. It appears that she had to walk for miles to reach us and since she was barefooted, she had done considerable damage to her feet. Before she told us what had happened, she fell ill with blood poisoning and malaria. Since then, she's been drifting in and out of consciousness, but last night she was a bit more with it, so to speak, and she was very anxious to get into contact with you. She kept saying, "Please ring Alistair Gordon who is in Scotland" and then she reeled off your mobile number. It was obviously important to her, but I didn't want to ring you in the middle of the night. The thing is, we, that's myself and the people caring for her, don't know who you are or what the relationship is between the two of you.'

'I'm her boyfriend,' said Alistair, and then he asked if Elizabeth had any other details about why his girlfriend had ended up in this state. He was horrified that Sharba had found it necessary to walk barefooted through the bush for miles; something was not right at all!

It soon became apparent to Alistair that the Ravens didn't really know what had happened to Sharba in the first place, but since she had been with them, they had been nursing her because she had become very ill. When they realised Alistair was now back in Zambia—and was not in fact in Scotland—they immediately invited him to come and stay with them so that he could be with Sharba.

'She's still asleep right now; I didn't want to tell her I was going to contact you until I knew that I could—and also find out who you were.'

They arranged to meet him at the Choma airstrip when he said he would be flying in.

❖

When Alistair entered the airy spare room where Sharba was being nursed, he found her propped up in her bed. Elizabeth had told him that this was the first day since Sharba had arrived that she had been fully conscious, and when she had been told that Alistair was on his way to see her, she had dramatically perked up! But when he first saw her, he was shocked by her appearance. She was clean and her long hair had been brushed out beautifully, but her skin was so pale it was almost translucent. It stretched over her features tightly, emphasising how much weight she had lost. Her beautiful eyes were sunken and deeply shadowed, and altogether she looked frail and very vulnerable.

Len and Elizabeth had suggested to Alistair that he go in alone and if Sharba told him what had happened to her before she arrived at Concord Estates, he could tell them later. Being the kind, considerate couple they were, they knew that the two young people would want private time together more than anything else.

'Oh my darling, whatever happened to you?' Alistair crossed to the bed and tenderly put his arms around Sharba and hugged her gently.

Tears flowed from Sharba's eyes as she hugged Alistair back.

'I was so worried when I couldn't get into contact with you,' Alistair told her as he perched on the bed so that he could hold her hand. 'I came back to Zambia early so that I could look for you because no one seemed to have a clue where you'd disappeared to. I should actually ring the Hubers now to let them know that you've been found.'

'No!' Although Sharba's voice was weak, her tone was emphatic.

'Please don't ring them!'

'Why, darling? Whatever has happened?'

Slowly, Sharba told Alistair of the events that led her to seek help from the Ravens. It took a while because it was a complicated tale, and Sharba decided she would have to tell him everything—with no omissions—right from the beginning if he was to understand properly why she had acted as she had.

'So that's where Oliver Naughton comes in,' said Alistair when she had told him about her previous boyfriend.

'What do you mean? It sounds as though you know him!'

'Oliver Naughton has been looking for you. He went to Arlo's hotel and when he didn't find you there, he went to my cottage to look for you there. After that, he turned up in Scotland at my parent's place asking for you. He said you're his fiancée.'

Sharba's pupils dilated in horror. 'I thought Oliver was one worry that I could discard,' she said in dismay. 'I'm *not* his fiancée, I never was, and I never will be! But he said if I left him, he'd never give up looking for me until he found me, and despite my best efforts it seems he almost did. Now I'm going to have to run again to avoid him.' Her expression became tormented, and Alistair could see her eyes were haunted and anxious.

'No, you're not going to run anywhere,' said Alistair emphatically. 'I'll keep you safe from Oliver Naughton and anyone else who upsets you. Now, forget this joker, Oliver Naughton, and tell me the rest.'

Alistair shuffled up on the bed so that he could sit with his arm around Sharba's shoulders. It made her feel safe, so she was able to forget about Oliver for the moment and continue.

'I didn't know I was Arlo's illegitimate daughter,' she said when she came to that part of the narrative. 'I promise I didn't. I would never have tried to get a job with Huber Enterprises had I known. But they'll never believe me, will they? They'll think it would be too much of a coincidence. They must all hate me now because they'll think I just worked for them to manipulate some sort of compensation out of the family.'

'They don't hate you,' said Alistair. 'But go on with the tale.'

Sharba could clearly feel the tension in Alistair's arm as she recounted what Karl had done to her on the night she had tried to take George back to his mother.

'I'll *kill* the bastard!' Alistair exploded. 'You could have died trying to find help, and that lying, murdering son of a bitch said he didn't know what had happened to you after you left the hotel! Just *wait* until I get my hands on him!'

'No, Alistair, just leave things be! The Hubers will already be hating me; I don't want to cause them any more trouble. I've got Oliver after me again and I don't want Karl seeking retribution as well!'

'Karl won't be able to seek retribution once I've sorted him out,' said Alistair hotly. 'There's absolutely no chance that he's going to get away with what he's done to you, I can promise you that. As for this man Oliver—well, he sounds a bit of a nutter, but I have a plan to bamboozle him as well.'

'What sort of plan?' Sharba was beginning to imagine her boyfriend turning into the incredible hulk and sorting everyone out!

Alistair removed his arm from around her shoulders and took both of her hands in his. Looking deeply into her troubled eyes he said, 'These last few days, when I had no idea where you were, have been the worst in my life. It really brings it home when someone you love suddenly seems to have been taken from you. I don't ever want to experience that feeling again—I love you so much. Sharba, will you marry me?'

Sharba stared into his eyes looking astonished, but then her expression turned to delight. 'Are you sure you want to marry me, knowing my past history?' she asked.

'Of course I do! I love you and want to keep you safely with me for ever!'

'Then yes,' Sharba said, a big smile spreading over her face. 'I'd love to become your wife, Alistair Gordon!'

Alistair leaned forward and kissed her. The kiss would have lasted a long time, but his mobile rang and reluctantly he pulled away so that he could answer it.

'Oh, hello Amanda,' he said, seeing it was she who rang. 'I've got good news, I've found Sharba—and she's just agreed to marry me!'

❖

Because Sharba begged Alistair not to leave her, he stayed with the Ravens for a couple of days while she convalesced. He was itching to go and confront Karl, but Sharba's need for him was more important and his being there helped her to stride back quickly to almost full health.

'I'm so sorry that I made you miss your parents' anniversary bash,' Sharba said to Alistair.

'Well, they haven't had it yet,' said Alistair. 'If you improve enough, we could perhaps fly back to Scotland together and still celebrate it with them. But first I need to fly to Livingstone because I have some unfinished business there.'

However, before he flew to Livingstone, there was a call from Arlo who had been told by Amanda that Sharba had been found. She had not filled him in on the details immediately because she didn't want him to have a relapse, but now he was better—and he wanted all the facts. Alistair told him everything and Arlo listened quietly, not interrupting at all.

'I'm sorry, Mr Huber,' Alistair concluded after he had told the older man everything. 'I'm coming down to have a word with your son and it won't be a pretty meeting. I'm also laying an attempted murder charge against him because Sharba could quite easily have died.'

'I'm sorry as well,' said Arlo. 'It's a bad business and I can't express how appalled I am at my son's behaviour. He deserves your wrath and he deserves to go to jail for what he did to Sharba, but he's gone. He disappeared on the day that Amanda discovered that Sharba had been found. I guess he didn't want to face the consequences of his actions, so he left that night without anyone knowing. I assume he went back to Germany, but as far as I'm concerned, he's no longer my son. I don't ever want to see him again and he'll have no inheritance at all. We'll look after Amanda and little George, and our grandson will inherit what could have been Karl's.

'I won't forget Sharba either. I also behaved badly when I was younger, but now I want to acknowledge Sharba as my daughter. I do hope she'll be able to forgive me for what I did to her mother and become part of our family. Please ask her to come and see us if she can possibly face this family again, so that we can apologise to her in person. I completely believe her when she says she had no idea she was my daughter when she applied for a job here. Having worked with her, I know she's a beautiful, principled, upright young woman who would never try to manipulate me or my family to her own advantage. That Karl would think she was capable of that only highlights his own way of thinking and it reflects badly on him.'

When Alistair told Arlo that he and Sharba were now engaged to be married, Arlo was delighted. 'You must come to the hotel so that we can throw you an engagement party,' he said enthusiastically.

'We were actually thinking of going to Scotland as soon as Sharba is feeling up to the journey, and then having a quiet wedding there,' Alistair told him.

'Well, when you return, we'll have the party then,' Arlo said. 'It'll be in lieu of a wedding reception and it'll also be a celebration to welcome both Sharba and yourself into the family.'

Sharba was amazed when Alistair told her of his conversation with Arlo.

'I thought he and the rest of the family would hate me,' she said.

'How could anyone hate you?' Alistair said looking at her adoringly.

'Karl made me believe that they would,' said Sharba. 'I'm so relieved he's gone now—I never want to see his face again!'

'He was the champion of liars and good riddance to him,' said Alistair. 'I'm only sorry I didn't get the chance to sort him out for what he put you through. Arlo thinks he's gone back to Germany and believes it's highly likely he'll end up in more trouble there and land in jail. Whatever happens to him, Arlo has disinherited him and never wants to see him again.'

❖

Sharba's recovery was rapid once she had been reunited with Alistair. As soon as she felt well enough, Alistair flew her down to Livingstone as Arlo and the family were very keen to see her. Rosa put on a special lunch and they all gathered to welcome her into the family. Arlo drove to the airport himself to meet them and take them back to the hotel.

'It's good to see you, Arlo,' said Sharba, who was surprised he hadn't sent a driver to collect them.

'It's good to see you as well, my girl,' said Arlo, his eyes twinkling as he gave her a hug. 'I wanted to come in person to say to you, before the celebration, that I'm so sorry for all that has happened. My son treated you atrociously and I apologise for that, but I also have to apologise for my own iniquities. I've behaved very badly in the past and I need to beg your forgiveness.'

'Arlo, please can we forget all that's happened in the past?' Sharba pleaded. 'What happened, happened. None of us are perfect. We all slip up, and I don't hold any grudges. Can we just go forward and enjoy the future without any further recriminations? That's what I would really like.'

'You're marrying an angel—did you know that?' Arlo said to Alistair.

'I know, I'm very lucky,' answered Alistair, putting his arm around Sharba.

When they got back to Arlo's house at the lodge, Rosa had put on a big lunch and everyone was there, including Charles.

'Oh my goodness, there's nothing left of you,' said Rosa when she greeted Sharba. 'Come on now, we'll have to feed you up and put some more meat on your bones!'

'Auntie Sharba!' George came running to greet her. 'Daddy's gone and now I'm the man of the house,' he told her proudly.

It was a happy gathering, and everyone seemed pleased to welcome Sharba and Alistair into the family.

'You're racing me to the altar,' Clara said accusingly. 'And none of us will be able to come to your wedding!'

'We're going to throw the party of the year for the wedded couple as soon as they get back, though,' said Arlo. 'Everyone must be invited!'

Sharba learned that Clara was training Amanda to be a receptionist. 'Well, you've left and I'll be leaving after I marry Charles,' Clara said. 'Actually, Amanda's shaping up to be really good at the job.'

'But she won't be able to do it on her own,' said Sharba.

'No, of course not; that's why I'm training up Uzma as well. Dad said he wanted an African girl in the job, and she is far too intelligent and well educated to be a maid, so we chose her. I think she and Amanda will do a brilliant job—they'll be almost as good as we were!'

After they had finished lunch, Sharba slipped away to go and see Uzma at the reception desk. She wanted to apologise to her for breaking her trust and revealing that it was Jackson who had abducted George and the village's involvement in keeping everything quiet.

'Oh Miss Sharba, don't apologise to me,' said Uzma with anguish in her voice. 'It is I who should be apologising to you for not coming forward the moment you disappeared and confessing what had really happened. I wanted to, but the people of my village pleaded with me to keep quiet. I was torn between doing the right thing and saving my village from a lot of recriminations. I'm so sorry.'

'Well, let's just leave behind everything that's happened in the past,' suggested Sharba. 'Everything has turned out for the best, hasn't it?'

'For us, yes. Mr Arlo did not want to discipline Jackson or chastise the village when he heard what Mr Karl had been up to. But you, Miss Sharba, you had to go through a terrible ordeal when you were trying to help us, and I see you're still hobbling about on bandaged feet. It makes me very ashamed and sad!'

'But it's all over now. I'm on the mend and Alistair and I are going to get married. You've got a good job and I believe you're doing it to a very high standard; the village is safe now Karl's gone, and I think this hotel will be a much happier place to work in now that he's not here. Let's just be happy with how things have turned out, Uzma, I don't want to blame anyone but Karl for what happened.'

When Sharba got back to the luncheon party, she found that Arlo had promised to clear the hotel of all guests when they threw the post-wedding party for her and Alistair. He wanted all the rooms to be vacant for their friends and family.

'It's going to be the party of the century,' he promised them.

❖

Sharba and Alistair flew back to Scotland a couple of days later, landing on the morning of the day before Alistair's parents' anniversary party. They were very pleased he had made it back in time and were delighted to meet Sharba. When the happy couple told them that they intended to get married as soon as possible while they were still in Scotland, they were thrilled.

'We've decided on a very small, low-key marriage ceremony,' Alistair explained to them, but when we get back to Zambia, Sharba's biological father is going to throw us a huge party. You're invited, of course, and you've got to come!'

❖

Oliver had been trying to commune with his dead father to plead his help in finding Sharba. While he begged, his hand continually caressed the cross that hung about his neck as he tried to figure out what to do. He wasn't a quitter and ultimately he always got what he wanted, but Sharba's continual ability to evade him made him wonder if some supreme influence wasn't at play. Maybe, despite his own conviction that they should be together, it was destined that they should not. He had always relied on a greater power to help him get what he wanted and up to now it had worked, provided he put in the effort. Now it seemed as though this power was hindering him, and since he was getting no answers from Father Hughes, it was probably time to concede defeat, he concluded miserably.

But over the next few days he kept imagining Sharba in another man's arms and it sent him crazy with jealousy. He felt driven by the need to win her back, so, despite his work piling up and the expense of flying halfway around the world yet again, he booked a flight back to Zambia. His first port of call would be Alistair Gordon's house because that was the only lead he had on Sharba at the moment.

Oliver was glad that Alistair's house wasn't far from the airport, and within a couple of hours of landing in Zambia, he once again arrived at the farm cottage. When Dixon saw who it was, he greeted him warmly, because he felt he had got to know this bwana quite well.

'Come in sir. Can I make you a cup of tea?' Dixon inquired politely.

'No thank you, I've just come to see Mr Gordon. It's very important.'

'Oh dear,' said Dixon looking sad. 'Mr Gordon has gone to Scotland.'

'What? Are you sure? I looked for him in Scotland at the address you gave to me last time I was here, and I was told he'd come back to Zambia!'

'He did come back,' said Dixon. 'He was looking for Miss Sharba because she was missing.'

'Did he find her?'

'Oh yes,' said Dixon happily. 'He found her, and they flew back to Scotland together. Yesterday Bwana rang me to tell me that they had just been married!'

Oliver went straight back to the airport. Wearily he booked a flight to Heathrow and as he boarded the aircraft, his shoulders were slumped. If Sharba was wearing a wedding ring given to her by Alistair Gordon, he knew he was beaten. Marriage was the one thing that he knew the supreme power that influenced his life considered irreversible, and for the first time in his life he realised he wasn't going to get what he wanted after all.

END

....

Also by Janet E. Green

Janet Green has enjoyed writing novels for a number of years. She was born and brought up in Kenya, East Africa, and also lived in central and southern Africa for many years. Now living in England, she draws on her memories of Africa, where her heart still remains, for inspiration. Most of the books she writes are sagas and some of them are seasoned by her strong Christian beliefs. You can find out more about Janet Green by visiting her website and blog at www.janetegreen.org.

A
HABARI
PUBLICATION

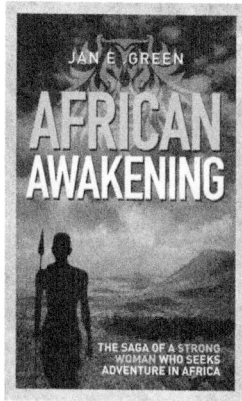

Kate drove her hire car at snail's pace down the dusty track, bumping over the crunchy coral bones that ridged on the surface of the narrow road, and she turned up a lane that was marked with the sign 'Bougain Villa'. With every metre she covered her heart seemed to pump faster and faster. She had searched for so long that she had almost despaired that she would ever find what she was seeking. But now after months of research and a trip half way around the world to Kilifi in Kenya, East Africa, she was sure that she was on the threshold of finding the person that she had sought for so long.

Dance of Jeopardy

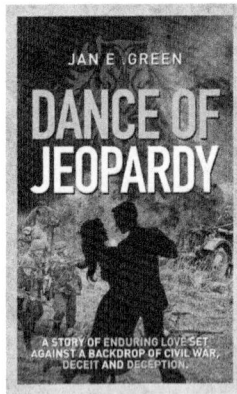

The man in my arms was the most important person in my life. Right from the time that I first met him when I was still very young, there had been a spark between us —a connection that had never been completely broken. It was there all through the years when he was seeking adventure in other parts of Africa—it was there when his life took a turn that excluded me completely, and it had lain dormant until the time was right for it to ignite once again. It seemed to me that too many years had passed while he was away striving to accomplish his dreams—the dreams of a man who craved action, danger, and adventure. His quest for adventure had, for so many years, seemed to draw us further and further apart, but now, at last, the man I loved so much was in my arms.

The Lunar Rainbow

It was one of those very rare days in England when the weather was decidedly un-British. The unusual pressure system that swirled over the British Isles that early summer's day drew in hot moist air all the way from Africa, causing the sun's rays to become magnified as they filtered through the moisture-laden atmosphere. It was so different from the normal British sunshine that would usually seep over a cool bracing dawn and highlight the countryside in fingers of bright warmth. This heat was humid and heavy, it felt like hot syrup, and I could feel my arms prickling as the fierce rays burned into the exposed skin. The sky was a steely blue, but to the east there was a huge build-up of cumulonimbus clouds under which the sky was almost black. Ominous growls of distant thunder rumbled every now and again.

Dangerously Unaware

As Josh hurried down the passage away from the dentists' rooms and towards the lifts, he felt a sense of relief. Although he was now a confident young adult, he still disliked going to the dentist for check-ups. He hated the feeling of vulnerability as the dentist tipped the chair back so that he was lying almost horizontal. It made Josh feel at the mercy of the dentist and his middle-aged assistant who hovered over him with their instruments of torture in their hands. He detested the sharp things that were poked around his teeth and gums and the shriek of the drill set his nerves on edge, while the sight of the dentist coming towards him with a syringe in his hand made Josh feel very apprehensive.

God's Timing

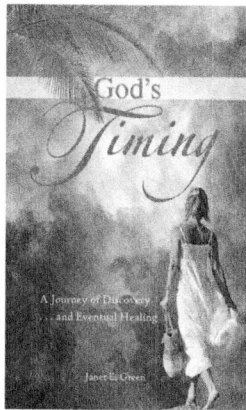

L ucy has suffered a crushing sorrow and now, to her, the world seems to be a place of chaos and disharmony. She is convinced that she or her family will sooner or later be caught up in some disaster and longs to know what the future holds so that she can be prepared. Although she is holidaying in one of the most beautiful places in the world, her dark thoughts drag her down to the point where she is almost overwhelmed.

Is it by sheer coincidence that she is introduced to someone who has the knowledge and absolute proof of what the future holds? Lucy finds herself going on a journey of discovery that almost blows her mind. And at the end of her holiday, there is one last surprise. . .

Printed in Great Britain
by Amazon